Seized by Love at Seaside

Sweet with Heat: Seaside Summers Series

Addison Cole

ISBN-10: 1-941480-89-6
ISBN-13: 978-1-941480-89-2

SEIZED BY LOVE AT SEASIDE

Cover Design: Elizabeth Mackey Designs

WORLD LITERARY PRESS
PRINTED IN THE UNITED STATES OF AMERICA

A Note to Readers

I have been excited about writing Blue Ryder's story since the very moment I met him, and when I met Lizzie Barber, I knew she was the perfect woman for loyal and loving Blue. They are outwardly sweet and secretly steamy—what could be more fun? I hope you love them as much as I do.

Seized by Love at Seaside is part of the Sweet with Heat: Seaside Summers series. Sweet with Heat books are the sweet editions of the award-winning, steamy romance collection Love in Bloom written by *New York Times* bestselling author Melissa Foster. Addison Cole is Melissa's sweet alter ego (pen name). The storylines and characters remain the same as the original titles. Within the Sweet with Heat series you'll find fiercely loyal heroes and smart, empowered women on their search for true love. They're flawed, funny and easy to relate to. These emotional romances portray all the passion two people in love convey without any graphic love scenes and little or no harsh language (with the exception of an occasional "damn" or "hell"). Characters from each series appear in future Sweet with Heat series. Sweet with Heat books may be read as stand-alone novels, or as part of the larger series.

Sign up for Addison's Sweet with Heat newsletter to be notified of the next release.
www.Addisoncole.com/Newsletter

For more information on Sweet with Heat titles visit
www.AddisonCole.com

Seized by Love at Seaside by Addison Cole is the sweet edition of the steamy Love in Bloom novel, *Seized by Love* (The Ryders) by Melissa Foster.

For Aimee Suter, for letting me borrow your precious lists

Chapter One

THERE WERE SOME nights when Lizzie Barber simply didn't feel like donning an apron, black-framed glasses, and high heels, covering her shiny brunette locks with a blond wig, and prancing around nearly naked. Tonight was one of those nights. Gazing at her reflection in the mirror of her basement bathroom, Lizzie tucked the last few strands of her hair beneath the wig and forced her very best smile. Thank goodness her elfin lips naturally curled up at the edges—even when she wasn't smiling, she looked like she was. And tonight she definitely wasn't in the mood to smile. Her oven had been acting up for the last few nights, and she prayed to the gods of all things sugary and sweet that it would behave tonight.

Tightening the apron tie around her neck and the one around her waist, to avoid wardrobe malfunctions, and tugging on the hem of the apron to ensure her skin-colored thong and all her naughty bits were covered, she went into the studio—aka the miniscule kitchen located in the basement of her cute Cape Cod cottage—and surveyed her baking accoutrements one last time before queuing the intro music for her webcast and pasting that perfectly perky smile back in place.

"Welcome back, my hot and hunky bakers," she purred into

the camera. "Today we're going to bake delicious angel food cupcakes with fluffy frosting that will make your mouth water." She leaned forward, flashing the camera an eyeful of cleavage and her most seductive smile as she crooked her finger in a come-hither fashion. "And because we all know it's what's *beneath* all that delicious frosting that counts, we're going to sprinkle a few surprises inside the thick, creamy centers."

Lizzie had mastered making baking sound naughty while in college, when her father had taken ill and her parents had closed their inn for six months to focus on his medical care, leaving Lizzie without college tuition. Her part-time job at a florist shop hadn't done a darn thing for her mounting school loans, and when a friend suggested she try making videos and monetizing them to earn fast cash, she drew upon her passion for baking and secretly put on a webcast called *Cooking with Coeds*. It turned out that scantily clad baking was a real money earner. She'd paid for her books and meal plan that way, and eventually earned enough to pay for most of her college tuition. Lizzie had two passions in life—baking and flowers, and she'd hoped to open her own floral shop after college. After graduation, *Cooking with Coeds* became the *Naked Baker* webcast, and she'd made enough money to finish paying off her school loans and open a flower shop in Provincetown, Massachusetts, just like she'd always dreamed of. She hadn't intended to continue the *Naked Baker* after opening P-town Petals, but when her parents fell upon hard times again and her younger sister Maddy's educational fund disappeared, the Naked Baker webcast became Lizzie's contribution to Maddy's education. Their very conservative parents would have a conniption if they knew what their proper little girl was doing behind closed doors, but what other choice did she have? Her parents ran a small bed-and-breakfast in Brewster, Massachusetts, and with her father's health ping-ponging, they barely earned enough money to make ends meet—and affording college for a child who had come as a surprise to them seven years after Lizzie was born had proven difficult.

Lizzie narrowed her eyes seductively as she gazed into the camera and stirred the batter. She dipped her finger into the rich, creamy goodness and put that finger into her mouth, making a sensual show of sucking it off. "Mm-mm. Nothing better than *thick, creamy batter*." Her tongue swept over her lower lip as she ran through the motions of creating what she'd come to think of as *baking porn*.

During the filming of each show, she reminded herself often of why she was still doing something that she felt ashamed of and kept secret. There was no way she was going to let her sweet nineteen-year-old sister fend for herself and end up doing who knew what to earn money like she did instead of focusing on her studies. Or worse, drop out of school. Madison was about as innocent as they came, and while Lizzie might once have been that innocent, her determination to succeed, and life circumstances, had beaten it out of her. Creating the webcast was the best decision she'd ever made—even if it meant putting her nonexistent social life on hold and living a secret life after dark. The blond wig and thick-framed spectacles helped to hide her online persona, or at least they seemed to. No one had ever accused her of being the Naked Baker. Then again, her assumption was that the freaky people who got off watching her prance around in an apron and heels probably rarely left their own basements.

She was proud of helping Maddy. She felt like she was taking one for the team. Going where no girl should ever have to go. Braving the wild naked baking arena for the betterment of the sister she cherished.

A while later, as Lizzie checked the cupcakes and realized that while the oven was still warm, it had turned *off*—her stomach sank. Hiding her worries behind another forced smile and a wink, she stuck her backside out and bent over to quickly remove the tray of cupcakes from the oven, knowing the angle of the camera would give only a side view and none of her bare butt would actually be visible. Thankfully, the oven must have just died, and the cupcakes were firm enough to frost.

Emergency reshoot avoided!

Smile genuine!

A few minutes later she sprinkled the last of the coconut on the cupcakes, narrating as she went.

"Everyone wants a little something extra on top, and I'm going to give it to you *good*." Giving one last wink to the camera, she said, "Until next week, this is your Naked Baker signing off for a sweet, seductive night of tantalizing tasting."

She clicked the remote and turned off the camera. Eyeing the fresh daisies she'd brought home from her flower shop, she leaned her forearms on the counter, and with a heavy sigh, she let her head fall forward. It was after midnight, and she had to be up bright and early to open the shop. Tomorrow night she'd edit the webcast so it would be ready in time to air the following night—*and* she needed to get her oven fixed.

Stupid thing.

Kicking off her heels, Lizzie went upstairs, stripped out of the apron, and wrapped a thick towel around herself. A warm shower was just what she needed to wash away the film of shame left on her skin after taping the webcast. Thinking of the broken oven, she texted her friend Blue Ryder to see if he could fix it. Blue was a highly sought after craftsman who worked for the Kennedys and other prominent families around the Cape. When Lizzie's pipe had burst under the sink in the bathroom above the first-floor kitchen while she was away at a floral convention for the weekend, Blue was only too happy to put aside time to handle the renovations. He was like that. Always making time to help others. He was still splitting his time between working on her kitchen renovations and the cottage he'd just purchased. He had work to do at his cottage tomorrow, but she hoped he could fit her in at some point.

Can you fix my oven tomorrow?

Blue texted back a few seconds later. He was as reliable as he was hot, a dangerous combination. She read his text—*Is that code for something sexy?*—and shook her head with a laugh.

Smirking, she replied, *Only if you're into oven grease.*

Blue had asked her out many times since they'd met last year, when she'd handled the flowers for his friends' quadruple beach wedding. Turning down his invitations wasn't easy and had led to more sexy fantasies than she cared to admit. Her double life was crazy enough without adding a sexy, rugged man who was built like Magic Mike and had eyes that could hypnotize a blind woman, but her reasons went far deeper than that. Blue was more than eye candy. He was also a genuine friend, and he always put family and friends first, which, when added to his drop-dead good looks and gentlemanly demeanor, was enough to stop Lizzie's brain from functioning. It would be too easy to fall hard for a caring, loyal man like Blue Ryder. And *that*, she couldn't afford. Maddy was counting on her.

She read his text—*Glad you finally came to your senses. When are you free?*—and wondered if he thought *she* was being flirtatious.

Time to nip this in the bud, she thought. Her finger hovered over the screen while her mind toyed with images of Blue, six foot three, all hot, hard muscles and steel-blue eyes.

It had been way too long since she'd been with a man, and every time Blue asked her out, she was tempted, but she liked him so much as a friend, and she knew that tipping over from friendship to lovers would only draw her further in to him, making it harder to lead her double life.

That was precisely why she hightailed it out of her house on the mornings before he showed up to work on her kitchen. Leaving before he arrived was the only way she was able to keep her distance. He was *that* good-looking. *That* kind. And *that* enjoyable to be around. Not only didn't she have time for a relationship, but she was pretty sure that no guy would approve of his girlfriend doing the *Naked Baker* show. Of course, the mornings after taping her shows, she left him a sweet treat on the counter with a note thanking him for working on her kitchen.

Even though Blue couldn't see her as she drew back her shoulders and put on her most solemn face, she did it anyway to strengthen her resolve as she typed a text that she hoped would very gently set him straight. *After work, but this is REALLY to fix my oven. The one I cook with! Thank you! See you around seven?*

She set the phone down and stepped into the shower, determined not to think about his blue eyes or the way his biceps flexed every time he moved his arms. Her mind drifted to when she'd arrived home from work yesterday and found Blue bending over his toolbox, his jeans stretched tight across his hamstrings and formed to his perfect rear end. She got aroused with the thought. He'd been the man she'd conjured up in her late-night fantasies since last summer. What did it hurt? He'd never know. She may not have time to date, but a little midnight fantasy could go a long way...

Chapter Two

SWEAT POURED OFF Blue as he carried the wood he'd just torn out of the second-floor bedroom down the stairs and into the late-afternoon sun. It had been a mild fall so far on Cape Cod, and as thankful as he was for the moderate temperatures, working on the second floor of a cottage without air-conditioning had him wishing winter would peek its head over the sandy stretch of land. He tossed the old wood into the dumpster and wiped his brow with his forearm, gazing out over the property he'd purchased weeks earlier, the Bowers Bluff Lighthouse and its keeper's cottage. Bowers Bluff was a mile-wide, eight-mile-long, dune-ridden peninsula on the north side of Cape Cod and the perfect location to one day raise a family.

Blue had fallen in love with it the first time he'd seen it two summers ago with his brother, Duke, a real estate investor. They had planned on jointly purchasing the property and renovating it to be used as a restaurant, but the more time Blue spent there, the more he became attached to it. Eventually he gave in to his love and told Duke of his desire to purchase the property himself. Duke, being the eldest of the six Ryder siblings, had been supportive and understanding, as always.

Blue had been working day and night renovating the cottage, until Lizzie Barber's kitchen was damaged and he began splitting his time between the two properties. The renovations on both were coming along nicely. And as a bonus, he was able to see Lizzie almost every day, at least for a few minutes. Lizzie was a sweet bundle of seductive energy. Her personality lit up the room, and Blue had a feeling that if she'd ever give in and go out with him, they'd find out that the friendship they enjoyed was just the tip of the iceberg. But Lizzie had turned him down more often than the sun set. That, however, didn't deter him. The more often she turned him away, the more he thought of her—and the more he wanted to make her his. Blue believed in following his gut, and his gut—and his heart— continually drew him to the petite, perky woman who could drive him crazy with a single smile.

He stood in the doorway of the cottage, admiring his hard work. He'd refinished the hardwood floors, renovated the kitchen, removed the old paneling, and installed drywall and decorative moldings on the first floor. With the first floor complete, the second floor seemed like a breeze. Everything about the old place already felt like home, despite the fact that he'd grown up just outside of New York City. Unlike most of his siblings, he had never felt drawn to city life. His family had visited the Cape when he was just a boy, and his love for it had stuck with him ever since.

He pulled out his cell phone to check the time. He was meeting Lizzie at seven to fix her oven, which he was sure was just a ruse, given that he was already renovating her kitchen and she had a brand-new oven. With any luck she'd finally come to her senses and would agree to go out with him. Every time he asked her out he was met with the same responses—she didn't have time to date or she didn't want to chance ruining their friendship. They did have an incredible friendship, but wasn't that how people got to know each other *before* dating?

Before heading back inside he noticed he'd missed two texts. That wasn't surprising. He was in the habit of giving his full focus to the quality of his work and letting everything else fall to the side.

The first text was from his younger brother, Cash, who was a New York City firefighter. *I'm with Jeremy. He needs a headcount for the wedding. Are you bringing a guest?*

Their cousin Jeremy, an attorney, was getting married next month to his fiancée, Susan, a fashion blogger. He'd love to take Lizzie to the wedding, but the wedding was in New York, and if she wouldn't go out on a date at the Cape, she surely wouldn't go away overnight with him. Normally, he'd take his best friend, Sky Lacroux, to the wedding, a little no-commitment arm candy to keep the single women at bay, but she'd recently gotten engaged, which meant Blue was on his own for the wedding. He'd never been a weekend hookup kind of guy, and his life was on the Cape. The last thing he wanted was to play the flirting game with women who meant nothing to him. Not when he'd had a certain feisty little brunette with a tight body and an effervescent personality on his mind every second of the day for the last year.

He returned Cash's text—*Flying solo. Thanks for checking*—knowing he'd likely spend the wedding hanging out with his family while his brothers checked out every skirt that passed and their sister, Trish, made fun of them. Not that he was opposed to checking out women, but while some of his brothers enjoyed one-night stands, Blue hadn't been into that for quite some time. He'd not only spent the last few years watching his closest friends fall in love and get married, and more recently, start families of their own, but he'd also been hurt by an ex-girlfriend who'd thought a one-night stand that had meant nothing to her wouldn't cut him to the bone.

Sarah Jane had been Blue's first love. They'd come together in the innocence of their youth, both just eighteen years old, and they'd stayed together for more than a year. She'd gotten a ride home from a coworker one night when Blue had been in an evening class, and when he'd shown up at her place and caught them having sex, Sarah Jane had tried to explain. *It didn't mean anything!* She'd been so wrong that even now the memory of being hurt—and of his broken trust—still stung. He'd sworn he'd never be in that position again, and it was an easy promise to keep. No long-term girlfriend left no room for agony.

The second text message was from Hunter, one of Sky's older brothers and Blue's buddy. *Bonfire tonight. You in?*

A bonfire sounded great, and assuming Lizzie was just going to turn him down again, he'd need a good distraction. *Definitely*, he responded, then added, *Fixing Lizzie's oven. May get there late.*

A few hours later he headed back to his cabin in the woods of Wellfleet, showered, and then drove over to Lizzie's. Blue parked in front of her house, thinking about how much he loved the feel of her place. The quintessential Cape Cod cottage exuded simple elegance. *Just like her.* The split-rail fence was laced with pink Knock Out roses, and the front yard had several beautiful gardens. He followed the slate walkway as it snaked through the gardens and heard Lizzie talking through the open window. Her laughter filled the air, and Blue paused to drink it in. It wasn't the feel of her house he adored; it was Lizzie. She was everywhere.

Lizzie answered the door with her cell phone pressed to her

ear, holding up one finger as she mouthed, *I'm sorry. One second*, and moved to the side for him to come in.

"Listen, Maddy," she said into the phone, "don't do anything you're not comfortable with, okay? Promise?" She held up a finger to Blue again, and even if he hadn't heard Madison's name, he'd know by the protective tone of Lizzie's voice that she was talking with her younger sister.

He tried not to let his eyes wander, but heck if he could keep from taking in her slim hips and tanned legs, revealed by a pair of sexy white cutoffs, or her smooth, lean shoulder peeking out from beneath a cream-colored, boat-neck sweater with a picture of an elephant on the front. The way the elephant hugged her curves made him a little jealous. What he wouldn't give to be that elephant.

He should've taken a *cold* shower before coming over.

LIZZIE ENDED THE call with her sister and slipped her cell phone into her pocket.

"I'm so sorry. That was Maddy, and she has a date tonight. She was a little nervous. I worry about her. I hope she doesn't get into a bad situation. I'm worrying over nothing, right? Please tell me I am." She blinked up at Blue, who was looking at her with amusement in his steel-blue eyes and a crooked grin that nearly made her heart stop. She always rambled when she was nervous. Better he thought she was nervous about Maddy than because of their close proximity.

"She's nineteen, Lizzie. She'll be fine."

"Right. Thank you." She exhaled loudly, trying to calm her racing pulse from the sight of him in his skintight T-shirt. He was truly beautiful, with a face that should grace the front of every magazine in the country and a smile that could melt butter.

"So, you have an oven that needs fixing?" He lifted his toolbox and cocked a brow, and she realized she was staring at him.

Great. Way to go, Lizzie.

"Yes. This way." She motioned for him to follow her down to the basement.

"You're going the wrong way."

"I have an apartment down here." She led him to the kitchen. Even though he was handling the renovations, she'd never given him a tour of the rest of the house.

She flipped on the lights, and her kitchen lit up too brightly. Perfect for her videos, not perfect for a basement kitchen.

"Wow, that's bright," he said.

"A properly lit kitchen is important. You know that." She smiled at him, hoping he'd buy that excuse.

Blue set his toolbox on the floor and eyed her laptop sitting open on the counter.

Thank goodness for power saver mode. She snagged it off the counter.

"Do you rent this space out?"

"No." She clutched the laptop to her chest, a shield between Blue and her secret.

"So..." He shifted his eyes to the oven and turned it on. "That oven looks older than you. You cook down here often?"

She laughed nervously, trying to think up something better than, *Only when I'm selling my body for my sister's tuition.* "Sometimes. I like to mix things up."

He leaned across the counter with a lazy smile. "If I didn't know better, I'd think you called me over just to see me, which I wouldn't mind at all."

She walked around the counter and stood beside him, staring accusingly at the oven. "The oven's really broken, Blue. Besides, if I wanted to see you, I'm pretty sure you'd be okay with me asking you to come over just for that."

He grinned, and her stomach fluttered. *Stupid stomach.*

"It really is broken." She pulled open the oven door and warm air rushed out. *Of course it did.*

"It's definitely heating up in here," he said in a low voice that made all her best parts take notice.

She sensed his heat behind her. If she leaned back a fraction of an inch she'd be pressed against him. The man oozed sexuality in the very best of ways, and he was in full-flirtation mode, which made him even hotter and more difficult to resist. His scent was potent, earthy and heady and purely male, and it was doing strange things to her resolve to keep a safe distance between them. She gripped the counter to keep herself from leaning in to him.

"I swear it wasn't working last night. It shut off all by itself."

"Maybe we should leave it on for a while and see if it turns off." He leaned against the counter, his eyes skirting over the white, builder-grade cabinets, dating back to the early eighties, and the Formica countertops.

Lizzie closed the oven door and crossed her arms to keep her greedy fingers from touching him. "What would make it turn off like that?"

He held her gaze as he answered. "I can't imagine anything turning off around you." Smiling with the flirtation, he added, "Probably the heating element."

How did he make *that* sound seductive? "Can we fix it?"

"Sure, *we* can fix it. It's an old oven, and if it's turning on and off, at some point you should probably consider swapping it out for a new one."

"You treat your women like you treat your ovens? When they start to break down you just swap them out?" *Yikes, where did that come from?*

His lips curved up in a wicked grin, and his eyes darkened. "I'd never swap you, Lizzie."

"I…" Great, he'd completely scrambled her brain. If he could do that with five words, what could he do with those capable hands and that sexy mouth of his? She had to stop. *This* was why she left before he arrived most mornings. *This* was why she turned down his invitations to go out. Blue was utterly irresistible.

"I'll tell you what. Hunter's having a bonfire tonight, and the hardware store closes in half an hour. Why don't *we* go to the hardware store and pick up the heating element, and then we can hit the bonfire for a little while? Afterward, we can come back and fix the oven."

Lizzie rolled that around for a minute in her head. She loved hearing *we* slide off his tongue full of innuendo, probably loved it too much, considering that she was still mulling over the idea rather than nixing it. She could tell him she had work to do, which was true. She still needed to edit her webcast, but she needed the oven fixed before she had to tape the next show, too. She couldn't do the *Naked Baker* webcast in her upstairs kitchen. On the off chance that anyone who knew her watched the webcast, they'd recognize her bright orange kitchen in a heartbeat. But if she tried to beg off this time, after hours, wasn't that rude? She was asking him to work on her oven late at night.

"Okay," she finally said.

Blue's brows lifted with surprise. "Okay?" He pushed from the counter and grinned.

"Yes, okay. I'll go to the bonfire. But it's not a date, so get that look off your face."

He turned off the oven. "Why do you always turn me down? I don't get it."

Neither do I.

She hated continually turning him down. It wasn't like she didn't *want* to go out with Blue, but the truth was, if she were to go on a real date with Blue, hold his hand, and kiss those full, delicious-looking lips of his, she *knew* she'd like it too much to walk away. She already knew that he treated her, and everyone else she'd ever seen him interact with, like gold. And right now Maddy was counting on her. She didn't need to get involved with a nice, gorgeous guy like Blue and then be forced to hide part of her life from him, or worry that someone he knew might watch the webcast and somehow figure out that she was the Naked Baker. Despite the income she gained from the show, she wasn't proud of prancing around nearly naked for money.

She finally met his gaze. "I just have so much going on right now. I barely have time to breathe."

He stepped closer and brought a heat wave with him. "Everyone has a little breathing room."

You just stole mine. "I'm running the flower shop, and..."

"And?" Blue looked around the kitchen. "Breaking ovens?"

"It's nothing personal."

He touched her arm, sending shivers of heat through her. She was sure he could see inside her to the part of her that was cuddled up in the corner, praying he didn't spot the Naked Baker.

"How can it not be personal? I've asked you out at least a dozen times and you always turn me down. A guy could get a complex." He slid his hand up her forearm and gently cupped her elbow.

How could such a benign touch make her whole body simmer? She knew she'd love the way it felt to have his hands on her, taking her to heights she couldn't reach by mere thoughts of him.

Great. Now she couldn't even respond. She was lucky she could walk after that voice slithered over her skin and his eyes held her prisoner. How on earth had her friend Sky spent time with him day after day without ever being more than friends with him? Lizzie forced herself to take a step back. Surely if Sky could do it, she could, too. Then again, Sky said she was never attracted to Blue in that way.

Therein lay the difference. From the moment Lizzie had seen Blue at the wedding, she'd been attracted to him. And the more she got to know him as a friend, the more she liked him and the more she fantasized about him.

She realized he was watching her, waiting for a response, and went with a tease to try to distract herself from her sexy thoughts. "We're friends, and I like our friendship. Besides, you're too good-looking to get a complex. And if we don't go soon, I might change my mind, but this isn't a date."

He grabbed his toolbox. "You're feisty when you're turning a guy down."

Blue's truck was so high off the ground Lizzie practically needed a stepladder to get in. As she gripped the cold metal doorframe, his hands landed on her hips from behind, and he lifted all five feet of her into the passenger seat.

"I'm glad my truck is so big," he said as she tried not to

think about how strong his grip was and how good his hands felt.

He turned on the radio and sang off-key on the way to the hardware store, which made Lizzie laugh and want to join in. He knew just how to put her at ease *and* just how to make her quiver. Another tantalizing and dangerous combination to contend with.

Inside the hardware store, despite a hand on her lower back that nearly burned her skin as they paid for the purchase, Blue didn't flirt with her as he had at the house. Lizzie wasn't sure if she was disappointed or relieved.

"Have you eaten dinner?" Blue asked as they drove toward the beach.

"No, but I'm okay." She hadn't eaten since that morning because the shop had been so busy, but she didn't want to make Blue late to the bonfire—and she was aware of needing to get home and edit her webcast.

An easy smile spread across his face as he watched the road, and she realized that this was the first time she'd really been alone with Blue. They'd gone out with their friends as a group, and he'd fixed broken pipes and built a few cabinets for her at the flower shop, and of course she saw him at her house after work sometimes when he was working on her kitchen, but she'd never been alone with him in a social situation. Being with Blue was comfortable and fun—except for the undercurrent of heat simmering between them, which made it hard for her to concentrate.

"Let's grab a quick bite before going to the bonfire." He turned into the parking lot of PJ's Restaurant, which had both a walk-up window and a dining room, and came around to help her from the truck. He reached his hands up and gripped her hips without saying a word.

The second his hands touched her, his eyes darkened. She liked the sensual look in his eyes and the feel of his hands on her hips way too much and forced herself to take a step away. She was so full of desire, she was sure he could taste it in the air between them.

The line for the dining room went out the door, and the picnic tables on the patio were full. With a hand at her back again, Blue led her to the walk-up windows. Lizzie wasn't as surprised by the heat of his touch this time, but she was confused by how much she liked it and by the possessiveness of it, the way it seemed natural for him to do it.

"What's your pleasure?" Blue asked.

"That's a dangerous question for a guy like you to ask."

He laughed. "A guy like me? What does that mean?"

"You ask me out, then you asked me what my pleasure is? What's a girl supposed to think?" Lizzie hadn't been out on a date in a very long time, and even though this wasn't a date, it was a lot more fun than editing her webcast, doing inventory at the shop, or planning her next recipe for the *Naked Baker*.

"You're supposed to think...Hm, which would I rather have? A lobster roll and fries or a hamburger?" He bumped her with his shoulder, and she keeled to the left.

"Whoa." He caught her with an arm around her waist and a killer smile that made her want to forget about the *Naked Baker* altogether and start working on her Naughty-Love list—a list she'd started in college when she was still trying to repress her naughtier thoughts. She'd been so used to fighting her changing hormones in high school, trying to stick to her rigid upbringing, that by the time she got to college she was near ready to burst. Instead of acting on the thoughts that came to her, she'd started her Naughty-Love list—all the things she'd like to lick off of a man and have him lick off of her—and her Naughty-Places list—the list of all the places she wanted to make love to a man. Somehow, getting those lusty thoughts down on paper gave her hope that one day she'd meet the right person, and then it would be okay for her to act on those desires. But she'd never met any man she wanted to explore with. Blue was an insanely tempting option.

Oh great. Now I'm thinking about licking you.

"Sorry about that," Blue said. "I forget how petite you are."

"It's okay." She shoved her hands in her shorts to keep from hanging on to him.

"So, what'll it be?" Blue asked.

Whipped cream and strawberries all over your abs. Holy cow. In a matter of minutes she'd turned into some sort of sexual deviant. She shook her head to clear the lust from her deranged brain.

"You choose," she finally managed.

Blue ordered two lobster rolls and fries, and they took them back to his truck.

"Let's eat at the beach," he said as he helped her in again.

She wondered if she could just spend all night getting in and out of his truck, because it felt so good when he held her.

They drove down the narrow road toward Cahoon Hollow Beach with the bag of food sitting between them. It smelled like heaven, and when Lizzie's stomach growled—*roared*—she wanted to curl up from embarrassment.

"Ah, you're a normal person after all." He smiled as he dug into the bag with one hand, withdrew a fry, and held it in front of her mouth. "Open up."

"I can wait," she lied, wanting to rip the delicious-smelling fry from his hand.

"How can you resist the smell of PJ's fries?" He waved it under her nose, and when she reached for it, he pulled it away. "Uh-uh. Open your *mouth*."

"Geez, you're a pain."

"The best kind of pain there is," he teased as he fed her the fry.

Chapter Three

THIS MIGHT NOT be a date, but this was the first time Blue had been alone with Lizzie since they met, and he wasn't in a hurry to share her with Hunter and their friends. He parked at the edge of the parking lot and circled the truck to open her door. Just getting in and out of the truck proved both entertaining and enjoyable. He loved the feel of Lizzie's sweet curves beneath his palms and couldn't resist helping her down by lifting her from the waist. Her heated stare was either a warning or an invitation, and for the first time in his life, he couldn't tell which. She definitely had a way of fogging his brain.

He grabbed the food from the cab of the truck and blankets from behind the front seat and carried them around to the back, where he opened the tailgate and reached for Lizzie's waist again to lift her up.

"We're eating in the bed of your truck?"

He lifted her easily and climbed in behind her. Gently turning her shoulders so she was facing the ocean, he said, "Look. This is why we're eating here."

The moon was almost full, glowing orange and yellow against the gunmetal sky, casting a streak of light across the dark water. A single light illuminated the tip of a sail as a boat moved past the shore, and on the beach, two bonfires cut through the night.

"It's gorgeous," she said just above a whisper.

He lifted her chin and gazed into her hazel eyes. "I'm not a bad guy, Lizzie. I'm not sure why you're dead set against dating me, but if you give us a try, you might enjoy spending time together."

He moved away from her to spread out the blankets and to keep from doing something or saying something he shouldn't. He'd wanted to get closer to Lizzie from the first moment he'd set eyes on her as she hustled around the beach preparing for their friends' wedding. Even when Bradley Cooper showed up at the wedding, she didn't falter for a moment. She had insurmountable grace, and there was something about the way she moved, with confidence and focus, that had sucked him right in, and it had only gotten more powerful every time he saw her.

She stood with her back to him, her arms wrapped around her middle as she ran her hands over her arms. Not only did she have grace and class, but there was no denying that she had a great butt, shapely legs, lean shoulders, and—*heck*, everything about Lizzie was exquisite.

He spread the blankets out in the bed of the truck and no-ticed she was trembling. He wanted desperately to tuck her against him to keep her warm, but he didn't want to chance moving too quickly and scaring her off. After all, this *wasn't* a date. Blue jumped from the bed of the truck and grabbed one of his zip-up sweatshirts from the cab, then climbed back in and draped it over her shoulders.

"Thank you," she said, turning to face him as he helped her slip her arms in.

He rolled up the sleeves four times, and she looked crazy cute. Curbing the urge to pull her into his arms and kiss her smiling lips was torture.

"You didn't have to go to all this trouble," she said as she sank down to the blanket to eat.

"Lizzie, seriously. How long have you lived here?" He handed her a lobster roll.

"I grew up here." She took a bite of the sandwich, her eyes quizzical.

"Then you know that eating dinner at the beach is never trouble. Toss a blanket in the truck, grab a sweatshirt, and you're good." He leaned in closer and said, "And if you're lucky enough to bring the prettiest girl on the Cape with you, then you're way better than good."

Lizzie smiled and her shoulders relaxed. "You do know how to flatter a girl. Blue, can I ask you something?"

"Of course."

"You were friends with Sky for years and you guys never took it further, or at least according to Sky you guys never did. She's beautiful, smart, funny." Her eyes rolled over his face, as if she were searching for an answer. "Why didn't you two ever date? And why do you want to date me so badly?"

Their friends often wondered why he and Sky had never dated when they were close enough to spend the night on each other's couch and before Sky met her fiancé, Sawyer, they'd hung out more often than he hung out with his guy friends. He didn't understand it very well himself, and he wasn't sure his answer would make any sense, but he had only one thing to offer Lizzie—the truth.

"That's like asking why someone likes chocolate ice cream but doesn't like vanilla. I'm not sure of the exact reasons, but from the moment Sky and I met, we were friends." He shrugged, because to him, it was that simple. "Sky is all those things you said, and she has been my best friend for a few years, but for whatever reason, I was never attracted to her in that way."

He touched Lizzie's hand, and when she didn't pull away, he held it. "Unlike what I've felt since the moment I saw you. I was, and am, attracted to everything about you. Not just your looks, Lizzie, although you're off-the-charts sexy and more beautiful than any woman I've ever seen."

She blushed, and it made his chest go warm.

"It's you, Lizzie. All of you. The way you were so focused and organized at the wedding. And when I come into the shop, you're always trying to tend to everyone so no one is left out. You watch over Maddy with a fierceness that belies your sweet personality. And the way you move like you have no idea you're the cutest girl on the planet—"

"Oh my gosh." She covered her face with her free hand. "Laying it on thick, aren't you?"

He pulled her hand away from her face and held it, too. Her hands were delicate and soft, and they fit perfectly in his, as he'd known they would.

"No," he said, holding her gaze. "I'm laying it on truthful-ly."

THE HONESTY IN Blue's eyes was captivating. How could he see so much in her? Then again, hadn't she seen as much in him from the first time she'd laid eyes on him? He'd been the most handsome man at the wedding, and she'd seen him eyeing her—felt the heat of his stare, the sultry effects of his smile. That's when she'd known she had to keep her distance. And since then, every time they were together she played a mantra in her head, reminding herself of her secret life and how much she didn't want to try to explain it to anyone. Certainly not to a man like Blue, who could have his pick of any woman around. He'd definitely want to steer clear of a woman who secretly played the Naked Baker in her basement.

The thought of him finding out made her feel a little queasy.

They finished eating in silence, the weight of Blue's confession hanging between them and somehow drawing them closer, then went down to the beach to join the others at the bonfire. Lizzie hadn't realized how many people would be there. She was surprised to see Sky. Sky owned the tattoo shop next to P-town Petals, and they usually saw each other for at least a few minutes each day, but today Lizzie had been too busy to stop by. Sawyer was playing the guitar, while Sky talked with her older brothers Hunter and Grayson.

Sky noticed Lizzie and squealed as she dashed across the sand and threw her arms around her. "I'm so glad you're here! Hunter called me an hour ago and said he was having a bonfire. I tried calling you, but you didn't answer."

"I must not have heard my phone. We were out buying something to fix my oven." Lizzie watched Blue spread out a blanket for them to sit on, still thinking of what he'd said in the truck. He'd opened right up to her, like he'd been thinking about all the things he'd said for a long time.

Sky lowered her voice. "And you're with *Blue*." She raised her brows as she zipped her hoodie. A breeze swept up from the ocean, sending Sky's long white skirt flying around her legs.

"It's not a date, Sky," Blue said flatly as he sank to the blanket and patted the spot beside him for Lizzie to join him.

Sky leaned down and hugged Blue as Lizzie sat beside him. "You're a buzzkill. This *should* be a date."

When he shrugged, Lizzie wondered why he didn't tell Sky that she was the one who wouldn't allow it to be called a date. She hadn't told Sky about Blue asking her out over the last few months because she didn't want to explain her reason for not going—or be pressured into accepting. As it was, at least once a week Sky urged her to go out with him. She could only imagine what she'd do if she knew he'd asked her out. She didn't keep much from Sky, just this and the *Naked Baker*. She didn't even want to think about what Sky would think of *that* little endeavor.

"I wondered if you'd changed your mind about the bonfire," Hunter said, tossing a drink to each of them.

"Nah. We just had to buy a heating element," Blue explained. Lizzie found it interesting that he wasn't pressuring her or flirting with her in front of their friends, and she wondered why. "Sawyer, that song is great. Is that a new one?"

Sawyer set his guitar down and pulled Sky onto his lap. "I wrote it last weekend, for Sky." He gathered her hair over one shoulder and kissed her cheek. Sawyer had retired from professional boxing and worked as a trainer, and songwriting was a hobby of his. He and his father, a published poet who had Parkinson's disease, had recently collaborated on a book of poetry.

Lizzie tried not to feel envious of their relationship, but there was no denying the longing she felt. She'd never imagined that by twenty-six years old she wouldn't have had a serious boyfriend. Then again, she'd never thought she'd be prancing around naked beneath an apron to pay for Maddy's education, either. Life had a way of throwing curveballs, and she was good at batting them out of the park, but that didn't mean that at a moment like this the tweak on her heartstrings didn't make her wish for more.

"Blue, when's Jeremy's wedding?" Sky asked.

"On the sixteenth." Blue smirked at Sawyer. "Thanks to you, I have no date. I'll be going to the Big Apple alone and will have to fend off women left and right."

Sawyer nuzzled closer to Sky. "She can go to the wedding with you. I'm marrying her, not putting her in jail."

"Like I'd take your fiancée away for a weekend so I don't have to go alone?" Blue shook his head. "I'm not that lame."

"Take Lizzie!" Sky's eyes widened with excitement, and Lizzie's heart nearly stopped.

The hopeful look in Blue's eyes tugged at the part of her that wished she didn't have the commitments of her webcast. A weekend in New York City with Blue sounded like the best escape ever.

"I have the flower shop to run." *And a* Naked Baker *webcast to film.*

"The wedding is on a weekend," Sky pushed. "I'll watch your shop for you."

Will you do the Naked Baker *program, too?*

Her show had picked up so much momentum that she couldn't even skip an episode. Doing so caused views and income to drop dramatically. How nice would it be to hand over the program to someone else and enjoy life without the embarrassment and constant commitment of it hanging over her head?

Pipe dreams.

She needed the money for Maddy, and she'd do the program for as long as it took. With every show she held out hope that it would be the big one. The one that earned her enough money that she could quit hosting it altogether. Her schedule was exhausting: She taped shows on Mondays and Thursdays and edited them on Tuesdays and Fridays. The show aired on Wednesdays and Saturdays, which meant watching the first few minutes to make sure there were no technical glitches, and that left Sunday as her only day off—and that was only if the programs didn't need refilming.

"I can't really afford to take off Friday or Saturday, and leaving you to watch my shop will cut into your income from your business." Lizzie felt Blue's hand brush over hers on the blanket. The hope in his eyes turned to understanding.

"It's okay, Lizzie. Sky's just being pushy." He glared at Sky. "I don't actually need someone with me. It'll be nice to focus on my family."

"I love your family," Sky said.

"Speaking of family," Lizzie said. "I just remembered that I have to pick up Maddy next weekend to have dinner with my parents." Maddy went to college in Harborside, about an hour away from the Cape.

"How are your parents?" Sky asked with a teasing smile.

Margaret and Vernon Barber had been stable forces throughout Lizzie's life. Her mother was sweet and never pried too deeply, and her father was a big man, weighed down with a strict set of morals.

"As proper as always," Lizzie answered. Every time she saw her family she worried that they'd find out about her webcast—and she knew her parents would not react well. The word *disown* came to mind, and that was not something Lizzie wanted to think about.

"You say that like it's a bad thing." Blue touched her hand again, and her insides warmed.

Blue was so attuned to her, to everything she said, and every time they were close sparks flew. She tried not to think about those things as she answered. "It's not a *bad* thing, just something I'm very aware of. My parents never let me or Maddy date, even in high school. They monitored what we wore—'Button up, girls; don't want to give anyone a show.'" She cringed at the memory. The Naughty-Love list had opened a door for Lizzie. When her father had taken ill and a friend had mentioned making money off of webcasts, she'd immediately nixed the idea. But later that evening, when she was adding to her secret Naughty-Love list, she realized that maybe she could help raise money for her education after all—with a secret webcast. It was a far cry from her upbringing, but it was also an outlet for a side of her she wasn't comfortable publicly playing with. And as the money came in, Lizzie became more and more embarrassed about what she was doing, and she feared her parents and friends finding out. But just when she was ready to give up the program, they'd needed money for Maddy's education. There was no way she could walk away from it then. She'd do anything for Maddy, even if it meant putting her own relationships at risk.

"I love my folks. I've just got a lot on my mind." She rose to her feet, feeling antsy thinking about her parents and the *Naked Baker*.

"Worried about your oven?" Blue asked as he rose beside her.

Not for the first time, she wished she had someone to confide in about her double life, but deep down she was so embarrassed by what she was doing that every time she thought about even confiding in Sky, she couldn't bring herself to do it.

She shrugged.

"I have an idea." Blue picked up the blanket and shook it off. "Hey, guys. I know we just got here, but we're going to go for a walk before we need to get back to fix Lizzie's oven."

A walk?

"Go. Have fun." Sky shooed them with way too much enthusiasm. "I'll see you tomorrow, Lizzie."

"Sounds good," Lizzie managed, trying not to think about taking a walk with Blue, or the way his hand had already taken up residence on her lower back again. She'd spent so many months avoiding a date with him, and in one night she'd already spent more time alone with him than she had in the last year. And to her surprise, she liked the fluttering in her stomach and the anticipation that was tickling up her spine.

Chapter Four

AS THEY WALKED away from the warmth of the bonfire, a breeze blew off the water, bringing with it the scents of the sea. Lizzie's brows furrowed, and Blue knew he was pushing her a little harder toward being alone with him than he'd planned, but she'd looked like her mind was going a million miles an hour. He knew her nature was to handle sixteen things at once, but even the Energizer Bunny needed a break sometimes.

"So, you grew up in a conservative home?" he asked to break the ice, loving the fact that she hadn't tried to shake off his touch yet.

"You could say that. How about you? I've met a few of your brothers, and they don't seem very conservative, but..." She obviously didn't want to talk about her childhood. Lizzie looked down at the waves crashing along the shore, and the moonlight caught her profile, highlighting her slightly upturned nose, her high cheekbones, and her incredibly distracting, kissable lips.

Blue took a moment to regain his focus before answering. "My father had strong beliefs about family loyalty and work ethics. He drove home the idea of what a man should be with each of us, and I think he forgot that my sister, Trish, was a girl, because he expected the same tough standards from her as the rest of us. That's probably how she's gotten so far in her acting career—on sheer will and wanting to be better than everyone else."

"I knew she was an actress, but when you say better than everyone else, do you mean stuck-up?"

Blue laughed. "No. My sister is anything but stuck-up. She's very competitive. Even growing up she tried to keep up with me and our four brothers, and we're a tough group. We were always roughhousing and racing around."

"It sounds like you had a lot of fun with your siblings. What do your parents do?" Lizzie stopped walking and gazed out over the water.

"My father is one of the founders of East Coast Search and Rescue." Blue had always been proud of his father and of the way he'd been raised. "I think it's safe to say that he has a no-bull policy on all things, ranging from taking responsibility to how we treat others. My mother was a little looser with us. She was a stay-at-home mom, and she was always baking and tinkering around with our school projects, building forts out of sheets with us. That kind of thing."

"That sounds wonderful. My mom isn't like that at all. She loves us, but she wasn't a sit-down-on-the-floor-with-your-kids type of mom. I'm going to be, though. I'm going to be the type of mom who bakes and makes forts for sure. I want my kids to smile every time they think of me."

"Don't you smile when you think of your mom?" Blue watched her eyes drop to the sand again, and his chest burned. He would do anything to give her a reason to smile. He wanted to fold her in his arms until she smiled again, go back in time and give her the childhood she wished she'd had. But he was thankful that she was here, taking a walk alone with him on the beautiful beach in the moonlight. He didn't want her to feel pressured for more, so he held back.

He'd been careful not to give any indication of his feelings toward Lizzie to their friends. She'd turned him down enough times that he didn't want to embarrass her, even though it had been torture fighting his desire to reach out and pull her into his lap, as Sawyer had with Sky. When Lizzie had first turned him down for a date, he'd purposely not told Sky he'd asked her out. What guy likes to admit defeat? The last thing he needed was Sky putting pressure on Lizzie to go out with him. He knew in his heart that if Lizzie ever came around and went out on a real date with him, she'd fall for him on her own, the same way he'd been falling for her all along.

"Sometimes," Lizzie answered, bringing his mind back to the moment. "But more often I worry about what she'd think of me if she knew who I really was." As if she caught herself saying something she shouldn't, she quickly added, "I mean, look how short my shorts are. She would totally think that's slutty."

"Slutty has more to do with attitude than clothing, and you're too beautiful a person inside to ever look slutty."

She shivered as a breeze swept off the water. The Cape was always cool at night, and the sea breeze made it that much colder. He'd like to have her in his lap now and to drape the blanket over her legs. He should have suggested that she change out of her skimpy shorts before going to the bonfire, but he hadn't been able to think past his shock of her agreeing to go with him. Blue draped the blanket over her shoulders and placed an arm around her to hold it in place, hoping the way it hung to the back of her knees would keep her warm. She turned to face him, no longer shivering.

"Thank you," she said softly. Her lips always seemed to be

smiling, but now they were slightly parted, and she was looking at him like she was trying to decide if she should lean in a little closer, the same way he was trying to decide if he should take the initiative and press his lips to hers.

"Lizzie." Her name came out as a whisper, surprising him, but standing there beneath the stars, with moonlight dancing on the water and Lizzie's sweet perfume surrounding them, there was nothing he could do to rein in the emotions he'd been trying to temper for more than a year. Being in a group made it easier to distract himself from all the ways he was drawn to her, but now, as Lizzie's hair blew across her cheek, he couldn't resist tucking the wayward strands behind her ear. She had the silkiest, shiniest hair, and he'd dreamed of tangling his fingers in it as he ravaged her mouth and kissed her breathless. That simple touch, the brushing of his fingers over her skin, heightened the desire that rushed through him.

She licked her lips, and it felt like an invitation, but Blue didn't want to mess this up. He fought to shift his brain off of the fast track to her lips and focus on something else. Anything else.

He reached for the two sides of the blanket and placed them in her hand. "Here. This will keep the wind off your back."

She watched him tuck the blanket into her hands, confusion riddling her brow and desire lingering in her eyes. "Okay. Thank you."

They started walking down the beach again, and he knew he was on his last shred of self-control. "We should probably head back to your place and fix your oven before"—*I take you in my arms and kiss you*—"it gets too late."

"Right."

Way to go, jackass. Now things are even more confusing.

By the time they made their way back down the beach, their friends were gone and the fire was out. Blue hadn't realized how long they'd been walking. On the way back to Lizzie's house, Blue silently cursed himself. He was a fool for not backing off before they got that close—and an even worse fool for not kissing her when he'd had the chance, but she'd made it clear that she didn't want to date him, which meant he had to have misread her signals.

Back at her house, he followed her down to the basement and knelt beside the oven to fish through his tools. Lizzie leaned against the counter, looking sexy in those skimpy white shorts and fidgeting with the edge of his sweatshirt, which she still wore. She smiled, and he rose to talk to her. *Well, that didn't help.* She was only a few inches away, and when she lifted her eyes to look at him, he swore they darkened seductively. As if his legs had minds of their own, he stepped closer. The air between them thickened with desire, and he couldn't resist caressing her cheek.

"I've been wanting to do that for so long." Was there truth serum in the drink Hunter had given him? What the devil was he doing?

"Blue..."

It wasn't a warning, and he was pretty sure she wasn't telling him to stop, but he needed to be sure.

"I can't help it, Lizzie. This is the closest you've let me get to you since we met. I won't take it further. I just..." *Want to kiss you.*

"I'm not good for you," she said so softly he almost didn't hear her.

He searched her eyes, but she wasn't giving anything away. "What does that mean?"

She held his gaze. "It means that we shouldn't get close."

"Lizzie—"

She pressed her finger to his lips. "This isn't easy for me. I had a nice time with you tonight. It was wonderful to spend an evening out and to get to know you better and to...*feel* so much."

He heard a *but* coming and was terrified of losing their connection. He slid his hand to the nape of her neck and stepped in closer. "I don't understand."

She dropped her eyes and closed them for a breath, and when she opened them, she said, "I'm sorry."

"You don't feel what I feel? Like there's a force pulling us together?"

"I feel..." She swallowed hard, as if she could swallow whatever it was that she felt. "I feel like if you kiss me, I'm going to tumble into you."

Thank my lucky stars for little favors. He couldn't suppress his smile.

"And...?"

She trapped her lower lip between her teeth. "And that's not good. For you. Trust me. I'll only let you down."

"Lizzie Barber, you are a smart, beautiful woman, but please let me be the judge of that."

LIZZIE WAS TRYING, *really* trying, to resist pressing her lips to Blue's, but the powers that be must have had it out for her. Maybe it was for keeping a secret from her family or living a double life, but she was sure this was some sort of test of strength. Blue smelled musky and earthy, and his hand was hot on her neck. He was thick and powerful, but his touch was gentle and somehow possessive at once. The feel of his calloused hand made her want to experience his touch all over. She wanted to know how his mouth tasted and if his kisses would be hard or soft, if he explored with his tongue or claimed and demanded. She wanted to go through every item on her Naughty-Love list and maybe even delve into her Naughty-Places list. She'd never met a man who made her want to be wholesome and dirty at once, but she could see it in Blue's eyes, the gentleman and the bad boy. It was a tempting combination, one she wasn't sure she could resist for long. But she owed it to him to try.

He'd asked her out for a year. *A year.* What kind of guy pursues a woman for a year?

What kind of woman turns down someone as wonderful as Blue?

"Blue—"

Before she could say another word, he pressed his lips to hers. Her mind went numb, and her legs followed. She clutched at his shirt for support as he slicked his tongue over her lower lip, teasing her there before dipping inside and stroking over her tongue. Blue didn't hurry the kiss. He deepened it, lingering over every surface of her mouth as if he were savoring every second of the hottest, most passionate kiss he'd ever experienced, the same way she was. It had been a long time since she'd kissed a man, but she couldn't remember ever feeling like this. Her entire body was aflame, and what the heck was her leg doing? Sliding up his thigh? Her hips pressed into his, and— *holy Moses*—he groaned. Groaned! Like, *Give. Me. More.* She clutched at his shoulders, but that wasn't nearly enough. As her chest tried to become one with his, her greedy fingers fisted in his hair and took the kiss deeper, but it still wasn't enough.

Her cell phone vibrated, and her fuzzy brain reluctantly began to come back into focus. He had one hand splayed across her back, the other tangled in her hair, and his talented mouth was doing everything it could to deaden her brain cells one by one.

Yes. Please!

Her phone vibrated again, and then the world spun away. She heard a moan and realized it came from her own lungs. She had no business leading him on. Lizzie tried to force herself to pull away, but it proved too difficult. His kisses were all consuming. She wanted to stay right there in his arms, with his mouth crushed to hers and his heart pounding so hard against her that it felt like it had climbed into her body.

They shouldn't do this. It couldn't go anywhere. He would never want a girlfriend who was the Naked Baker, and she couldn't give that up until Maddy had her degree. Reality refused to be shoved aside. Reality sucked. She pressed her hand firmly to his chest, forcibly pushing him away as she gulped in air. He blinked several times without saying a word, and she gripped his shirt in fisted hands.

"Say something," she pleaded. *Oh no, what have we done?* Their friendship was at stake, and the longer he remained silent, the worse she felt. "Blue!" She didn't mean to raise her voice, but she was mad at herself for giving in to her desires—and equally as angry at herself for pulling away and making them stop.

He shook his head and narrowed his eyes, as if she were just coming back into focus.

"Sorry. I'm sorry. I thought..." He scrubbed a hand down his face and took a step back, but she was still clutching his shirt. He covered her hands with one of his and smiled.

"We can't do this," she managed in a thin voice she didn't recognize.

"Why?" He stepped closer again, and she pressed back against the counter, afraid if she didn't, she'd kiss him again.

"Because."

"That's not an answer," he whispered as he slid a hand down her side to her waist, leaving a trail of renewed heat.

"I can't," she said, despite the voice in her head telling her to shut up. "My life is crazy."

"So is mine."

"It's complicated." It was a lame excuse, but the best she could muster while still reeling from their kiss.

"We'll figure it out." His face was serious, his voice earnest, and his hand on her waist was sending little shock waves of desire zinging through her. "Lizzie, I've wanted to go out with you for a year. How can you say no after that kiss? I know you felt the same fury of emotions that I did. I could feel it in the way you kissed me."

Fury of emotions? She'd never felt such fierce desire, been so completely lost in a man. She pried his fingers from her waist and forced the words from her lungs. "We should fix the oven."

"There's a reason I didn't stop asking you out." His tone was gentle, but his words were confident. "I knew we should be together, and after that kiss, I'm sure of it. I'm not walking away from you, Lizzie."

"I'm not asking you to walk away. Just…We can't do *that*."

His brows furrowed. "So, you aren't asking me to walk away? You'll go out with me again?"

"This wasn't a date." *I'm so messed up.* Fantasizing was totally not going to cut it after *that* kiss.

"Right." He smiled. "Go out with me tomorrow."

"Blue…"

He took a step back and held his palms up in surrender. She instantly missed the heat of them on her skin.

"As friends," he said. "Go out with me tomorrow as friends."

She still had to edit her webcast. She should have had it done already, but she'd wasted all evening. *No, I didn't waste a second of it.* She'd be up all night editing, and then she'd be exhausted Saturday. She definitely should not agree to go out with Blue.

She shouldn't say yes. She shouldn't smile. Why was she smiling? Why was she touching his arm? *Geez!* What was wrong with her? She tried to pull her hand away from his muscular forearm, but his skin was warm, his muscles hard, and his seductive eyes were stealing her ability to think straight again.

Oh, the heck with it. One more outing. As friends. She could do this, couldn't she?

"Okay."

Chapter Five

BLUE PACED THE bedroom on the second floor of his cottage on the bluff with his cell phone pressed to his ear and a grimace on his face as he listened to Duke complain about Trish's newest role. It was late Saturday afternoon, and he'd already finished laying the hardwood floors in the bedrooms. He should be exhausted after staying at Lizzie's to fix her oven until nearly one o'clock in the morning, then getting up to work at the crack of dawn. But he wasn't exhausted; he was invigorated.

"I just don't see what the issue is," Blue said as he walked down the stairs. "She's an actress, Duke. What do you want her to do? Turn down the most lucrative roles?"

"Hold on a sec, B." Blue's siblings had called him B for as long as he could remember.

While he waited for Duke to return to the line, Blue went into the kitchen and admired the cabinetry he'd built, and his mind drifted back to Lizzie and the kiss they'd shared. Even though he was no longer into meaningless hookups, he'd had his fair share of women over the years. Blue adored the intimacy of kissing. He loved the closeness, the feel of a woman's breathing going shallow, the pressure of her lips on his, the urgency or languid enjoyment of the kiss. From a single kiss he could tell how deep their connection would go. There were surface kisses—the kind that he doled out to end a date when there wouldn't be another. Then there were hurried, urgent kisses as a precursor to sex. Hot, steamy, let-me-take-you kisses. He loved those. But the most glorious kiss of all was the very first one. The kiss where both people were testing the waters, feeling for their bodily reactions and sensing those of their partner. Waiting to see if the first few seconds of coming together had the ability to obliterate everything else in the world. Twenty-four hours ago Blue would have sworn that his first kiss with Sarah Jane had been the most intense kiss of his life, but after kissing Lizzie, he realized that every other kiss, every other woman, paled in comparison.

"I'm back. Sorry, dude." Duke's voice brought Blue back to their conversation.

Blue pictured his brother running a hand through his thick hair. It was a mannerism all of the Ryder men shared. A frustrated hair rake they'd picked up from their father.

"No worries. Look, Duke, all I was saying about Trish is that she's an adult. She's in a competitive field. She's going to take the best roles that come to her. She's not a teenager anymore. You can't control what she does."

Duke laughed. "No one could *ever* control Trish. You know that. I just don't want her to be known forever as that actress who played a role the equivalent of that girl in *Fifty Shades of Grey*."

Blue walked outside. "Well, get over it. She's secure in who she is, and things change quickly in Hollywood. A year from now no one will even remember this role."

"Maybe you're right. Hey, have you heard from Jake? He

left two days ago for that plane crash out in Colorado, and I haven't heard from him since. I'm getting worried." Jake was their youngest sibling. He'd followed in their father's footsteps as a search and rescue professional and traveled often. He always kept in close contact with family, and with Duke in particular. As the eldest, Duke tended to keep closer track of his siblings than the rest of them did, though they were all close.

"No, but they're still dealing with the aftermath out that way. He'll get in touch when he can." Blue made a mental note to text Jake after they got off the phone. He stood back and admired the cottage. "You should see the cottage. Man, does it look great."

"I can't wait to see it. Did you decide what you're going to do with the lighthouse?"

"Not yet. One thing at a time."

"One thing at a time?" Duke laughed. "B, you've been talking about the lighthouse since the day you first saw it. Why the sudden halt?"

"I've got something else on my mind right now. Guess who I have a date with tonight?" Blue grinned just thinking about Lizzie. He and Duke had both spotted Lizzie at the same time at the wedding. All of the Ryder men were six three or six four and blessed with athletic builds and smart minds. Blue had to admit that when they'd first met Lizzie, he'd felt a stroke of competition with his older, very successful brother. And it felt awesome to come out on top.

"No kidding? Lizzie finally agreed to go out with you?"

"Yes, although she's not calling it a date. I hope to change her mind on that point, though."

"You've been courting her for a year. I haven't heard you sound so sure about a woman since *you know who*."

Blue's family had the decency not to speak of Sarah Jane often, and when they did, it was rarely by name, which he appreciated. "I know. Let's not bring her up, okay?"

"That was more than a decade ago. That woman's probably got five kids by five different guys and boobs that sag to the ground by now."

"Duke." Blue winced. "No need to slam her like that."

"You really did get Mom's genes, didn't you? I'm telling you, you should have slept with every one of her friends back then. It would have made you feel a heck of a lot better."

Blue had never been a vengeful person. He'd walked out of Sarah Jane's apartment without a word after catching her with that jerk, and he'd never looked back or taken revenge.

He and Duke talked for a few more minutes, and when they ended the call, Blue sent a text to Jake, trying to elicit at least a smart-alec response.

Dude, you still alive?

Knowing Jake, he was probably holed up in a hotel room with a woman—his form of stress relief.

Blue locked up the cottage and headed back to his house, thinking about Lizzie and how glad he was that she'd agreed to go out with him again. He'd tried to distract himself from thinking about her too much today, which was why he'd worked at his cottage instead of on her kitchen, but with every board he'd installed, the hope that she'd want to go on another date, and another, and another, grew. Now he couldn't shake the mounting desire that she'd want even more than that. When it came to sweet and sultry Lizzie Barber, one kiss was definitely not enough.

LIZZIE LOVED EVERYTHING about owning her own flower shop, from meeting new people every day to being surrounded by the scents of nature and the glorious colors of the plants and flowers. But by far, the best thing about owning P-town Petals was the location. Provincetown was an eclectic town that was home to about three thousand people in the off-season and nearly burst at the seams with upward of fifty thousand tourists over the summers, and it had always been Lizzie's favorite place on earth. Provincetown was known for its harbor and beaches and the extensive diversity of artists and the community. Excitement vibrated through the town each week with an onslaught of tourists and a variety of shows and street entertainers. Even now, in October, there were still a large number of tourists. But Lizzie knew that in another month, the streets would be nearly empty and the buzz of excitement that made the town come alive would be tamped down to the gentle hum of residents reclaiming their quiet streets.

Lizzie rang up a bouquet of flowers for a customer and walked him out. "Thanks for coming in." She inhaled the cool afternoon air, admiring Sky's tattoo shop next door. Sky had recently renovated Inky Skies and painted the outside bright yellow. It fit in well with the other vibrant shops on Commercial Street, like the graffiti-covered Shop Therapy and bright orange sweets shop down the street. Lizzie's shop was painted pale blue with flowers and greenery winding around the columns.

She waved to Sky through the open door. Her friend was absolutely beaming as she came outside wearing one of her long skirts and a soft purple sweater. Her dark hair was piled on top of her head in a messy bun, with long tendrils framing her face. But it was the mischievous look in her eyes that had Lizzie also grinning like a fool. She knew Sky wanted details about her evening with Blue, and just thinking about him made her insides go wild. It had been Sky's text she'd missed last night when she and Blue were making out, and when she'd finally returned it two hours later, after editing her webcast, she'd still been confused about how to handle things with Blue, and she'd been vague in her reply to Sky.

"Is your place as crazy as mine today?" Sky asked, eyeing the tourists milling about in the streets. "Don't they know it's October? I mean, I'm thankful for the business, but *sheesh*! What a busy season it's been."

"It's been insane. This is my first break, and I'm beat." She'd been on such a high after kissing Blue that working through her edits hadn't been as exhausting as normal, but then she'd lain wide-eyed in bed, her body vibrating, her mind reeling with thoughts of Blue, until she finally drifted off to sleep in the wee hours of the morning. She was surprised she had any energy at all.

"I bet you are." Sky raised her brows. "You didn't text me back until three fifteen. I guess you and Blue had a *really* good time."

Lizzie laughed. "Not that good of a time. He fixed my oven and then I just couldn't sleep."

"Fixed your oven. Seriously, Lizzie? This is me you're talking to, remember?" Sky smiled and nudged her shoulder. "Details, woman. Come on."

"I don't have details. We kissed. Once."

"One kiss? Was it that bad?" Sky's disappointment was evident in her flat tone.

"No. It was *that* good." She pulled Sky away from the busy sidewalk to the doorway of her shop and lowered her voice.

"The man kisses like it's his profession. I think he's perfected the art of seduction through one mind-blowing kiss."

"That's good, right? So why did you stop? When Sawyer and I first kissed, I could barely think, much less stop."

"Yeah, well, it definitely wasn't easy." That was putting it mildly. She'd kicked herself all night for dragging her lips away from his. She wished she had a normal life, without secrets hanging over her head, but she'd made her bed—alone, unfortunately—and now she had to sleep in it. "But Blue is your best friend. Well, he was until you met Sawyer, and we both know that he's not a player, and he'd give the shirt off his back to a stranger. He's…perfect."

"And?"

"And he doesn't need *me* complicating his life."

Sky rolled her eyes. "You're the best thing that ever happened to him. You're the total package. You're gorgeous, smart, a great big sister to Maddy. You're an amazing friend, and I'm sure you'll be an incredible girlfriend."

Lizzie smiled at a couple as they stepped inside her shop to admire the string gardens hanging in the front window. She wondered how incredible a girlfriend or friend Sky would think she was if she found out about her secret.

"I better go in and help them, but I did tell Blue I'd see him again tonight."

"Really?" Sky hugged her. "That's great. Perfect. See? Blue knows you're the best woman around. You two will be great together!"

Lizzie wasn't worried about their being great together. After last night's kiss, she knew they had amazing chemistry. It was the rest of her life colliding with his that she worried about.

She headed inside to greet the young couple that was admiring her string gardens. The woman reached up and touched the ball of moss. Her long dark hair was tied back in a low ponytail, and when she went up on her toes, the man touched her back in the same manner Blue had touched Lizzie. She had to work hard to push past the jolt of desire that ran through her at the memory of his touch.

"Those are called string gardens. Are you familiar with them?" Lizzie asked.

"No," the woman answered. "But they're really cool."

"They are cool. String gardens are essentially balls of soil held together with moss and string rather than pots. They aren't difficult to make once you understand the process, and I actually give a free class once a month. This month's class is on Wednesday evening, if you're interested." Lizzie had at least a dozen string gardens hanging from the ceiling, and not only were they a great conversation starter, but they fed right into her love of creating unique plantings. She explained the process of making a string garden to the couple, and before leaving, they bought two of her favorite plants and signed up for her class.

After they left Lizzie had an onslaught of customers. She was on her feet all day, and by the time she closed the shop, she was running late to meet Blue. She leaned her back against the door, the heaviness of fatigue suddenly settling in. She was so tired, she wouldn't have her wits about her tonight, and it had taken every bit of her strength to stop kissing Blue last night. If they kissed tonight—and boy did she hope they would—she might not be able to stop.

She had a good feeling about Blue. Being with him was not just easy, but he'd looked at her like she hung the moon over the sea when they were on their walk, and she couldn't remember the last time anyone had looked at her like that, if ever. She wanted to get closer to him, but at the same time, she knew she needed to keep her distance. Maybe she should cancel their date. *It's not a date.*

Her mind traveled back to the look in his eyes when he said he wasn't going to walk away from her, not after that kiss. *That kiss.* The kiss that left her head spinning and her excited in places she didn't know could be turned on. If he could do that with one perfect kiss, what would it be like to go further? To feel his mouth traveling down her neck as his hands caressed her bare skin? A thrill rushed through her at the thought.

She grabbed her purse and fished out her cell phone, mulling over the idea of canceling before she got in too deep. She noticed she'd missed a text from Blue, and her heart leapt despite her concerns.

Are we still on for our friendly outing tonight?

Her webcast aired tonight, and she liked to watch the first few minutes to make sure there weren't any technical issues, but she could do that on her phone in the privacy of a bathroom while they were out. She didn't *want* to cancel seeing him. In fact, the more she thought about it, the more excited she became.

She replied with a quick *yes* before she could change her mind, silently praying that there would be no technical difficulties to deal with. There rarely were, but it would be just her luck to have something go wrong this evening. She pushed away the nerve-racking thoughts and retrieved the flowers that hadn't sold, debating what she'd do with them. Lizzie didn't believe in wasting anything and gave to others as often as she could. That was why she dropped off the goodies she baked for her webcasts at the homeless shelter on the way to work the mornings after she filmed. When it came to doing something with the flowers that hadn't sold and would soon wilt, she had several options, but today was cemetery day.

Her phone vibrated with another text from Blue. *Great. Looking forward to getting to know you even better. See you in twenty mins?*

The truth was, she wanted to get to know him better, too. Her chest tightened with the reality that there was a whole side of herself that she couldn't share with him or anyone else, but just this once she wasn't going to let that stand in her way. She'd had a great time last night, and didn't she deserve just one more night out with a friend? It's not like she was going to jump in the sack with him—even though the idea had run through her mind a thousand times today.

If he really wanted to get to know her better, why not start right now? She typed in a quick response.

I'm running late. Sorry! Heading to Shore's Edge Cemetery before going home. Meet me there? She sent it off and gathered the flowers in her tote. As she walked out the door, she realized she was way too excited to be going to a cemetery—and she really needed to get her emotions in check now, because as she found out last night, getting her emotions in check around Blue was not an easy feat.

Lizzie pulled into the parking lot of the cemetery and parked beneath an umbrella of trees. She gathered the tote of flowers she'd brought, and as she stepped from her car, Blue's truck pulled into the lot. A shiver of delight ran through her as he parked and stepped from the truck with that sexy smile that made her forget to keep her distance.

"This wasn't what I imagined when I asked you out, but I'm game." He pressed a hand to the small of her back and kissed her cheek. He smelled fresh, as if he'd just showered, which made Lizzie realize that she hadn't.

She'd been so intent on getting to the cemetery—and seeing Blue—that she hadn't slowed down enough to think about proper dating etiquette.

Way to go, Lizzie.

This isn't a date.

Maybe not, but it sure felt like one.

"I can't believe you came," she said honestly.

He stepped in closer, sucking all the air from the space around her.

"You don't think I'd pass up time with you, do you?"

She inhaled a jagged breath, filling her lungs with his fresh, manly scent, and smiled, which was about all she could muster at the moment. *This* was definitely a date. She may have been able to fool her mind into accepting the offer, but her body knew the difference.

Her body craved the difference.

Her body craved Blue.

She cleared her throat and tried to shake off the craziness that was sending her thoughts into overdrive. "I'm glad you did."

"Are we visiting a particular grave?" Blue fell into step beside her, and they walked up the slight incline and across the lawn, toward the sea of headstones.

"Sort of. When I have flowers that don't sell, sometimes I bring them here and place them on the graves that go unattended." She'd never shared this with anyone before and wasn't sure how he'd respond—or why she had invited him to join her when she'd always kept this private.

He placed his hand on her back again and didn't say a word. She liked his quiet acceptance—and the feel of his hand sending heat and awareness through her like live wires.

"Some people find cemeteries scary at night, without the sunshine to give them a feeling of safety," Lizzie said as they weaved through the headstones. "But when I come here I think about all the people who are buried, and I can't help but feel like they would have wanted to be remembered."

"Everyone wants to be remembered by those they love. Which graves do you put the flowers on?"

She liked that he was interested enough to ask. "I've been coming here for years, so I've gotten to know which graves are visited and which aren't. Some people leave painted stones or letters, but some graves never have anything left on them. It can be tricky to figure out, but, for example, that one over there." She pointed to a child's headstone. "That one looks like all the others, right?"

His eyes slid over a line of headstones. "Sure."

She walked over to it and crouched. Blue crouched beside her, their thighs brushing as their eyes met and held. He was doing it again, looking at her like she was all that mattered, like she was his total focus. She forced herself to focus on the explanation, when all she really wanted to do was get lost in the depths of emotions she saw there.

"This grave gets visited every other week. Sometimes I find remnants of flowers." She pointed to the grave beside it. "But that one? I've never found anything there." She pulled a rose from the tote and laid it across the headstone. Her fingers lingered on the cool marble. "I wonder what they were like. Was this person pensive and shy or aggressive and obnoxious?"

They walked between the headstones, his hand resting on her back, and it felt natural to share her thoughts with him. "I wonder if they were loved and who they left behind."

Blue took a flower from the tote. "May I?"

She smiled and nodded.

He crouched before a headstone, his eyes running thoughtfully over the engraving. "I don't see any remnants of flowers. This is for you, Helen Craft. I hope good feelings reach you." He took Lizzie's hand in his as he rose to his feet. "I never imagined you doing this, but it doesn't surprise me."

"I'm sure I do lots of things that you never imagined I would." The way his lips tipped up told her that he thought she was implying something naughty. She loved that glint of wickedness in him, but she was too aware of her secret to let the mistaken innuendo go. "I didn't mean it that way."

"I'm sure you're full of surprises, and I can't wait to learn about each and every one of them."

Wanna bet?

THE GOLDEN GLOW of the moon cast shadows like memories across the grass, and in the distance, the Pilgrim Monument stood sentinel behind a buffer of trees. Blue had driven by this cemetery hundreds of times, but he'd never given it a thought. He watched Lizzie crouch before another grave in her jeans and P-town Petals shirt, the moonlight dancing off her thoughtful eyes as she placed a flower in front of the headstone, then rose beside him. He reached for her hand and she laced her fingers with his. This might not be a typical date, but holding Lizzie's hand, with no distractions, in such an unexpected place, seemed like a perfect evening.

"Why are you looking at me like that?" She fidgeted with the seam on her jeans.

Unlike other women, Lizzie didn't need special outfits or lots of makeup. She was a natural beauty, and after a year of wanting to be closer to her, Blue couldn't imagine being more attracted to anyone. He stepped closer and brushed his thumb over her jaw. "This is a little embarrassing. I was just admiring how beautiful you are, and how thoughtful."

Even in the moonlight he could see her cheeks flush as they began walking again.

"How often do you come here?" He wanted to get to know so much more about her, but even though she was holding his hand, he saw something in her eyes that told him she was still wary of getting too close.

"About once or twice a week. I also bring flowers to the assisted-living facility in Wellfleet, and sometimes I give them to tourists outside my shop, or I take them to the police station or the firehouse." She shrugged like it was no big deal, but Blue knew how she raced around every day at work. He'd seen her in action, and he knew how big of a heart it took to make time after a long, busy day, when she had to be tired, to do something like this.

"Oh! Come with me." Her eyes widened with excitement as she dragged him around a big tree to an old cracked headstone green with moss, and kneeled in front of it, tugging him down with her. Her smile was so bright that he was sure this was someone special's grave. "This is Henry."

"Henry?"

She traced the unreadable engraving on the headstone. "That's what I call him. I sat here one night for a long time trying to figure out his or her real name, and as you can see, you can't read a thing. But while I was sitting here, the name Henry came to me. So, this is Henry."

She took the last flower out of her tote and laid it across Henry's headstone with a sigh. Then she patted the headstone and smiled at Blue. "I'm glad you're here with me. I've never brought anyone here before." She shifted her eyes to the headstone again. "It feels good to do this, doesn't it?"

"Better than you can imagine. I'm honored that you're sharing this part of yourself with me." Blue reached for her hand again, giving it a little squeeze to underscore how grateful he was to be included. He did a lot for other people, but it was rare to know someone who did for others without expecting an acknowledgment of some kind. He had a feeling there was a lot more to Lizzie than met the eye.

They walked back toward the parking lot hand in hand, and when they reached the edge of the lawn, Lizzie stopped walking and said, "I'm glad you showed up." She smiled up at him, and like every one of her smiles, it reeled him in even more.

"I'm glad you asked." He stepped in closer.

"I'm sorry I haven't had a chance to change or shower or anything."

"Lizzie, you could be covered in mud and you'd be beautiful." He searched her eyes and saw a flicker of embarrassment. "You're beautiful, Lizzie, no matter what you wear." He brushed his fingers over her cheek and felt her skin heat up with his touch. He fought the urge to press his lips to hers but couldn't keep his emotions from coming out in words.

"I want to kiss you, but I'm so afraid of scaring you off that I'm fighting it every second." He held her gaze, not wanting to steal the kiss as he had last night. This time, he wanted her consent, needed to know she was in this, too.

"You do? You are?"

"More than you can imagine." He wrapped her in his arms,

and she gripped his shirt as she had last night. "What do you want, Lizzie? Tell me what you want."

She took tiny steps to the side, turning them as one, until Blue was standing on the low slope of the hill and they were eye to eye.

"I want you to kiss me." She pressed a hand flat on his chest, keeping his efforts at bay. "But only if you can promise me we won't go further, because I don't trust myself, and I need to know I can trust you."

His heart squeezed. Trust was everything to him. "You're very brave."

"How on earth does that make me brave?"

"And so cute with your brows all pinched together. It takes courage to admit that to a guy. What if I wasn't someone you could trust? You could be taken advantage of so easily."

She tightened her grip on his shirt, her eyes sharp and as-sessing. "But you are someone I can trust. I've known you for a year. I know the man you are, Blue, and I trust you. That's the whole point."

"And what about you, Lizzie? Are you someone I can trust?"

Warmth filled her eyes. "Are you asking if I'm going to take advantage of you?"

He'd like nothing better than that, but he kept that thought to himself. "No, I mean in general. If we were dating, could I trust you?"

Her brows knitted a little tighter, and something he couldn't read flickered in her eyes. "I'd like to think so."

He touched her hand, which was still pressed to his chest, and she opened her fingers, lacing theirs together.

"You can always trust me, Lizzie. I'll never do anything to hurt you."

She went up on her toes, and when their lips were a breath apart, she said in a tremulous whisper, "Then kiss me, Blue. Please, kiss me."

Every muscle in Blue's body flexed as he reined in the urgency mounting inside him and pressed his lips to hers with heartrending tenderness. His mouth moved over hers, devouring its softness while trying not to ravage her with the intensity thrumming through his veins. Her hand slipped from his, settling around his waist, and as he gathered her in closer and deepened the kiss, he felt her soft, pliant curves melting against him. He moaned at the sheer pleasure of their bodies coming together. He'd waited so long to kiss her, to feel her against him. And this kiss was so much more than a second kiss.

He felt her opening up to him, giving herself over to him. She had to feel the effect she had on his body, to understand how difficult it was to be this close, knowing it wouldn't go further, to taste his desire in every stroke of his tongue. She had to realize that it took every ounce of his self-control to keep his hands from roaming over her luscious curves. He was lost in his own reveries of Lizzie giving herself up to their kiss, but true to his word—he'd always remain true to his word to Lizzie—he forced himself to draw back, pressing soft kisses to her lips, before finally pulling away completely.

His heart thundered at the sight of her half-lidded eyes, her body free of tension, completely unguarded and relaxed. He needed more, if only another kiss, another taste, to be closer to the woman he'd dreamed of becoming one with for months on end. He brought a hand to the nape of her neck and pulled her closer again.

"Lizzie," he whispered against her lips, needing to know she wanted this, too. Her eyes blinked open. "Do you want me to ask every time I kiss you, or do you trust me enough to let me?"

Her dimples appeared as she said, "I trust you."

"Thank you," he murmured before recapturing her mouth, more demanding this time. He felt her entire body sink into him, and he welcomed the heat of her as their tongues found their rhythm once again. Her mouth was even sweeter, hotter this time, like she was just as lost in him as he was in her. But he'd made a promise.

"I will never get enough of kissing you," he said as they parted again.

"Yeah." Her breathy whisper brought images of her saying it while lying beneath him.

It took every bit of his self-control not to take her up by the dunes and love her until neither one of them could think.

She circled her arms around his neck and pressed her cheek to his chest, and Blue knew in that moment, with the stars shining brightly above them and the sounds of the sea in the distance, that they were meant to be together.

When she drew back with a seductive look in her eyes, it took all his willpower not to kiss her again. Instead, he brushed her hair from her shoulder, needing even that small connection, and asked, "Are you ready for our outing?"

"Um…" She smiled up at him. "How about if we call it a date?"

"A date. Really? You want to go on a date with me?" He reached for her hand as they walked down the hill toward the lot.

She pushed him playfully. "*You* want to go on a date with *me*."

He pulled her against him again and kissed her. "You're darn right I do."

They dropped Lizzie's car off at her place. Before driving away from her house, Blue reached around her and lifted her across the bench seat of his truck, casually draping one arm over her shoulder as she sat, slack-jawed, gazing up at him.

"You *moved* me."

"Aw, babe, you move me, too. Better put your seat belt on so we don't get a ticket," he said with a smile.

Lizzie put on her seat belt. "Do you do this to all your dates?"

She had no idea how special she was. He gripped the steering wheel tighter and admitted, "Actually, I've never done that before."

"You literally scooped me up and moved me." She narrowed her eyes. "It felt very practiced."

"Seriously, I've never done that before. I'm not sure why I did it, but it felt right." He started the truck, so thankful she was out with him again. "Just like this does." He slanted his mouth over hers, immediately swept up in her taste, her scent, the sexy little sigh of surrender she made as he deepened the kiss.

"Wow," she whispered. "Kissing you is a purely sensual experience."

"Well, enjoy it, because that's all you're getting. Sensual kisses, nothing more. I made a promise to someone I respect, and I don't intend to break it."

She giggled, and it was the sweetest sound on earth.

Chapter Six

BLUE PARKED IN front of the Paintery, a restaurant that doubled as an art house, occasionally hosting comedians and musicians in addition to offering painting lessons while customers dined. The building was painted graffiti style, with colorful flowers paired with dark, haunting images of animals and greenery that looked like it belonged in a tropical rainforest, making the building feel alive.

"I never would have pegged you for a Paintery guy. What a fun surprise," Lizzie said. "I've never been here."

"Neither have I, but I figured that since this wasn't supposed to be a date, we'd better go someplace that felt platonic." Blue held the door open, and as she passed through, his hand found hers again.

Sometime between Blue telling her she could trust him and their last kiss, Lizzie had gone from needing to keep distance between them to wanting to be closer and wanting to enjoy the evening as a real date. Being with Blue, kissing him, opening up to him, had reminded her what it was like to *feel*, to allow herself to get close to someone. They'd crossed the platonic line into sensual and scintillating territory, and Lizzie felt herself wanting to explore all of it, which scared her and excited her at once.

She'd kept such thick walls around herself for the past few years that even accepting this evening as a *date* was a huge deal. And, as her mind skipped off track and reminded her that her webcast began in half an hour, she reminded herself that letting down those walls was also a huge risk.

They followed the hostess past a number of round tables with easels set up on them to a booth in the back, also sporting two easels and paints facing either side of the booth.

Blue turned an assessing gaze to the table. "Well, this isn't right, is it?" He moved the easels so they were beside each other, then shifted the paints and paintbrushes to one side of the table and scooted the whole thing away from the edge, making room for them to eat and paint sitting side by side.

"Much better." He motioned to the bench. "After you."

"That doesn't look very platonic to me," she teased.

"You gave me the okay to call this a date, so I'm taking full advantage of wooing you until you take it back." He slid into the seat beside her and leaned in close. "And by the time tonight is over, you won't ever want to take it back."

"You're pretty confident." As well he should be. Blue wasn't just more handsome than any man alive, but he was also a gentleman and probably the world's best kisser.

He stretched an arm over her shoulder, opened a menu, and moved it in front of her so they could both look it over. She loved that, too.

They ordered drinks and decided to share an entrée— another bonus point for Blue. Lizzie loved sharing meals. Everything tasted better when it belonged to someone else. A few minutes later the waiter brought their drinks and took their dinner order.

Blue held up his glass in a toast. "To our first date."

They clinked glasses, and Lizzie sipped her drink, taking a moment to admire the incredibly sexy, confident man beside her. She'd worked so hard to fight her attraction to him that she'd succeeded in seeing him as *Blue Ryder, friend.* She'd put him securely in that category with a continuous mantra of all the reasons why they couldn't be more, a list that started with their friendship and ended with the *Naked Baker.* Now, as she looked at him, all she could think about was how many kisses she'd missed over the past year, how many chances to hold his hand, to see that smile when it was meant just for her—and to get to know him even better.

"So, how does this work?" she asked, eyeing the paints.

"It's a pretty hard concept. We pick up the brushes"—he handed her a paintbrush—"and then we paint."

"It's good to see that being on a date didn't dampen your ability to be a smart-alec." She smiled with the tease. "I'm a truly sucky painter."

"I somehow doubt you're a truly sucky anything." He leaned in and kissed her, and she closed her eyes, willing him to kiss her longer.

She'd known it would be like this, that it would feel right, and good, and incredibly natural to fall under Blue's spell. Just another reason she'd fought going out with him for so long. She'd known she'd never have a chance of resisting him once that door was opened. His lips lingered on hers, drawing out the kiss, so that by the time he pulled away, she was breathless for more.

He ran his fingertips through her hair and touched his forehead to hers. "I really like kissing you."

Afraid if she tried to respond she'd say something like, *Then don't stop*, she opted for silence instead.

"Do you want to join the others or do our own thing?"

Her mind was still spinning from their kiss. He must have sensed it in her silence, because he went on to explain. "When I called to make reservations, they said we could paint what the instructor is painting." He pointed at a tall guy who was walking from table to table, looking over the paintings and commenting on each one. "Or we can go totally rogue and do our own thing."

"That's what I want to do," she said, feeling silly for being so awestruck. "Our own thing."

"A woman after my own heart." He held her gaze, and when his phone vibrated with a call, it reminded her that she needed to check her webcast.

"Why don't you take that call while I run to the ladies' room, and then we can paint."

Blue slid from the booth and reached for her hand, pulling her against him. "Is it cheesy to tell you that I'll miss you while you're gone?" He cracked a smile, but she was too lost in the feel of his arms around her and the press of his muscles against her chest to care if it was cheesy.

"I kind of like cheesy."

His lips met hers in another sensual, sizzling kiss, and then he held her hand until she'd taken too many steps to keep holding it, and that fraction of a second, with his eyes on her, his fingertips grazing the tips of hers, felt like a scene from a movie, and it made Lizzie even dizzier.

She walked in a daze to the ladies' room, coming back to the present the moment the door clicked shut behind her. She pulled out her cell phone and tried to find a signal. Nearly all of the lower Cape had spotty Internet and cell service. She held the phone over her head. Still no signal. *Darn it.* She stepped from the ladies' room and into the hall, holding her phone high above her head, glad the hallway turned a corner so Blue couldn't see her. Her phone finally picked up a signal. She navigated to her *Naked Baker* site and clicked play on the newest show.

She paced the narrow hall, holding the phone over her head and praying no one came in from the dining room. Her heart hammered in her chest as she stared up at the video loading as slowly as molasses dripping from a jar, and suddenly her sexy voice filled the air.

Shootshootshoot. She pressed the volume button to mute as Blue came around the corner.

"Hey there. Everything okay?" He eyed her phone as she clicked off the video and shoved it into her back pocket.

"Yeah." *Thinkthinkthink!* "Maddy called, but I lost the signal." She hated lying at all, but lying to Blue felt like the biggest, most painful lie she'd ever told. Even worse than when she'd snuck out of her parents' house to meet a boy in high school, and that was pretty darn bad.

"Do you want to call her back? We can step outside to get a signal."

He was so thoughtful and considerate, and she was still keeping her secret. She couldn't do this to him, not when everything he did was with her best interests at heart. It wasn't fair to either of them. She'd make it through this date, and then she'd end it. She couldn't play with his trust, and she couldn't reveal the *Naked Baker* to a guy like Blue, either.

I hope you appreciate all that I do for you, Maddy.

She forced a smile, knowing Maddy appreciated everything she was ever given. Her younger sister wasn't selfish like many teens. She was considerate to a fault, which was one of the reasons Lizzie was willing to put herself out there to give her a leg up in life. It wasn't Maddy's fault their parents couldn't afford college for her, and Lizzie knew how school loans would strap her sister down after college. Thank goodness for *Cooking with Coeds*, and in turn, for the *Naked Baker*.

"No, it's okay," she answered as they walked back to the table. "Did I take that long?"

"Not that long. The waiter brought our dinner."

She *had* taken a long time. At least she'd seen and heard the very start of the webcast, which meant it was probably playing properly.

They shared their meal and drank wine while they talked. It was nice being alone with Blue, just as she'd known it would be.

"I knew you and Maddy were close, but I never realized she called you about dates and stuff. That's nice," he said.

"It is nice. We talk about everything. But you seem just as close with your siblings." He was so easy to talk to. He listened so intently to her while watching her with those piercing eyes of his, she was unable to resist falling right back into their intimacy. She speared a piece of steak with her fork and fed it to him.

"Mm. I like this arrangement." He swallowed the steak and said, "We talk about everything, too. There are lots of us, though, so we tend to be close in pairs, and those pairings vary based on what's going on in our lives." He fed her a tomato from the salad and followed the fork with a quick kiss that made it taste a million times better.

"Pairs?"

"Yeah. Like when Jake visits, we'll be close for a few weeks afterward. Then he'll get busy with his own thing, and then

Gage or Duke will have something to talk about, or an issue to work through. It sort of goes in cycles. Big family dynamics, you know."

"And what about Trish? Where does she fit in?" Lizzie knew his sister was an actress and that she was close with her family, but she hadn't met her, and she wondered what it was like growing up with so many brothers.

"Where *doesn't* she fit in?" Blue laughed as they finished eating, then set the plates aside so they could paint. "She weasels her way into everyone's business, like any sister would, I guess. Nosing around for details on our personal lives."

Lizzie picked up a paintbrush and started to paint. "And do you guys do the same to her?"

"I don't want to know the details of her personal life. I just want to know she's safe and happy. When she was in high school, I'm sure we scared off a lot of her dates, but once she went away to college, she pretty much set us straight." Blue dabbed his brush in blue paint and held it in front of the picture of flowers in a vase that Lizzie was painting. "May I?"

"Sure."

He smoothed out the edges of the vase, then added shading that made the vase look like it was three-dimensional.

"Trish set us all straight except Duke. Duke is relentless when it comes to being protective. He watches over all of us like it's his job. I think it's an eldest thing."

"I think I'd agree with that. I was pretty protective of Maddy when she was younger." And even now, wasn't she being protective by taking care of Maddy's tuition so her sister wouldn't have to? She tucked that thought away, not wanting to think about the webcast or the fact that she'd seen only thirty seconds of it and that there could still be technical issues.

She turned her attention back to the easel, painting flower petals falling from the flowers in the vase. Blue painted a window behind the vase that looked so real she could practically feel the sky beyond.

"Where did you learn to paint like that?"

"Just something I picked up in school. Who knew that architecture skills carried over to art?"

They painted together, teasing each other and laughing, while talking about families and friends and life on the Cape. Lizzie set her paintbrush down to watch Blue paint. His dark brows knitted together and his jaw clenched. He was usually so relaxed that seeing him so intent on the painting was almost like seeing a whole different person. She imagined it was what he must be like when he worked without anyone else around.

She stifled a yawn, her long day catching up to her.

"I kept you up too late last night." Blue set down his paintbrush and pulled her in close, pressing a kiss to her forehead. She loved the intensity of their wild kisses as much as the tenderness of his softer ones, and even though she knew they could only share this one date, she wanted to enjoy every second of it, of him.

"No. I'm okay." She looked at the painting and realized he'd painted two string gardens beside the vase. They were drawn in perfect perspective and looked strikingly similar to two of her favorites.

"Are those mine?" she asked softly.

"Yes. You told me they were your favorites the day I came in to buy the aloe vera plant."

"But that was months ago. You remembered?"

He rubbed the back of his neck, inhaling a deep breath before finally answering. "Lizzie." He met her gaze with an intensity of heat and honesty that made her whole body warm up. "I don't think there's a thing you've told me that I haven't remembered."

Her heart ached with desire and longing. Blue was, without question, the most honest man alive, and no part of her wanted to put distance between them again. But she knew she had to. She reached for his hand, wanting to enjoy their closeness for the rest of the evening. Even if she couldn't have him forever, she'd take one night. One night of tender kisses that made her head spin, and the most perfect date she'd ever been on. And then she'd go back to the way it was.

BLUE KNEW HE was in too deep the moment he'd first pressed his lips to Lizzie's, and he had no desire to swim to the surface. When they left the restaurant, Lizzie climbed into the truck and moved beside him without his urging. Everything felt natural and right, just as he'd known it would. He felt closer to her than he'd ever felt to a woman, and as they drove away from the Paintery with their painting propped against the seat, he didn't want the night to end.

"I had a great time tonight," Lizzie said. "It's been so long since I've been on a date. I had forgotten how much fun it can be to connect with someone."

"Me too, and I knew we'd hit it off. No matter how many times you refused to go out with me, I always knew we'd end up together. I think that's why I never told Sky that I'd asked you out and that you'd turned me down."

"Oh gosh." Lizzie gasped. "You didn't tell her either?"

He laughed and shook his head. "You didn't tell her? I

thought girls talked about everything."

"Usually we do, but I never told her that you asked me out. I didn't want to feel pressured into accepting."

"And I didn't want her to pressure you." He hugged her against him and kissed her again. He hadn't worn his heart on his sleeve for years, but with Lizzie, there was simply no other way to wear it.

"See how alike we are?" he said. "I know it's late, and you're probably too tired, but I have something else planned if you're—"

"Blue, I don't want our date to end either, so whatever you had planned is great with me. Tomorrow's Sunday, and I usually take the day off, so I can rest then."

"Don't you want to hear what I had planned?" he asked as he turned off the road toward his house.

"It doesn't matter." She rested her head on his shoulder like they'd been dating forever. "Whatever it is, I'm sure it's going to be perfect."

Blue lived about as simply as a person could while still having creature comforts to enjoy. His modest cabin was set down a narrow and winding road, deep in the woods of Wellfleet on the way to Cahoon Hollow Beach. He parked in front of the one-story, cedar-sided cabin and helped Lizzie from the truck, holding her close and soaking in the feel of her as he set her on her feet. She surprised him again by snaking her arm around his waist as they walked up to the front door. Again he had to wonder how he'd gotten so lucky to finally break down her defenses.

"I guess I should have warned you. My place is pretty small."

He unlocked the front door and flicked on the lights, illuminating the cozy cabin. He watched her eyes roll to the right, past the kitchen and up to the vaulted ceiling, then travel to the loft above his bedroom. There were no interior walls in the cabin, other than the ones separating the bedroom and bathroom. Blue loved the open floor plan. As he watched Lizzie running her fingers along the marble bar that separated the living room from the kitchen, he wondered what she was thinking.

She smiled as she took it all in. "This feels very much like you. It's rugged and gorgeously built, of course." Her voice held a flicker of flirtation. "And it feels safe. Like you. You feel safe."

He wrapped his arms around her from behind and kissed her neck. "Just what a guy wants to be called. *Safe.*"

She craned her neck to the side, giving him better access to nibble her soft skin. He traced the shell of her ear with his tongue and felt her shiver against him.

"Okay, safe just went out the window," she said, turning toward him. "You promised me just kisses, remember?"

"That was like a kiss." He took a step back and made a sweeping gesture with his hand as he bowed. "Your wish is my command."

She laughed. "My wish is definitely *not* to only kiss, but this *is* our first date…"

He walked around the counter to put some space between them before he was unable to stop touching her and selected a bottle of wine from the rack.

"I'm glad you like my place. I built this cabin when I first moved to the Cape." He'd always loved his cabin, and although Sky had been there many times, he'd never brought a woman he was dating home with him.

"But you just bought that lighthouse property. Are you

going to move there?"

"When I bought this land, I fell in love with it. It was one of those moments you never forget." *Like the first time I saw you.* "I could smell the ocean coming over the ridge and the woods buffered me from the outside world. And when Duke and I went to see Bowers Bluff, I had that same feeling. I knew I wanted to be there."

He poured them each a glass of wine, and they went into the living room, where she looked over family photographs on the mantel while he queued up a movie.

"So, you'll move there?" she asked.

He shrugged as he came to her side. "I'm not really sure. When I'm out on the bluff, it stirs another part of me. The part that's ready to start thinking about the future, having a family someday."

"Aren't most guys trying *not* to get tied down?" she asked.

"I'm not most guys." He drew her in close again, and her eyes darkened as she met his gaze.

"No, you're definitely not."

He set their wineglasses on the mantel and lowered his lips to hers, gently covering her mouth and taking her in a slow, drugging kiss. Her lips parted instantly for him, and every stroke of their tongues brought a thrum of desire.

"I love your mouth," he whispered against her lips before kissing her again. "I've dreamed of kissing you for way too long." He didn't want to stop kissing her, even as he sealed his lips over hers again, knowing he needed to pull back or he wasn't going to be capable of honoring his promise. She kissed him hungrily, as if she couldn't stop either. This was totally unfair. Why did he have to be the good guy? Being the good guy totally sucked.

Tearing his lips from hers, he managed, "I made you a promise." Lust laced each syllable.

She pressed her hands to his cheeks, went up on her toes, and kissed him again. Her body fell against him, as if she'd lost her balance, and he wrapped her in his arms, holding her there, aching to feel every inch of her softness with nothing between them.

"Lizzie," he warned.

"I know," she said between kisses.

"Movie." He forced himself to step back. They were both breathing hard, and he had no doubt that he could sweep her into his arms, carry her into the bedroom, and make sweet love to her all night long. But he'd promised her they'd only kiss, and if Blue was one thing, it was trustworthy.

He moved their wineglasses to the coffee table, and she settled in on the couch. How many times had he envisioned coming home with her, feeling her presence in his home? He slipped off his shoes, then helped her do the same, and as she tucked her feet beside her, he dimmed the lights. The movie started as he sat beside her and pulled her in close again, loving the feel of her against him.

"You have *Love Actually?*" She lifted her head from his shoulder and looked at him with curiosity in her eyes.

"Yeah, don't tell any of my buddies or I'll never hear the end of it." She giggled, and he kissed her again. He knew that bringing her home to watch a movie wasn't a big, exciting date, but he'd craved time alone with Lizzie for so long, and since he'd never brought a woman home before, it felt like a very big deal to him. And now that he knew how tired she was, he was glad he hadn't planned a more exciting first date. "You're dangerously addicting, Lizzie."

"Don't go there," she said softly.

"Why? What's so bad about my liking you?"

She gazed up at him again. This time her eyes held confusion, and unless he was reading her wrong, a tinge of sadness. "There's nothing wrong with you liking me. Just don't get addicted to me. Addictions aren't safe."

He kissed her again. "Well, as you said yourself, you're safe with me. I made a promise, and even if it kills me, I'll keep it."

She stifled a yawn and snuggled against him again. "Sorry. I think the late night and the wine are hitting me after all."

"You can lie down if you want to be more comfortable." He knew she must be exhausted.

"Why are you so nice to me after I turned you down for so long?"

"Why wouldn't I be?" He smiled. "I'm a nice guy. Don't you know that yet? Do you really think I'd change because you agreed to go out with me?" He pressed his lips to hers again. "I only want to make you happy, make your life better, and be closer to you."

"That's actually why I didn't want to go out with you." She dropped her eyes, and he lifted her chin so he could see her face.

"Because I'm nice? I'm not that nice. There's a huge difference between being *beta* and nice, you know."

She smiled at that. "You are so *not* beta. I didn't go out with you because I knew how easily I could fall for you, and my life is complicated. I told you that." She shifted her eyes away and asked quietly, "Will you lie down with me?"

As Hugh Grant played in the background, they stretched out on the couch. Blue spooned Lizzie, one arm draped over her waist, his knees tucked behind hers, and her sweet rear pressed firmly against him. Pure. Torture. The fact that she'd just told him that she knew she'd fall for him only made it more difficult to hold back his emotions. She was painfully honest, even when she gave away her hand, and that made her even more lovable.

She nuzzled in closer and whispered, "Thank you for being trustworthy."

For once in his life he wished he could break a promise, take her in his arms and love her like he wanted to. Instead, he did the right thing.

"Always."

Chapter Seven

LIZZIE AWOKE WRAPPED securely in Blue's arms. It had been so long since she'd felt the hardness of a man's body touching hers that she reveled in it. She closed her eyes and relaxed against him, telling herself that their date could go on a little longer before she pulled the plug. It was Sunday, after all, the one day of the week she didn't need to film or edit her webcast, or even go into the flower shop if she didn't want to. And what could be nicer than spending the next few minutes snuggled up against Blue?

From her horizontal vantage point, she took in his cabin. It was small but tidy. The cedar ceiling and hardwood floors gave it a masculine, rustic feel. She was surprised to see plants from her shop on top of the refrigerator and on the small kitchen table. Blue was always in and out of her shop, but she hadn't realized that some of the plants he bought were for himself.

Blue stirred behind her. His unshaven cheek brushed over her skin, and his lips followed. Oh, how she loved his lips and the feel of his stubble against her skin. He pulled her flush against him and kissed her neck again while his hands pressed flat against her stomach and ribs. She loved his big, strong hands, and his sexy moans were heating her up in places that hadn't heated without her help in a very long time. She couldn't resist turning to face him. His eyes were heavy with sleep, and his thick dark hair was tousled. He looked too delicious not to kiss. He still tasted faintly of wine, and the second their tongues touched, shivers of electricity rippled through her. He pressed a hand to the small of her back.

"Do you know how long I dreamed of holding you like this? Kissing you like this?" He kissed her again, and she slid her hand over his muscular back, taking pleasure in the firmness of him, the surety and safety of him.

"Tell me," she whispered against his lips.

He kissed her again, then pressed scintillating kisses along her jaw as his hands smoothed down her back, over her hip, sending ripples of awareness through her with every touch.

Blue whispered, hot and lustful, in her ear, "Every night since the first day I laid eyes on you."

When he shifted his weight, bringing one thigh over hers, she moved further beneath him, wanting to feel the weight of him, to feel what it would be like if she had a normal life and could allow herself to give in to her feelings and fall for such an amazing man. Her fingers traveled down his back, trembling by the time they reached his firm behind, which she couldn't help but hold on to.

"You're beautiful in the morning. Sorry about the morning breath." He reached into his pocket and pulled out a piece of gum, then ripped it in half, placing one piece on her tongue and the other on his.

"I love a man who's prepared." She wanted to stay right there all day long.

He sealed his lips over hers, and she tried to tuck the gum between her cheek and teeth, making them both laugh. He plucked it from her mouth and set it, and his piece, on a magazine on the coffee table.

"Now we taste minty." He pressed his lips to hers. "But just for the record, that gum was so I didn't gross you out. I love the way you taste in the morning. No gum necessary."

"You're such a sweet talker." She pulled him into a greedy kiss, wanting to feel more of him, to forget that she had to go back to real life—which she'd already decided could wait another day—and just disappear into him.

His mouth was hot and commanding, his hands were heavy and possessive as they played over her hips and waist. She could only imagine how good it would feel to make love with him.

"*Blue*...We should slow down." She panted, arching her neck, giving better access to his skilled mouth while she tangled her hands in his hair and held him in place, his teeth grazing over her skin, sending chills down her spine.

"Okay." He started to pull away.

"No." She pressed his mouth to her neck again. "*Yes.*"

She felt him smile against her skin, and when his lips met hers in another soul-searing kiss, she melted against him, her mind blurry with desire.

"Blue," she whispered urgently.

He lifted lust-filled eyes and met her gaze.

"I'm sorry." His hand slid from her chest. "You said only kisses. I shouldn't—" He tried to pull away again, but she covered his hand and held it on her chest.

"I wasn't saying, *Blue*, like *stop*. I was saying, *Blue*, like, *Ohmygosh, Blue, you feel so good.*"

He smiled and touched his forehead to hers. "Still. I got carried away. You trusted me, and—"

"And I want this. I want you."

"Lizzie, if we keep going like this, there's no turning back."

She held her breath, trying to grasp her fraying resolve and come back down to earth, trying to make a decision she didn't want to make. Her heart was pleading for more. Her head was teetering between doing what she knew she should and ending this right here and now and doing what she so desperately wanted and what felt so very right that it couldn't be wrong. She searched his eyes for answers he couldn't possibly have, and her heart overruled her head.

"Kiss me, Blue. Touch me."

He hesitated for only a second before a flash of unbridled passion burned in his eyes and their mouths crashed together, shattering their last bit of restraint. Even through their clothes she could feel his heat penetrating her skin. She shouldn't do this. Couldn't do this. She had to stop.

But he felt *oh so good!*

He gripped her hips, pressing against her, and searching her eyes for approval before taking her in another heated kiss.

She loved the way he was careful with her, making sure he had the green light, and then he took control. This wild, unbridled man could have whatever he wanted. She loved the way he claimed her mouth as if he were branding her as his—and *boy*, did she want to be *his*. She was on a bullet train and she wanted to ride it all the way to heaven. He lifted her shirt over her head and stripped off his own. The skin-to-skin contact was almost too much too take.

"Blue. *Goodness, Blue.*"

"Too much?" He pulled back. He was so thoughtful it made her want to give even more of herself to him.

"No." She pulled his mouth to hers. "Maybe," she said between kisses. "No," she corrected herself. "Definitely not."

"You're gonna give me whiplash," he teased, and kissed her so long, they both came away breathless. "Lizzie, we can stop. I don't want you to regret this."

She felt another pang of guilt about hiding the *Naked Baker*, and she couldn't be sure if that guilt would lead to regret or not, but she wanted Blue more than she wanted to figure it out right now, so she answered with hope. "I'm not going to." She pulled him into another kiss.

Being together felt so right, she didn't want to stop. Time failed to exist as they kissed and touched, greeting the morning in the sweetest way she ever had.

After what felt like hours of reveling in his sweet kisses and loving touch, when she finally opened her eyes, the look in Blue's was so caring that she had to close hers against the emotions she saw there, for fear of her own tumbling out.

He pressed another kiss to her lips. "Spend the day with me."

She opened her eyes, reality creeping back in. This was her moment of decision. She knew she should end it here. Take what he'd given and go back to her secret life. But how could she do that when the man she'd wanted for so long was looking at her like she was truly all he ever wanted? She hadn't counted on this, even though she'd known the dangers of allowing herself to go out with Blue. She hadn't counted on feeling as if every moment sucked her deeper into him. Reality waited outside these cabin walls. Monday would bring the need to film her webcast. Tuesday, the commitment of editing...She stopped those thoughts by sealing them beneath a hard, painful swallow.

Reality, it turned out, was no match for her heart.

"Okay."

BLUE COULD HARDLY believe his luck. After a year of asking Lizzie out, not only was he blessed with the most amazing night, but now he was given the gift of another day with her. And that's how it felt, like a gift. How could an afternoon that had yet to come feel so special? He didn't need to pick that apart, because he already knew the answer. He'd been falling for her every time he saw her. Falling harder every time she turned him down. He'd seen the way Lizzie looked at him, and he knew it took a strong woman to fight the attraction that had simmered between them for so long—and that strength was just one of the things he admired about her, even if he still didn't understand why she'd fought it for such a long time.

"Okay? You're not going to fight me on it? Or give me stipulations?"

"Only one," she said, wrapping her arms around him. "I need to go home and shower."

"Darn. I thought I'd convince you to shower with me." He pressed his lips to hers again. He'd never get enough of her lips, and seeing them pinked up, swollen from their intense kisses, her skin flushed from the heat between them, made her even more alluring.

"If we get naked, we won't be doing anything today but *naked* things." She giggled, and he raised his brows.

"And that's a problem because...?" He was teasing, but her eyes turned serious.

"Because, we're not there yet."

"Agreed. We *are* still partially dressed, but we could be there pretty quickly."

She rolled her eyes.

"We moved too quickly. I'm sorry, Lizzie." He reached for her shirt and helped her dress.

"No, we didn't. You're so careful with me. I appreciate that. But it makes it easy to forget…"

He rose to his feet and brought her up against him. "Forget?" He searched her eyes, and she had an *uh-oh* look in them that made his gut clench tight. "What is it? What's wrong?"

"Nothing. It's just easy to forget that my life is complicated."

"You keep telling me that, but I just don't see it. So you run a business? So do I." He brushed her hair from her face and kissed her again. "Lizzie, we both have busy lives. So what? I love being with you, and you seem to enjoy being with me."

"Too much. That's the problem." She was clutching his waist like she had last night. He could feel her desire in the firmness of her grip, which was in stark contrast to the worry in her eyes. He wished he knew why she was holding back. He didn't want to just be with her. He wanted to know everything about her, to care for her, for her to be his and for him to be hers.

"Why?"

"Because my life isn't about going out with a great guy." Her voice escalated. "Or sleeping on his couch, comfortable and safe against him, or making out in the morning and wanting to laze the day away in his arms."

"Whoa." The harsh regret in her voice startled him. He held her against his chest, feeling her heart beating fast and hard. "You're really upset." He tipped her chin up and looked into her confused eyes. "Talk to me."

She swallowed hard, as if she could contain whatever was creating distance between them, and silently shook her head.

"Do you want me to take you home? We don't have to spend the day together." The last thing he wanted was to cause her pain of any kind. Even if he didn't understand why she needed space, he'd give it to her. He'd give her anything she needed.

"No." She clung to his arms. "More than anything else, I want to spend the day with you."

"Well, that makes me happy, but we'll go back to only kissing." *Even if it kills me.* "I never want you to regret being close to me."

She pressed her cheek to his chest and wrapped her arms around his waist. "I will never, *ever* regret being close to you." She gazed up at him and smiled, but he swore he saw something else there. Maybe not regret, but something curious. "I've never felt so much for someone so fast, and I'm sure it's because we were friends for so long before we decided to become more. I've never had that type of foundation with anyone else I've gone out with. I feel so comfortable with you. It's easy to skip all those early, awkward moments. And that's amazing, but scary, too."

Fear, that had to be the flicker he'd seen in her eyes a moment ago.

"You're scared." He breathed a little easier. This he could handle. This he understood. Sarah Jane had left him scared of letting anyone too close, and Lizzie had touched something in him that made him willing to push past that fear for the first time in more than a decade. "I'm scared, too."

They held each other for a long while, and Blue knew they were each contemplating their fears and the goodness of what they felt. When Lizzie's breathing calmed and she took a step back, they left the cabin to take her home, so she could shower and change as Blue had promised—but hopefully not change her mind.

In the truck Lizzie moved beside him and rested her head on his shoulder. It already felt like *her* spot, and as he drove to her house, he found himself opening up to her.

"I haven't been in a relationship in a very long time, and I'm not sure what the rules are. Or how fast we should go, or any of that. All I know is that for the first time since I was in college, I want a relationship, and I want it with you. I want to figure out the complicated things, and I want to know what scares you." He stopped at a red light and gazed into her eyes. "I want to be the guy you can count on. The person you trust with your secrets and the guy you let in here." He pressed a kiss over her heart.

"You make it all sound so easy." She fidgeted with the edge of her shirt.

"It's not going to be easy, but we both know that nothing worth anything is easy. I want happy, not easy, and I know we can have that together."

Chapter Eight

AFTER BLUE DROPPED Lizzie off at her house with more heart-stopping kisses, she showered and dressed as quickly as she could, thinking about the things he'd said. He wanted a relationship with her, and just as she'd feared, going out with Blue had unearthed the feelings that had been seeding and growing over the past year. And overnight they'd bloomed into something beautiful and desirable. But looming above her, dark clouds threatened, clouds that only she could see.

She couldn't figure that out right now. Blue was coming back in less than an hour, and she still had to check the *Naked Baker* email, review stats on last night's show, and figure out what she was going to bake for tomorrow's program.

She pulled up her email and readied herself for the on-slaught of lewd and suggestive messages that had become the bane of her existence.

One hundred and seventy-seven new emails.

Fun.

Not.

She riffled through them, scanning for anything important. Sometimes viewers sent in baking ideas, and she was thankful for the ones that weren't looking for naughty-shaped cakes or cookies, although those *were* interesting to bake. It had taken her a while to get past her own hang-ups on inappropriately shaped food, but once she got into her *Naked Baker* mind-set, just about anything went. The sexier the shows, the longer viewers watched, and the longer they watched, the more money she earned. *Oh, the joys of monetizing videos.* Not to mention that her website was also completely monetized. There were months when she raked in more than ten grand, making up for slower months, when she made just a few thousand dollars. Of course, being the good girl Lizzie was, she reported the income to the IRS and paid her taxes diligently. She wasn't about to be caught with her pants down, so to speak.

With offers ranging from the greatest sex she could imagine to a guy who was willing to lick whipped cream from between her toes—*ew*—she made it through with one golden nugget. *MrWhipIt@whipmegood.com* requested a cake in the shape of handcuffs. That, she could do!

She checked her website stats next. Views were up, as was length of viewing time. She must have done something right in the last show. She noted the stats in the ledger where she kept track of these types of things. She'd watch that video again tomorrow and compare it to the others that did well and the ones that didn't, noting the differences. Lizzie was always trying to figure out what the viewers liked best. It seemed to be a moving target.

That thought brought images to her mind of potbellied guys pleasuring themselves while watching her videos, which she *tried* not to think about, but sometimes it was impossible to push those images away.

Her phone rang, startling her. *Mom.* She closed the laptop and headed upstairs as she answered her mother's call. She wasn't even comfortable talking to her mother in the same room where she made the videos.

"Hi, Mom."

"Hi, Busy Lizzie. How are you?"

She smiled at the endearment. "Fine. Sorry I haven't called lately. Things have been crazy."

"That's okay, sweetheart. I know how busy you are with the flower shop. We were just wondering if you were still planning to pick up Madison this weekend or if you needed Daddy to do it."

"I can do it. I'm picking her up Friday night and coming straight there for dinner. She wants to stay with me and then she'll take my car to see you Saturday." Lizzie closed her eyes as silence filled the airwaves. This was a recurring theme. Madison liked to stay with Lizzie. Who wouldn't prefer staying with a sibling rather than eagle-eyed parents whose idea of a wild night was watching CNN and discussing current events?

"Oh." Disappointment rang in her mother's tone.

"Mom?" Lizzie went into the bedroom and checked her outfit one last time. She had on her favorite crushed-cotton skirt and a long-sleeved V-neck shirt that was soft as butter. Since she'd decided to give herself one more day with Blue, she hoped he'd find her irresistible and want to keep her close—even if she wasn't going to sleep with him. She'd drawn that line in her head, and now, as she looked in the mirror, she wondered if it was fair to want him to find her irresistible. No, she reasoned. It was one thing to enjoy another day together before cutting ties, but a whole other thing to become even more intimate and *then* try to go back to real life. She ran her fingers through her hair, remembering the exquisite sting on her scalp when Blue had tangled his fingers in it. She flushed with the memory.

"That's fine," her mother finally said, bringing Lizzie's mind back to their conversation. "We'll enjoy our time together when you get here. We love you, honey."

Familiar guilt settled around her as she ended the call. Not guilt over her sister staying with her, but the feeling that she was hiding part of herself from her own family. She wished she could talk about the show, and Blue, and that her parents would be supportive and understanding. Maybe even thankful that she was helping Maddy financially and thankful that she'd done such a miraculous job of helping herself. But knowing what their reaction would be, that wasn't an option, which was why she hadn't even told Maddy or Sky. She couldn't take the chance of her parents finding out about the *Naked Baker*. She couldn't take the chance of losing them.

A knock at the door startled her back to the moment, and a new type of guilt found her. She glanced at a photograph of her and Madison, both sticking their tongues out at the camera, and she reminded herself that these lies of omission were just her way of doing what she had to do to help her sister. Her flower shop earned her a good living, but the desolate Cape winters meant stretching every penny, and she didn't earn nearly enough to pay for four years of college for Madison. She'd never dipped into the *Naked Baker* income for herself or her flower shop, but if she were honest with herself, even knowing it was an option helped her through the rough winters.

She pulled open the door and found Blue casually leaning one arm on the doorframe, holding the picture they'd painted together in the other. Her breath caught in her throat, but it was her heart, once again, that pulled her under. It wasn't just the way his inky hair magnified the rugged edges of his cheeks and jaw, or his athletic physique that she'd slept beside, touched, and practically memorized. She knew her heart wasn't skipping to a new beat because of Blue's innately captivating presence. What she felt went too deep for just good looks. It was the depths of emotion in his eyes that had her stepping forward, going up on her toes, and kissing him like he was hers. And when he wrapped his strong arms around her waist, holding her as close as two people could be, and kissed her possessively, she knew she'd crossed an invisible line. She was already *his*.

"That was the longest hour of my life." He kissed her again. "Let's not do that again."

She laughed. "How will we go to work?"

"Work is highly overrated." He squeezed her to him. "This is where we should always be. Right like this."

He captured her mouth again in a slow, sensuous kiss, leaving her powerless to resist his charms—and unwilling to even try.

AFTER HANGING THE picture they'd painted between her kitchen and living room, so she could see it from either area, they drove out to Yarmouth, stopping for muffins and coffee along the way. Blue wished Lizzie had accepted a date with him a year ago. Despite her claims that her life was too complicated for them to date, she was warm and openly affectionate, holding his hand and kissing him without his prompting. He could only assume she'd somehow waylaid those worries in the hour they'd spent apart.

She was acting different, even more relaxed than last night and when they were making out this morning. More present and less hesitant. Not only was she not afraid to join him in singing off-key like a goof on the way into Yarmouth, but she tortured him—in the very sweetest way—with the silliest knock-knock jokes known to man. He loved seeing that uninhibited side of her almost as much as he loved seeing the unguarded sensual side of her.

They spent the morning perusing arts-and-crafts booths at the annual Seaside Festival. The grounds were lined with large blue vendor tents, selling everything from handmade furniture to used books and children's toys. Lizzie gravitated toward the more crafty exhibits, like homemade quilts and pottery, which didn't surprise him, given her creativity with flowers and plants.

Children ran around the lawn, and a clown entertained a group outside the largest tent. Lizzie pulled Blue over to watch.

"When I was little I was afraid of clowns," she confided as the clown made balloon animals for the children.

"Because of the whole strange man dressed up in a costume and playing with little kids thing?"

She laughed, and he tugged her in closer for a kiss.

"That scares me, too. But I'll protect you."

"I bet you will," she said with another sweet laugh.

After watching the clown, they meandered through a few more booths, then wandered over to listen to the band playing by the beach. Lizzie pulled Blue into the center of a crowd of people who were dancing.

"I suck at dancing," he said, holding her close and hoping she'd stick with a slow dance.

"You couldn't suck at anything. Just let yourself go." She pushed away and swayed her sexy little hips, awakening his entire body. "Come on, move with me." She stepped in closer and placed her hands on his hips. Pressing her body against him, she guided him to the beat, instantly arousing him. "See?

You *can* dance. You just needed the right motivation."

He clenched his jaw against his mounting desire. She was so sexy, with those dimples beckoning to be kissed as she smiled up at him, oblivious to what she was doing to him.

"Only with you, Lizzie."

Her fingers trailed over his chest, making it impossible to take his mind off of her seductive dancing. And when she lifted her hands over her head and swayed, it was all he could do to keep from taking her right there.

"Lizzie," he warned.

Her eyes narrowed, darkened, and a wicked smile split her lips. She was clearly aware of the effect she was having on him. He took her hand and led her out of the crowd.

"Where are we going?" She stumbled to keep up as he pulled her too quickly behind the stage and gathered her warm, pulsing body against him.

His hands traced over her curves as he took her in a punishingly intense kiss, knowing it was all they could have. She pressed her body to his, moaning with pleasure, making him want to go further despite the fact that they were outside at a festival with hundreds of people walking around just out of eyesight.

"I'm sorry," he said against her mouth. "I had to kiss you."

"You don't have to take me away from people to kiss me, Blue. I'm *with* you."

He loved the sound of that, although he would have liked it even more if she'd said, *I'm yours.* "I didn't take you away just to kiss you." He stepped back, and her eyes dropped to his very noticeable arousal.

"Oh." She covered her mouth with a giggle.

"Get over here." He kissed her again, and she rocked against him. "You're not helping."

"Oh, I think I am," she said with another sinful laugh. "You'll be sure to think about me all day long after this."

He took her hands in his and backed her up against the wall, pinning her wrists beside her head. "You don't think I've been thinking about you every day since the moment we met?"

She pressed her lips between his pecs, then went up on her toes—a move he'd already come to love—and whispered, "Kiss me again."

A tormented groan tore from his lungs. Knowing he was only going to be more tortured, more desperate to have her, he sealed his lips over hers and released her hands so he could clutch her fine rear end and press their bodies firmly together.

"You feel incredible." He kissed her neck, and she lifted her chin, spurring him on to take more. He buried his fingers in her hair—he *loved* her hair—and sealed his mouth over her flesh.

She brushed her hips against his.

He gripped her hips. "Lizzie, I won't be able to walk out of here if you keep doing that." His eyes darted to the grounds around them. They were tucked behind the stage among wires and technical equipment, out of eyesight from passersby, but still, as badly as he wanted her—and he did, desperately—he felt possessive and protective of Lizzie. He didn't want to take a chance of anyone seeing them when they were being intimate.

She trapped her lower lip between her teeth, looking even more adorably sexy. He'd never met a woman who could look equally seductive and innocent—and it was a total turn-on.

"You're too freaking sexy." He kissed her again, weighing the urge to take her home and make love to her, with the part of him that remembered her plea for him to be strong when she couldn't.

"I've never been this attracted to anyone in my life, and I'm afraid of crossing a line if we don't get out of here." He forced himself to take a step back.

"But I love kissing you," she said, reaching for him again.

He cupped her face and gazed into her sultry eyes. "Lizzie, I want you so badly I ache, and if I keep kissing you, I'm going to pin you against that wall, and take my fill." She smiled, and her cheeks pinked up. He added, "Which would be incredibly hot, until I killed some guy who happened to notice us and we got arrested for indecent exposure—and murder—and you had to explain to your parents why we were in jail."

She laughed. "Well, I do have a Naughty-Places list we could work on, and this plays right into it."

"A *Naughty-Places* list? Holy cripes, woman, who are you?" He stepped in closer again, even more aroused.

She dragged her finger down the center of his chest. "It's a list of all the places I want to…you know." She licked her lips, and he gritted his teeth.

"You're every man's darkest fantasy come true, but I want you as *mine*, Lizzie. I'm not good at sharing."

"No sharing. Got it." She went up on her toes and kissed him again.

A surge of desire drew him further in to her. "Lizzie," he growled against her lips, and reluctantly took another step back, trying desperately to stand up to his promise of behaving. "I cannot wait to work on that list, but in light of keeping this PG, stay here while I walk this off." He glanced down at his obvious arousal and shook his head.

"Don't think of me," she whispered. "Think of math or science."

He closed the distance between them again. "I could think

of seaweed, and if it's your voice I hear, I'm a goner."

"Oh, the power," she said with another wicked grin.

He captured her mouth in one final kiss and said, "Try not to sound sexy."

A very long and painful time later, they finally returned to the festivities.

"I love being out with you," Lizzie said as they walked toward the arts-and-crafts booths.

"I love being with you, too." He swept her into his arms and kissed her again, knowing he was kissing her way too much but so utterly taken with her, he was unable, and unwilling, to stop. "I love being with you. It should be illegal to taste this good." He kissed her again. "And feel this good."

She giggled and, holding his hand, ran toward the tent. "Come on. Otherwise I'm going to make you do things to me you really *want* to do."

"Wait. You think *that's* a threat?"

They decorated a pumpkin and gave it to a little girl who admired it. Then they ate hot dogs while they walked through more arts-and-crafts tents. All the while, they kissed and touched and teased. It was the most wonderful date Blue had ever been on.

"I need something sweet," Lizzie said.

"There's a pie-eating contest in five minutes. Want to try?"

"Really?" She was already dragging him toward the tent. "I love pie. Will you do it with me?"

"Sure, but you can't possibly eat more pie than me. I'm twice your size."

"Watch me," she said with a challenging stare.

Donning plastic bibs, they joined a long table full of hungry spoon-yielding contestants.

"I'm *so* going to beat you," Lizzie declared. "Even if I don't beat everyone else, I'm still going to eat more pie than you."

Blue laughed. "You wish."

She rolled her eyes.

The whistle sounded, signaling the start of the contest, and while Lizzie gobbled down blueberry pie, Blue tried not to think about that naughty list she mentioned.

"I have a Naughty-Love list, too. If you're lucky, maybe you can help me work through it." She shoved more pie in her mouth.

"Naughty-Love list?" His fork paused on the way to his mouth. "Is that...?"

"Things I'd like to lick off a man's body." She licked her lips and gobbled down more pie. "And things I'd like to have licked off mine."

"Holy..." The dichotomy of the heat in her words and the flicker of innocence in her eyes made his body fully alert again. "I think I found the perfect woman."

They finished their first pies at almost the same time. Lizzie leaned closer to Blue as they started on their second. She lifted the spoon to her mouth and made a seductive show of licking the sweet filling off of it.

Who cares about the contest?

He pushed his hand around the back of her neck and pulled her into a blueberry kiss, which he intensified until he drew a lusty moan from her lungs and left her breathless. "Paybacks are torture." He finished his second pie slowly, savoring every bite as she recovered from their scorching-hot kiss.

When the whistle signaled the end of the contest, he dipped his finger into the sugary blueberry and brought it to her lips. "I won't leave you hanging, babe."

She swirled her tongue around his finger, then drew his finger into her mouth and sucked it.

"No, but I will," she said as she rose from her seat. "That'll teach you not to cheat."

"Cheat?" He scooped her into his arms as she giggled and squirmed. "You just got even hotter, but be warned. Second-time-around paybacks are even worse."

"I'm *so* looking forward to it."

He kissed her again before setting her feet back on the ground. "I love that you're not bashful about eating like most girls are, and I love that you challenge me back with the naughty stuff."

"I think you'll find I'm nothing like most girls."

He pulled her against him again. "Sweetheart, I've known that since the day I met you."

"I have no idea how. I'm nothing special." She gazed up at him with the most innocent expression of disbelief in her eyes, and his chest tightened.

"How did I get lucky enough for you to finally agree to go out with me? You're not just special, Lizzie. You're unique in every way. You make rules about kissing, and sometimes you catch yourself enjoying us too much, and I see you trying to pull away, but I can feel how much you don't want to. You have a personality that lights up a room. You're smart and funny and insanely sexy. How can you think you're nothing special? I've never met a woman like you."

She wrinkled her brow. "You can feel when I'm enjoying myself *too* much?"

"Not today, but I did last night and this morning. I thought you were just getting used to giving in to your emotions, the same way I was."

"And you think I light up a room?"

"When I got back home this morning after dropping you off, my cabin felt like it had less life in it. Your absence was tangible, like part of me was missing. I realize that might be the craziest thing I've ever said after two dates." He searched her softening gaze, seeing the disbelief slowly melt away. "It's true, Lizzie. We spent a year building a friendship. A foundation, as you said. It makes sense that we'd fall hard and fast."

She clutched his shirt just above his waist, and her eyes went serious again.

"You make me want to give in to what I feel and not worry about how complicated my life is."

He touched his forehead to hers, basking in the knowledge that she wanted to give in to the emotions between them. "We'll uncomplicate it together. Nothing is too much for us to handle."

"I want to believe you." Her grip tightened, snagging his skin in her clutches.

He covered her hand possessively and reassured her. "Trust in me, Lizzie, like I trust in you. We belong together. I've known it since we first met, and it's only gotten stronger every day since."

Chapter Nine

IT WAS AFTER eight by the time they left the festival. The sun had long ago kissed the horizon, leaving a chilly evening behind, but Lizzie was warm and happy sitting beside Blue on the drive home, tucked beneath his arm. She'd already decided to forgo trying to end their relationship—because in the space of a day that's exactly what it had become. *A relationship.* She struggled with how to tell him about the *Naked Baker*, because she knew Blue trusted her, and the guilt of hiding that part of herself was eating away at her. Maybe it was selfish that she didn't want to ruin this beautiful day by blurting out something that might totally turn him off, but as she snuggled closer and he kissed her temple, she knew she would never get enough of him. How could she? Blue was everything she'd always known he'd be, and so much more.

"I would really like to see the place you bought out on the bluff. You've talked about it, but I've never actually seen it."

"I'd love to show it to you." He squeezed her tighter against him. "How about if we make a fire and we can chill on the beach for a while?"

On the way to Bowers Bluff, Blue's brother Jake called. Blue put the call on speakerphone. "Jake, good to hear from you and to know you're alive."

"Dude, do you expect anything less? It was a mess. Sorry for not being in touch." Jake's voice was as deep as Blue's. "We got about two hours' sleep each night before heading back out. Am I on a squawk box?"

"Yeah, sorry. I'm driving, and keep it clean. Lizzie's with me." Lizzie had met his younger brother last summer, when Jake had come to visit. He was tall and fit, like Blue, and a total flirt.

"Hi, Jake," Lizzie said.

"Hey, Lizzie. How's it going?"

"Great, thanks."

"What're you doing with B? Slummin' because I'm not in town?" Jake asked with a laugh.

"I can still kick the tar out of you," Blue teased.

"Yeah, yeah," Jake scoffed. "We'll see if that's true when we get together at Jeremy's wedding. Are you going, too, Lizzie?"

She said, "No," at the same time Blue said, "Maybe."

"Okay, then," Jake said. "Listen, I was just calling to let you know I'm okay. I've got to give Duke a ring. He's called me about fifty times. I'll see you at the wedding. Have fun, and don't do anything I wouldn't do."

"Great. No restrictions, then. Love ya, bro," Blue said casually.

"You too."

Blue was smiling when he ended the call. Lizzie had seen Blue with Duke and Jake, and she knew how close they all were, but hearing Blue say he loved his brother struck her in the center of her chest.

"I like that you guys say you love each other," Lizzie said.

"Family's everything," Blue said. "Don't you tell your family you love them?"

"All the time. But I've never heard guys say it so freely." She glanced out the window as Blue pulled down a dirt road. "This is really private."

"Just the way I like it."

He parked the truck in front of an adorable white cottage with a red roof, set at the edge of a sandy beach streaked with long dune grasses whipping in the wind. There were no trees or bushes to buffer the breeze as it swept off the water. To the right of the house stood a stately white lighthouse with a balcony around the top and a peaked black and glass cap.

"This is beautiful."

"Thank you." Blue lifted Lizzie from the truck.

Lizzie had never been the type of woman who felt like she needed taking care of, but being with Blue, having him lift her to and from the truck, watching his eyes dart around them, like he was always making sure she was safe, felt good and made her feel special. She'd put so much energy into hiding part of her life for so many years that she'd forgotten what it felt like not to feel so alone. And she hadn't even realized she'd been lonely, but Blue touched a part of her that made her see how lonely she'd been. Every minute they spent together brought them closer, magnifying the reasons they were meant to be together.

"I can't believe you bought a lighthouse. This is so different from your cabin."

"I know. But as I said, it spoke to me. The inside still isn't quite finished." He unlocked the cottage door and moved aside for Lizzie to walk in.

She slipped off her sandals and stepped onto the shiny hardwood floors. The wide foyer opened to a dining room to the right and a great room straight ahead. A stone fireplace graced the center of the back wall, flanked by two glass doors that led to a deck. Lizzie walked through the living room, taking in the decorative moldings and dark cherry mantel over the fireplace. A stone surround led up to the cathedral ceiling. A railing overlooked the living room from the second floor. Knowing Blue's capable hands had brought this place to life, she felt him all around her.

"This is gorgeous. Did you take out the second floor above this room, or was it like this?"

Blue came to her side, pride beaming in his eyes. "I removed the second floor here and kept two bedrooms on the other side."

"This is a work of art," Lizzie said as they passed through an archway into the kitchen, where she admired the custom-built cabinetry. Blue never flaunted his talents. He was as modest as he was generous, and those traits only added to his allure. "I love how you used the muted greens and earth tones. I can just imagine how beautiful it would be with the bay window open and the breeze coming off the water while you're cooking." She sighed. "Heaven."

He wrapped his arms around her from behind and kissed her cheek. "I'm glad you like it. You're the first to see it, you know."

"I am?" She turned to face him. "I'm honored that you'd share it with me."

"I want to share so much more with you, Lizzie."

A thrill rushed through her at the thought of sharing her life with Blue, but that thrill was chased by a nagging voice reminding her of the parts of her life she couldn't share. It had become the constant push-pull she'd worried it would, and now she had to figure out how to deal with it.

"When the house is done, we'll throw open the windows

and cook something wonderful. Come on, I'll show you the upstairs and then the lighthouse."

They followed the hardwood stairs up to the second-floor hall overlooking the living room, which led to two bedrooms, complete with full baths.

"I just finished the hardwood floors. I'm working on the closets and moldings next."

"It amazes me how much you can do, and you have such great vision." She thought about the incredible job he was doing in her kitchen, which brought her mind back to the basement kitchen and to her webcast. For a second she wondered if she really could share her secrets with Blue. If he might be able to overlook what she did. She walked to the window and gazed out over the water, deciding to leave that thought unanswered for a little longer. "This is just lovely. I can see why you were so drawn to it."

"Wait until you see the lighthouse."

A few minutes later they stood at the bottom of the circular iron staircase in the lighthouse. The steps had molded iron risers with intricate designs, the type that they could see straight through. Lizzie's heart beat so fast she felt like she might hyperventilate.

"I'm not great with open staircases like this." She hated how weak she sounded. She'd forgotten the panic that filled her at open staircases. There was no reason for it that she'd ever been able to put her finger on, but the fear was very real, clutching at her chest and squeezing her lungs.

"It's okay. We don't have to go up." Blue reached for her hand, and she stood stock-still.

"I want to. I *really* want to."

"Okay, then let's do this." He moved to the side with the

railing and wrapped one arm firmly around her from behind. His other hand pressed to her belly. She felt secure, safe. "I've got you. Are you afraid of heights?"

"No. There's just something about these types of stairs that freak me out. I haven't been in many places like this. Otherwise I would have warned you."

They made their way up the stairs slowly. Blue was patient, taking each step at her pace and not pushing her to ascend them any quicker than she was able. When they reached the doorway to the balcony, he stopped and held her close.

"You never need to warn me. There's nothing I can't handle. Are you sure you'll be okay on the balcony? We're really high up."

Nothing you can't handle? Again, she wondered if that were really true.

"Yeah, I'll be fine. It's just the open stairs that rattle me."

He opened the door and a gust of cold air rushed over them. Lizzie pressed herself closer to Blue, stealing his warmth as they stepped outside and took in the breathtaking view of the water and the miles of unencumbered shoreline.

"Thank you. I'm sorry about that."

"Lizzie, you never have to apologize for being scared. We all have fears."

If only he knew her greatest one. Losing him because of what she did. She tamped down that thought and focused on the here and now—being with Blue in this incredible place.

"Thanks for understanding. It's crazy that you *own* this. What will you do with the lighthouse?"

"I'm not sure yet. I thought about restoring it to its original condition."

"Makes sense, I guess. But if it were mine, I'd do something really different. You've got this spectacular view. Why not make this into livable space? I'd put a floor between the top and bottom with another balcony and windows. Or maybe that's not structurally possible, but how cool would it be if it was?"

He stood behind her with his arms wrapped around her waist. "I love your vision. You don't see what everyone else sees. Like with your orange kitchen and your string gardens, you put your personal touch on everything."

"Is that a nice way to say I have weird taste?"

The brisk air stung her cheeks and Blue's warmth heated the rest of her.

"No, it's me telling you that I am attracted to everything about you, Lizzie, and I'm totally falling for you." He turned her in his arms and gazed into her eyes. "I'm picturing you here with me all the time. In the house. In the lighthouse. On the beach."

Her heart was beating so fast she was afraid if she opened her mouth it would come racing out.

"Does that freak you out?" he asked.

She shook her head, envisioning the same things, despite the devil on her shoulder whispering, "*Naked Baker.*" Her hair whipped across her face in the wind. Blue gathered it in his hands and held it over her shoulder as he leaned down and kissed her, sealing her secret away.

THEY TOOK A walk along the beach, kept company by the sounds of waves rolling in. They were barefoot, and the sand was cool beneath their feet. When they returned to his property, Blue spread out a blanket on the beach and made a fire to keep them warm, then joined Lizzie, reclining on his side and propping himself up on his elbow.

"I can't remember when I've had such a great day. I still don't know how you fit almost two full pies in that tiny body of yours."

She laughed as she stretched out beside him. "My mom used to tell me that one day I'd wake up weighing six hundred pounds, and I used to say that that would be okay. At least I'd enjoy getting there."

He placed his hand on her hip. "You'd be just as gorgeous, no matter what size you were. Your beauty comes from within."

She blushed and dropped her eyes. When she met his gaze again, her eyes were serious. "Blue, you're such a great guy. You're open and honest in a way that most guys aren't, and you're romantic and thoughtful. Why are you still single?"

"Why? Well, for the last year I've been trying to get a certain woman's attention." He knew she was asking for more, and although he hadn't ever shared his past with anyone but family, he wanted to let Lizzie into his world. He didn't want any secrets between them.

"Before that, I guess it was a combination of not meeting the right person, and the past."

"The past?"

His gut knotted with the memory, but he wanted to be honest with her. "I dated a girl for a little more than a year, and I thought she was it, you know? We were young, and honestly, she probably did me a favor, but I caught her cheating on me, and…" He shrugged, hoping that would suffice.

"And it hurt," she offered.

He nodded.

"That sucks. I never understand why people cheat instead of

just breaking up. I'm sorry you went through that. Although I can't imagine anyone ever cheating on *you*."

He moved closer, bringing their bodies together, and draped an arm around her, holding her to him. Her feet snuck between his legs, and he knew she was seeking warmth. Reflections of the fire danced in her eyes, and when she smiled, he felt it in the center of his chest.

"What about you? You're gorgeous, you have your own business, and you're sweeter than that pie we had this afternoon. Why hasn't some guy scooped you up by now?"

"I told you, my life is complicated. After college I opened my flower shop, and that was really time-consuming. And lately…I'm just so busy all the time."

"So no horrible breakups? No stalker ex-boyfriends?" He hadn't heard about Lizzie dating since he'd known her, and he'd wondered why.

"No, thank goodness. I've been focused on other things."

"It seems like it's paid off. P-town Petals is *the* place for flowers in Provincetown. Maybe now it's time to focus on you for a while. To focus on us."

"I'd like that," she whispered.

Blue lowered Lizzie to her back as he pressed his lips to hers.

"Do you have any idea what torture it is to work in your house? To smell your perfume as you walk by? To know that everything I build is going to have your hands on it?"

She inhaled a ragged breath.

"I want to be those cabinets and feel your hands on me every day." He pressed his lips to the corner of her mouth. "I want to be the countertop that you trail your fingers on every time you walk by." He kissed the delicate line of her jaw. "I want to make love to you on every surface, so every time you reach for a glass, or prepare a meal, you think of me. Of us. Of how good we feel together."

"Oh, yes," she whispered.

His mouth covered hers hungrily, and she succumbed to the forceful domination of his lips, meeting every stroke of his tongue with her own. He'd been reining in his desire since their very first kiss, and now, as she clutched at his back, pressing her body against him, he didn't want to hold back anymore. He slipped a hand beneath her shirt, needing to feel the weight of her against his palm.

"You feel so good," he said before kissing her again.

His lips trailed over her jaw to the hollow of her neck. She arched back. His promise came rushing back and he stopped, breathing hard, needing her approval to take them further.

"Don't stop," she urged.

"I'm not sure I'll be able to." He searched her eyes. "Are you sure?"

"I've never been more sure of anything in my life."

He pressed his lips to hers in another soul-searing kiss, need pulsing through his veins, hot and urgent. He wanted to go slowly, to pleasure her in every way, tease and taunt her until she was begging for him, but his body had a mind of its own. And it was on a mission, moving south, and lifting up her shirt.

"You feel so good," he rasped against her neck. "This. Here. *Now*," Blue panted out. "Every moment of my life has been leading up to this. To *you*."

"Stay with me," she whispered.

He'd never heard so much emotion in three words, and as he touched his forehead to hers and whispered, "Always," he knew she'd fallen for him every bit as deeply as he'd fallen for her.

Chapter Ten

LIZZIE DRIFTED THROUGH Monday morning feeling like her whole world had changed. When Blue had shown up at her house to work on the renovations, he'd swept her into his arms, and it had taken all of her focus not to throw caution to the wind and stay home with him instead of rushing off to the shop. But her supplier was due to bring fresh flowers, and Blue had enough on his plate between her kitchen renovations and working on his own place. He didn't need her slowing him down, no matter how enjoyable it would be.

"Knock, knock." Sky breezed through the door wearing a short dress, knit stockings, and knee-high go-go boots and carrying a to-go cup in each hand. "I brought liquid energy."

"You're a goddess." Lizzie sipped the delicious coffee as she moved through the shop putting together displays and primping flowers.

"So? I texted and left messages and you totally ignored me." Sky pushed herself up and sat on the counter, watching Lizzie whip around the shop. "Either you've turned antisocial or you were with Mr. Blue Eyes, and from that freshly loved glow you're sporting, I'm thinking it's the latter."

Lizzie set her coffee down on the counter beside Sky and

stared at the colorful bouquet in front of her, sighing dreamily.

"Sky, he's so…" She sighed again, because words to describe Blue were not coming easily. She felt so much for him, so fast, and everything about him was in high focus. If she closed her eyes, she could see his, full of wicked sensuality and something far deeper. Knowing Sky was still waiting for her to finish her thoughts, she finally said, "He's everything. Hot, sexy, sweet-but-*all*-male."

"I know he is. I told you!" She kicked her feet excitedly. "So. Did you two…?"

"Did we *ever*." Lizzie felt her cheeks flush, and when Sky jumped from the counter and barreled into her, hugging her so tightly she could barely breathe, she couldn't help but laugh.

"I'm so happy. Two of my best friends, together. What the heck took you so long?" She pushed her long dark hair over her shoulder and hugged Lizzie again. "So, you guys are a couple now, right? Like, not dating other people?"

"We didn't talk about it, but yeah, I think so." She looked at her friend and wanted desperately to confide in her about her webcast and see if she had any idea how Blue might react. She knew that if they were going to be together, she needed to tell him about it. He was so good, so honest and trusting, but as much as she wanted to tell him, she also didn't want to lose him over it.

"What's that look?" Sky asked. "Your smile faded."

"I…um…" Just thinking about telling Sky that she pranced around in nearly nothing for money made her feel cheap and ashamed. She couldn't do it. Not yet, anyway. Right now she wanted to revel in what had been swelling in her heart for two days.

"We've only gone on two dates, and I feel like we've been

dating forever. I'm so comfortable around him. That's weird, right? That it's so fast?" She walked to the back of the shop to keep herself distracted from what she *wasn't* sharing with her friend and filled a watering can. Sky followed on her heels.

"That's not weird. When I met Sawyer I felt like I'd known him forever by the end of our first date, and you've known Blue for a year. How does he feel?"

Lizzie watered a peace lily, remembering the look in his eyes when he'd told her he was falling for her, and later, when his eyes had heated even more and he'd said that everything in his life had led up to the moment when they'd made love. A shiver tickled up her spine with the memory.

"He said he's falling for me," she admitted.

"I knew it. I should be a fortune-teller." Sky smiled and Lizzie laughed. "What? I knew you guys were perfect for each other. I never understood why he wasn't asking you out for all those months."

Oh no. That was something else she'd kept from Sky. She felt like such a heel. At least this she could come clean about without feeling cheap or risking her parents finding out about the *Naked Baker.* "Sky, he *was* asking me out. The first time he asked me out was right after your friends' wedding, but I said no."

"What?" Her jaw hung open and her eyes narrowed. "You never told me that."

"I know, and I'm so sorry. But I didn't want you to pressure me. You know how crazy my life is, between the flower shop and—"

"Busy or not, you should have told me. Oh my gosh, Lizzie. I gave him such a hard time all year long for not asking you out." Sky crossed her arms angrily. "How could you keep me in the dark like that?"

The hurt in her eyes seared straight to Lizzie's heart.

"I'm sorry. I really am. I just wasn't ready to say yes, and if you were pressuring me and telling me how wonderful he is all the time, I would have caved." She reached for Sky's hand, feeling her friend's resistance and wishing she'd told her sooner. "Now that I've gone out with him, I *wish* I had accepted his offer sooner. I'm so sorry, Sky. I only kept it from you out of self-preservation." Guilt settled heavily around her shoulders. If Sky reacted this way to not being told about being asked out by Blue, how would she react to the *Naked Baker*? How would Blue?

"Self-preservation?" Sky rolled her eyes. "Whatever. Am I that pushy?"

"No." She smiled. "Maybe."

Sky shook her head. "Well, if I am, it's only because I knew you'd be good together. I guess I'm just glad that you're together now. What else haven't you told me?"

"Nothing." Lizzie closed her eyes for a moment, fully expecting to be struck by lightning in the next ten seconds.

"Okay, but you owe me a drink. Want to catch open mic night at the Governor Bradford?" Governor Bradford was a restaurant and bar in town.

She needed to film her show tonight, and she wanted to spend time with Blue before that, although she didn't know his plans for the evening.

"I really want to see Blue before working through my inventory tonight." *Inventory.* Not only would she be struck by lightning, but her nose was probably growing, too.

"Don't you ever get tired of being the good girl and doing everything on a schedule, checking off your to-do list without fail?" Sky asked.

Yes, only every day of my life. "It makes life easier"—*and views to my webcast higher, which means higher profits*—"if I follow a schedule."

Sky looked around the shop. "Well, you do earn a boatload of money, so you're doing things right. That's for sure."

Or very wrong.

"How're your kitchen renovations coming along? Oh! I just realized how often Blue's at your house. That's convenient."

Except when I'm filming. "Yeah, very. He's doing an amazing job. The kitchen is already stunning."

"We knew he would. He's so talented. I need to get back to the shop—Cree's watching it for me—but I'm so happy for you guys." Cree was a waitress at Governor Bradford, and Sky had done several tattoos for her. "She wants me to teach her how to do tattoos."

"That sounds like fun." Sky hugged her again and waved on her way out of the shop, and Lizzie's mind traveled back to Blue.

She didn't have much time to linger on thoughts of Blue, as a steady stream of customers kept her busy throughout the afternoon. By the end of the day, her feet were killing her. She groaned at the thought of shoving them into a pair of heels for her webcast, when all she really wanted to do was curl up with Blue and have him kiss the long day away. He'd called her twice when she was with customers, and as she gathered the flowers that hadn't sold and would soon wilt, she finally returned his call.

"How's my favorite girl?" His voice sent a river of heat through her.

"Missing you. Still flying around, getting ready to take flowers over to the firehouse."

"Lucky firemen," Blue teased.

"How about you?" How had he become so important to her so quickly? Just hearing his voice rejuvenated her. "Are you sick of being in my kitchen yet?"

"Never. But I'm sick of being without you. Can I take you to dinner?"

She glanced at the clock. By the time she closed up and dropped off the flowers, it would be nearly eight o'clock. She hadn't had time to prepare for filming tonight's webcast, but she desperately wanted to spend time with Blue.

"I would love that. I'd offer to cook for you, but this hot guy has my kitchen torn apart."

"Why don't we cook together at my place? Or we could go down to the pier and grab something at Mac's if you'd rather."

Being alone with Blue was just what she needed. "Dinner at your place sounds perfect. What can I bring?"

"Just you, babe. I'll grab what we need on the way home."

Lizzie swallowed past the guilt that clogged her throat. She needed to tell him about the webcast. *Tonight*, she promised herself. Tonight she'd tell him.

BLUE LIT CANDLES and set them in the center of the table, turned on the stereo, and as Lizzie came up the front walk, he went outside to greet her. He'd just seen her twelve hours earlier, and still his pulse ratcheted up at the sight of her in a miniskirt and strappy sandals. He drank in her smile and the sultry look in her eyes. He was one lucky guy.

He gathered her in his arms and touched his lips to hers,

intending to give her a tender welcome, but tender went out the door when her luscious curves melted against him and she kissed him back with fervor. How would he ever make it through dinner when every time he was near her he wanted to devour her? Desire radiated from her body, her eyes, her breath, and he knew she was on the same page. Was all this passion, all this desire, just the culmination of a year's worth of wanting, or was this something bigger? Something even more powerful? Something that made him want to sweep her off her feet and make her his forever?

"I missed you," he said against her lips before capturing her mouth in another kiss.

"Me too." She ran her hand up his back and pressed on his shoulder blades, holding him as close as she was able. "It was so hard to walk out of my house this morning knowing you were staying."

"It was even harder for me to let you go."

They walked inside, kissing every few steps. At the sight of the candlelight dinner, Lizzie's eyes widened, and her smile followed.

"You did all of this? For me?"

She turned to him, and he couldn't resist gathering her close again. Their mouths met in a spark of fiery kisses. He lifted her in his arms, and her skirt slid up her thighs as her legs circled his waist.

"Do you want to eat?" he said breathlessly.

"Dessert first," she said as she lowered her mouth to his neck, sucking hard enough to blur his thoughts.

He pressed her back against the door. "You feel like heaven."

His teeth grazed over her jaw, and she let out a sexy little sound that drove him wild.

"I love the sounds you make." Her head tipped back, giving him better access to her neck, which he licked and kissed, making her squirm with desire. Her fingernails dug into his back as he pressed against her.

He buried his tongue in her mouth, probing, taking, starving for more of her. Knowing she was craving him as much as he craved her, shredded any chance at staving off his desires.

"Damn, Lizzie. I can't wait. I need to be with you."

"Yes," she said in a heated long breath.

He turned off the stove, blew out the candles, and in a few determined steps they were in his bedroom. He set her feet on the floor and she reached for her skirt.

He set his hand over hers. "Let me."

He cupped her cheeks, kissing her with all the love in his heart and all the emotions that had been mounting for so long.

"You own me, Lizzie. Heart, body, and soul."

Chapter Eleven

LIZZIE BLINKED SEVERAL times, her thoughts slowly coming back into focus. Blue's arms were wrapped tightly around her. Even in sleep he held her possessively, and she loved it. His bedroom was silent, save for the peaceful cadence of his breathing. Her eyes were drawn to the digital clock, glowing like a beacon in the darkness.

Oh no!

It was after midnight and she still needed to film her show—and now she needed to shower first. She slid as quietly as she could from Blue's arms, feeling the fatigue in her muscles. The type of fatigue that came only from a night of incredible sex. Wow, did he know how to love a woman.

She sat on the edge of the bed, torn between cuddling up beside Blue again and staying the night and going home to film her show. She knew her ratings sank by at least forty percent when she missed posting a new show on time. She'd trained her viewers like Pavlov's dogs. They knew when to expect their next episode of bakery porn. She'd tracked the income, and the few times she hadn't been able to film the show, views and income had both tanked. Maddy needed books next semester, and Lizzie held on to the shred of hope that one month she'd hit it really big and she wouldn't need to continue filming. All she needed to earn was enough money for Maddy's last two years of school—times two, to allow for taxes.

Every time she taped a show she hoped it would be the one that found twice as many viewers and went viral. The one that would make it possible for her to stop doing the show altogether. One lucky break.

Like that's ever going to happen.

She had no choice. She had to leave and tape the show. Her eyes skirted around the room, searching for answers that wouldn't come. They caught on a streak of moonlight streaming through the curtains and the string garden she'd given Blue for his birthday a few months earlier. She smiled, loving that he kept it in the bedroom and that he'd cared for it well enough for it to still be alive. Why would she have doubted that he would look after a plant? Wasn't that who he was? Look how well he cared for her. Whether they were out or he was loving her, he always had her best interests at heart.

She glanced over her shoulder just as he rolled toward her and wrapped an arm around her waist, pinning her against him.

"Sneaking out?" He shifted to her side of the bed and kissed her spine.

"Not sneaking, but I do need to go."

"Stay. I'll make you breakfast in the morning." His voice was thick with sleep and rich with comfort.

She turned and kissed him. "I wish I could, but I have to be up early tomorrow and I still need to go through my inventory lists tonight." She was going straight to hell for lying to the best man on the planet. *A gentleman on the outside and a beast in the bedroom. The perfect man.*

Her perfect man.

He tugged her down on top of him and kissed her again. "Okay, if you must, but I'll miss you."

Forty-five minutes later, alone in her own home, Lizzie stepped from the shower, dried her hair, and wondered what on earth she was doing with her life. She had the most amazing man begging her to stay in bed with him, and here she was, putting on makeup at one thirty in the morning, tying an apron around her back, and putting her feet into a confining pair of heels.

This sucks was the first answer that came to mind, followed by, *I'm doing this for Maddy.*

She carried her laptop down the basement stairs, wishing she were walking back into Blue's bedroom instead, and went about setting out her baking supplies while giving her laptop the evil eye. She had no right to sneer at the stupid thing. The *Naked Baker* was the only reason she'd been able to pay off her school loans and buy her flower shop. And she really did love baking. She loved the smell of sugar, flour, vanilla, and other scents blending together and warming to the perfect temperature. She loved putting her heart into anything—her flowers, baking...now Blue.

She pushed thoughts of him aside, or at least she tried, and focused on what else she loved about baking, to try to get into her *Naked Baker* frame of mind. Of course the outcome of baking was utterly delicious almost every single time. But then there was this part of baking—baking for the show—that tainted baking as a whole for her. This was the part she disliked, the part that sucked all that goodness from it and made her feel like a video prostitute.

She glanced at the picture of Madison she kept on the wall

on the other side of the room for motivation.

Forcing her best smile, she pointed at the picture and said, "This is for you, Maddy." She turned on the camera, thrust out her chest, and gazed seductively into the little black camera lens, and saw Blue's eyes looking back at her.

She quickly turned off the camera, breathing hard at the shock of the image. Closing her eyes tightly, she exhaled and said under her breath, "I can do this. This is for Maddy."

She turned the camera back on and once again mustered her most seductive voice.

"Welcome back to the *Naked Baker*. I've been thinking about you." She trailed her finger over the edge of the counter, remembering what Blue had said about wanting *to be* her counter, and as she dragged that finger down her neck, she buried the thought as deep as she could. She had to. For Maddy.

"Have you been thinking of me?" she purred to the camera.

Suddenly keeping a sexy facade while filming the episode was like treading water with no arms. Every time she gazed into the camera with a sultry look, she thought of Blue. Every sensual movement she made was chased by guilt. Every word out of her mouth was pushed by self-loathing. This had to be her worst episode yet, and by the time she was done baking the yellow cake in the shape of handcuffs, she felt like she'd been run over by a train—or chased by one. It didn't matter which, because the outcome was the same. The ecstasy that had laced every breath, every thought, just hours earlier when she was with Blue was gone. Tarnished. Ruined.

She took another shower, feeling dirty and unworthy of the only man she wanted. Under the hot water she tried to wash the guilt from her body. Tears streamed down her cheeks, and she scrubbed her skin raw until they finally subsided. By the time she dried off, she'd wiped all the goodness of Blue away, and buried the filth of her dirty secret a little deeper.

Chapter Twelve

HOPING TO CATCH Lizzie before she left for work, Blue arrived at her house early Tuesday morning, but despite the early hour, her car was already gone. It had been so wonderful to start his day by seeing her yesterday morning before work that he'd hoped for the same again today. And after the incredible evening they'd shared, he was having thoughts of going to sleep with her in his arms every night and waking with her every morning. Disappointment washed through him with a force he hadn't expected, and he found he had to work hard to move past that unfamiliar feeling. Falling for her didn't begin to touch on what he really felt.

He set his tools down and surveyed his work. He'd replaced the water-damaged ceiling, refinished the hardwood floors, and installed most of the custom cabinetry, which Lizzie had insisted remain orange. He'd wondered at that when he'd first seen the brightly colored kitchen, but now he saw how the happy color fit her personality perfectly. He still had another few days of work ahead of him, setting the island, installing the moldings, painting, and setting the appliances.

His eyes landed on a piece of yellow cake with pink frosting sitting on the counter with a note propped up beside it. He smiled at the familiar sight, wondering when she could have possibly had time to bake. Before they'd started going out, the notes she'd left him in the mornings, accompanying a muffin, cupcake, or some other sweet treat, said things like, *Thanks for working on my kitchen!* or *It looks amazing!* This morning's note read, *Naughty-Love list #1, Licking frosting off your washboard abs. Want to choose who licks what off of which body part for #2? Xo, Lizzie.*

Heat spread through his body just thinking about Lizzie licking him.

She was the epitome of sweet and sensual, and he couldn't wait to see her again.

He texted her in response to her note before starting work. *Naughty-Love list #2…Combine with your other list. Whatever your #1 is on that list, I'll bring the whipped cream.* He pressed send and couldn't temper the foolish grin plastered on his face.

LIZZIE BROUGHT THE handcuff-shaped cake, minus the piece she'd saved for Blue, to the homeless shelter before work. She'd sliced it and rearranged it on the tray so no one could tell what shape it had been, and like every other time she'd dropped off goodies at the shelter, the director, Paul, gave her a big hug.

"You're so good to us, Lizzie. Thank you." Paul was tall and slim with thick blond hair and eyes the color of grass. He was always appreciative of the things she brought, and he never minded that she whipped in and out in a matter of seconds the mornings she stopped by.

"It's nothing, really. I'll be back Friday morning with more goodies!"

"Thanks, love." Paul waved as he closed the shelter doors.

She drove up the highway toward Provincetown. She'd always loved the stretch of land where Truro ended and Provincetown began, where the residential area gave way to a shoreline dotted with summer cottages. Once again her mind traveled back to Blue. It had taken all of her willpower not to wait for him to arrive before leaving for work, but the battle going on between her head and heart was too difficult to manage in his presence. She knew that if she was in his arms again, feeling him holding her like he never wanted to let her go, she'd fall right back into the luxury of *them*. She needed a clear head to figure out how to tell him about the webcast, and when she was around him, a clear head was not possible—not when he made her feel so good, made her hope for more, for a future without the webcast in it.

And Maddy couldn't afford for her to make that choice.

As she drove toward her shop she marveled at the artsy little town coming to life. The people strolling with a pet's leash in one hand and coffee in the other, early-morning joggers, and shop owners opening their businesses.

She couldn't imagine running her flower shop anywhere else. Even when she was growing up in Brewster, she'd always known she'd end up here. Provincetown was full of life, and she thrived on the energy that buzzed through the town. Thinking about how she'd ended up in the place she had always wanted to be made her wonder about destiny and fate. She didn't put much stock in those things, because she'd had to fight her way through everything in life to get where she was. When she was taking on student loans, every thousand dollars she borrowed felt like another shovel of dirt burying her deeper in debt. Deeper into the reality of working for minimum wage and never seeing the light of day.

No, fate and destiny were not her friends. They were notions that people who had it all believed in. She believed in creating her own life. Making life happen the way she wanted, with her own determination and sheer will. It wasn't fate that brought her *Cooking with Coeds* or destiny that kept her locked in her basement making the slightly naughty videos. It was the need for a better life and the drive to get it, no matter what the stakes.

Her life path had seemed pretty clear to her until Blue appeared dead center, blocking out the feigned simplicity of it—and showing her just how complicated her life really was. Blue was like an unexpected tollbooth in the center of the road. *Time to pay the piper, confess my sins if I want to get through.* The problem was, she didn't know how to get around it, and going through it was risky at best.

She parked behind the shop and walked over to the Portuguese bakery, thinking of the text she'd received from Blue. Would he still want to combine her precious lists after he found out that she was the Naked Baker? Would he still want to be with her?

Maybe she was overthinking the whole thing. Maybe the webcast *wasn't* that big of a deal, and he'd laugh and think it was sexy or fun.

Or totally slutty.

Pushing the awful thought away, she bought two coffees, then headed over to Inky Skies, to apologize again for not telling Sky about Blue asking her out so many times. Sky was an early bird just like Lizzie—up at the crack of dawn and ready to take on the day. Lizzie heard Sawyer's guitar before shading her eyes to see him sitting on their apartment balcony above the tattoo shop, basking in the morning sunlight.

"Hey, Sawyer," she called up. From the moment Sky had met Sawyer, the two of them had been inseparable.

"Hi, Lizzie. Sky's already in the shop."

"Thanks." She eyed the coffee cups in her hand. "Want one?"

"No, thanks. I have to run down to the fight club for a training session in a few minutes." Ever since retiring from boxing, Sawyer had worked as a professional trainer at the fight club in Eastham.

Lizzie was thinking of Blue again as she walked into Sky's shop. Sky had fallen just as hard for Sawyer as she was falling for Blue. If only the timing were as right for Lizzie and Blue as it had been for Sky and Sawyer. Then again, Sky and Sawyer had had their own hitches. With the threat of brain damage following a concussion, they'd had to make life- and career-changing decisions. Maybe there simply was no right time for love.

Sky walked through the hanging beads in the back of the store and smiled as she reached for a cup of coffee. "You are a savior. I was just thinking about how I needed something hot and wet." She laughed and lowered her voice. "That's what Sawyer says every morning when I come out of the shower."

"TMI." Lizzie laughed. "I love that he sits up there and plays his guitar in the mornings." She sat on the couch in the reception area, and Sky plopped down beside her.

"Yeah, me too."

"Now that he got his advance for the poetry book he and his father published, do you think you'll move out of your apartment?" She knew Sky loved her little apartment above the shop.

"No, not yet. But after we're married, probably. I want to have a family, and we can't really do that upstairs with Merlin's beds in every corner and barely enough room for our own bed." Merlin was Sky's very spoiled Persian cat.

A stroke of jealousy skittered through Lizzie. She hadn't allowed herself to contemplate her own future beyond making it through the next two years with enough money to help Maddy. Once Maddy was out of college, then she could put serious thought into what else she wanted in life, but now, hearing Sky talk about having a family tugged at something inside of her. And if she were honest with herself, being with Blue had also nudged open that door.

She changed the subject to distract herself from the unfamiliar longing.

"Did you guys set a date for the wedding?" Lizzie asked.

"We're thinking about the spring, when Matt can come up over his break." Sky's brother Matt was a professor at Princeton and rarely took time off. "Can you do a spring wedding, or is that too busy of a time to fit us in?"

"I can do whatever you need me to do. Have you decided where you're getting married?" She smiled at her friend, wondering for the millionth time what it would be like to only have the flower shop and her relationship with Blue to worry about, and not Maddy's tuition or the webcast.

"Not yet. Maybe at Sawyer's parents' house, so it's easier for his father." Sawyer's father had Parkinson's disease, and it was becoming more and more difficult for him to get around. Sky sipped her coffee. "When do you need specifics?"

"Whenever you're ready. Normally I like as much lead time as possible to prepare and to make sure I can get in the flowers you want, but I know you're not really a *prepare* type of girl, so give me three weeks and I'll make your wedding beautiful."

"I know you will. How's your man?" Sky asked with a cocked brow.

"*My* man." She loved saying that. Thoughts of last night came rushing back, chased by the reality of her needing to tell him about the webcast. Being with Blue was not only bringing Lizzie's future into focus, but also clarifying her present. Faults and all. "Speaking of Blue, I'm really sorry for not telling you sooner about him asking me out. I feel bad about keeping it from you."

Sky waved a dismissive hand. "*Pfft.* I'm over it. We all do stupid things."

"I think I'm falling for him, Sky." Her heart squeezed with the admission, knowing it was far more real than just a thought. "I actually think I've been falling for him all year. He's such an amazing person. I knew that if I went out with him I wouldn't be able to keep from falling for him. That's why I didn't go out with him when he asked all those times."

"How could you *not* fall for him?" Sky smiled and hugged Lizzie. "Seriously, you two were meant for each other."

Lizzie's pulse quickened with hope. She felt that way, too, but how could it be? What a cruel joke, giving Blue a woman who had a secret like hers and giving her a man like Blue, who was making her reevaluate her two-year plan at every turn.

"Sky, can I ask you something?"

"Sawyer's really talented in bed." She flashed a cheesy grin. "What else?"

"Again, TMI," Lizzie teased, but she wasn't in a teasing mood. She rested her head back and looked up at the clouds and stars Sky had painted on the ceiling. *Do you think you always have to be one hundred percent honest with the person you love? Even if it might hurt him and someone else in the long run?* She held back those questions and instead asked, "Do you tell Sawyer everything?"

"Always."

They watched a group of people walking past the shop laughing. Lizzie wondered how many lies they were carrying around. Funny, the *Naked Baker* never used to feel like a lie. It had only felt like a secret of the most embarrassing kind.

But now that she was with Blue, it had somehow morphed into a lie that felt wrong to hide from him.

And too risky to reveal.

Chapter Thirteen

THAT EVENING LIZZIE worked as fast as she could to edit the webcast, but as she watched herself prance around the computer screen, sucking her finger seductively and bending over at just the right angle so viewers would see the curve where her butt met the back of her thighs, she felt even more ashamed. How could she tell Blue that she did this? She'd been fooling herself earlier, thinking that he might find it sexy or fun. She didn't find it either of those things—and at the same time, she couldn't be upset with herself for doing it, because it was what made it possible for her to live her life, and Maddy would soon have a college degree without being strapped with school loans.

It was worth the internal struggle and embarrassment.

If only she'd met Blue two years from now, when she could close the doors on this endeavor of hers forever.

Blue was working at his cottage on the bluff tonight, and they planned on meeting later and spending the evening together, but the more Lizzie edited, the more she felt compelled to tell Blue about the show. She had at least another half hour of editing to do before she was done, but every second she watched drove the guilt deeper. With her heart in her throat, she packed up her laptop and headed over to Blue's.

The property was dark, save for the lights inside the cottage. She stepped from the car into the cool night air, spotting Blue through an upstairs window, and paused to watch him for a moment. She wondered if he was thinking of her and what else might be on his mind. The longer she watched him, the deeper the pain of her reality cut. He was so loving, so trusting, and she was about to turn the lights out on the best relationship she'd ever had—and the only one she wanted. Blue had been hurt before, and she didn't want to be the woman who hurt him again.

I already am.

She closed the car door and crossed the sandy path to the front door, feeling like she was walking a plank with no blindfold. Her eyes were wide-open—and she almost wished he'd happened across the show, or someone would tell him about it, because wouldn't that be easier to deal with? She knocked on the door and waited, fighting the urge to retreat.

She heard music coming from inside and knew he couldn't have heard her knock, so she pushed open the door. "Blue?"

The music drowned out her voice. She mounted the stairs feeling the oppression of her confession clinging to her. Blue was standing on a stepladder, painting the room the color of French-vanilla ice cream. The muscles in his shoulders bunched beneath his shirt as he painted along the edge of the molding. She could turn around and tiptoe out and he'd never know she was there. Just forget the whole idea and go back to the bubble she'd allowed herself to inhabit with him.

At the tail of that thought, Blue stepped from the ladder and turned to dip his brush in the paint, startling when he saw her. A smile spread across his lips. He was *so* sexy.

"Hey, babe. I wasn't expecting you. Did I lose track of

time?"

He strode across the floor with a warm look in his eyes. It was a look she'd already come to love, a look that said, *I'm so glad you're here. Kiss me.* His arm swept her possessively against him as his lips claimed hers. Her entire body heated. He gazed at her with so much emotion in his eyes that she felt her resolve slipping away. Her breathing hitched, and her heart followed.

Oh my gosh.

She'd already fallen.

She grabbed his arm to steady her wobbly legs. *I love you.* She tried to evaluate those emotions, to pick them apart, but her mind was spinning. Maybe it was all the emotions coursing through her because of what she'd come to tell him. She looked into his eyes, and the side of his mouth curved up, sending a spear through her heart. No. It was him. All of him and all of her. It was the way they were together, the fun they had, the love they so easily shared. She loved him. There was no doubt, no hesitation, only heartfelt emotions.

"I'm so glad you're here." He pressed his lips to hers again.

Being in his arms was like coming home.

"Every time we're apart," he said, "I miss you more than I did the last time."

Nothing had ever felt so right—and she'd never been so wrong. This was worse than walking the plank. This felt more like committing hari-kari.

The urge to change her mind and not tell him the truth was too strong, like she was battling a tangible presence. A literal skeleton that had moved out of the closet, looming behind him and waiting to be revealed with a few words. Words she didn't want to say, words that would bring it to life, so the darn thing could move between them and drive them apart.

"I missed you, too," she said honestly. "I'm sorry to interrupt your work."

He closed the paint can and put a hand on the small of her back as they walked downstairs.

"You're never an interruption. I can't think of a better reason to stop working."

Did he have to be so positive? Couldn't he be a jerk for once and tell her that she was a big pain in the neck for interrupting or something else that was equally as jerky? That would make this much easier.

Blue washed out the brushes in the mudroom, while Lizzie paced the hallway trying to talk herself *out* of chickening out of coming clean.

He joined her a minute later with open arms, gathering her in close and smelling like heaven on legs. Why, oh why, did everything about him turn her inside out?

"Did you bring the whipped cream to work on your lists?" The spark in his eyes told her he was teasing, but that didn't stop the realization from hitting her anew—she'd finally found someone she cared enough about, felt comfortable enough with—*loved* enough—to want to explore those lists.

She felt her cheeks flush when she met his heated gaze. "I was in such a hurry to see you…"

"You sure are cute when you're embarrassed." He pressed a tender kiss to her lips. "I was only joking. Was your evening okay?" Blue asked. "Did you get everything done that you hoped to?"

"Um…Not really, but I wanted to come see you." *Because I'm an idiot.* For the first time in Lizzie's life, she wished she were one of those people who could live a lie without remorse.

No.

Not really.

But it would make things easier.

Ohmygosh. No, it wouldn't. Wasn't that what she'd been trying to do for years?

He kissed her again. "I love that you came over. Do you want to go back to my place?"

"No." She said it so quickly his brow furrowed. If she went back to his place, she'd want to cuddle up with him, which would lead to kissing him, and kissing Blue was never enough.

"I mean, let's take a walk."

"Sure." He grabbed a blanket, and they walked down to the beach. "Are you okay, sweetheart? You seem a little jumpy."

No. Not even close to okay. "Uh-huh."

He spread out the blanket and held Lizzie's hand as they walked along the water's edge. Everything felt so natural with Blue, so easy. Just thinking about telling him her embarrassing secret made her feel queasy.

"I was thinking." He played with the ends of her hair. "I was actually *hoping* you'd reconsider going to Jeremy's wedding with me. I hate the thought of being apart for the weekend."

She wanted to say yes so badly she ached, but she knew that once she told him about the webcast, he might not want to see her at all.

"I want to go, but there's a lot on my plate right now."

Walking along the shore, the scents of the sea surrounding them, the comfort of their relationship warmed her despite the evening breeze. She wasn't ready to let this go—to let him go. Would she ever be?

A sense of relief washed over her, and she clung to it like a lifeline, pushing away the gloom of her reason for being there. She would tell him, but not on such a perfect night. Not when he was so happy to see her, or when even just holding his hand made her this happy. She did so much for others. Was it really too much for her to want to take a little more for herself?

BLUE'S MIND WAS running all over the place. He'd been thinking of Lizzie the whole time he was working, and as if she'd read his mind, here she was, making his evening a million times better. He'd felt tension all around her when she'd arrived, but it seemed to fade quickly, and now she was smiling and as relaxed as she usually was. He worried about her. She did so much every day, between the flower shop and making special efforts to drop off the flowers after work so someone, somewhere could enjoy them, or so people wouldn't be forgotten. Her generosity was just one of the things he adored about her. And adore he did. He wanted to make her life wonderful.

"Thanks for letting me drag you away from work," she said.

"Sweetheart, you can drag me away from anything, anytime." He stopped to pick up a conch shell, brushed the sand from it, and held it up to her ear. "What do you hear?"

"You, whispering how much you want to kiss me."

They both smiled as he sealed his lips over hers, and she melted against him. That was what he'd craved all day, the feel of her giving herself over to him, the way he instantly gave himself over to her. The press of her body, the sweet sigh of surrender, and the way she looked at him like she'd been waiting for him her whole life, made his head spin.

"Mm. This is just what I needed tonight. To be with you." She pressed a kiss to the center of his chest.

"It's such a beautiful night, isn't it? Soon it'll be too cold not to be by a fire."

She leaned her head on his shoulder as they walked hand in hand. "Then we should enjoy this while we can."

Blue imagined taking walks with Lizzie years from now, maybe with a child or two in tow. His chest tightened, as if his heart had actually swelled with the thought.

Lizzie sank down to the sand, pulling him down beside her. It didn't matter that the sand was cold and damp or the breeze off the water was chilly. Being with Lizzie made everything seem new and somehow *better*.

She began piling sand up in a mound. "I love the beach so much. When I was little I spent most of my free time at the beach, but I never did much else." Her eyes turned thoughtful. "I wasn't very rebellious."

"Well, as a guy, rebellion sort of came with being a teenager. Was there something you never did but you wish you had?" Blue asked.

"Do you want the truth or a safe answer?" She piled more sand on top of a mound.

"With a question like that, I can only imagine what I'm in for. Truth." He leaned over and kissed her.

"I just wish my parents would have caught me doing bad things so when I did things after I left home, I didn't feel so guilty or like I had to hide it from them."

"That's a pretty big regret. Should I expect you to hit a midlife crisis a little early, like when you turn thirty?"

She laughed. "No, but my parents are so conservative. I think it would have made some things easier for me if my parents had *expected* me to do questionable things instead of always assuming I'd do the right thing. Maybe I wouldn't have kept so many secrets if I'd known they would roll their eyes and say, *That's just Lizzie.*"

"Secrets? Care to share?"

She patted the sand castle she was building into a peak and sighed. "You know, normal stuff like making out with guys when I was in college or going to parties. If Maddy were older, I could have confided in her, but she was too young." She shrugged. "So I learned to keep things to myself. It's not a bad thing, just…a *lonely* thing."

His heart ached for her. He'd always had an open relationship with his family, and with so many siblings, there was always someone to talk to about girls or problems, or anything, really.

"I'm sorry you went through all those years without having someone you felt close enough to talk to about those things." He moved closer to her. "But I'm here now, and I want to share your secrets. And if you want to be rebellious, I'll be right there by your side."

She turned curious eyes to him, her dimples in full adorable force. "You'd do bad stuff with me?"

"I would walk to the ends of the earth with you. I'd lick chocolate off your entire body if you'd like. What other kinds of *bad* stuff did you have in mind?"

The sand she was holding fell from her hands. "Wait. I'm thinking about the chocolate." She raised her brows, and that little invitation had his fingers twitching to pull her in close and kiss her again, but before he could, she said, "Nothing too bad."

He thought he saw a hint of restraint in her eyes, as if she was holding something back, but then she smiled and the look of restraint washed away as she said, "But you know Sky and her friends go skinny-dipping. I've never even done that." She walked to the water's edge, brushing the sand from her hands.

Thinking about how sexy she would look running naked into the water made the twitching in his hands travel to more aroused parts of his body. He joined her by the water. "Sure, I'll go skinny-dipping with you. Want to go now?"

"Now? What about sharks?" She reached for him.

"That's the reaction I was hoping for." He nuzzled against her neck. "We'll go skinny-dipping in a heated pool when you go with me to my cousin's wedding."

"I'm going to your cousin's wedding?" She smiled up at him. "But my shop?"

"Your shop? I didn't hear any concern for your boyfriend having to go all weekend without you if you don't come with me," he teased.

"My boyfriend," she said in a dreamy voice. "You can't imagine how much I like to hear that."

"Actually I can, because I'm sure you get the same feeling I do when I think of you as *my girl*." He held her hand as they walked toward the blanket. "I really do want you to come to New York with me and meet my family. Sky already said she would watch your shop."

"I've never asked anyone else to watch my shop. I could close it for the day, actually, and that way I'm not imposing on her. Do you really want me to go meet your family? That's kind of serious."

"Are you kidding? I never want to go a day without seeing you. And in case you haven't noticed, we're very serious."

She gazed up at him and said, "I've noticed, and I never want to spend a day without you, either."

That sounded *real* good to him. They sank down to the blanket and Blue asked, "What other types of rebellious things would you like to do? Because I can think of a few naughty things you might enjoy."

She leaned in to him. "I bet you can, and I want to do them all with you."

"You don't even know how naughty I can be. You might regret giving in so easily." He felt himself getting aroused.

"Tell me." Her tongue swept over her lower lip, and her eyes darkened seductively.

She had no idea how she stirred his deepest desires. Desires he'd never played out with anyone before. "Maybe we should table this discussion for a while. I wouldn't want you to think I only want to be with you for sex."

"I think we really are made for each other," she said with a coy smile. "I've never felt close enough with anyone else to get *really* naughty, but I want to with you."

Their eyes held, and the air heated up about fifty degrees despite the cool breeze coming off the water.

"Lizzie, you have no idea what you do to me."

She climbed over him, straddling his lap. "Then tell me all the naughty things you want to do to me." She pressed her lips to his chest.

It was one thing to play out a fantasy in the bedroom when they were both into it, but another to hear it spoken when they weren't in the heat of the moment. He worried that despite her willingness to play along, he might cross a line that shocked her. "One day I will show you."

Her lower lip came out in a hard-to-resist, sexy pout. "You're a tease."

"I'm anything but a tease, but if I tell you what I want to do, I doubt we're going to *talk* for long." He was already aroused, and thinking about what he wanted to do to her only made him want her more. He slid his hand to the nape of her neck and brought his lips to hers, deepening the kiss.

When their lips finally parted, her eyes remained closed in that hazy state lovers found when they'd hit a sweet spot and didn't want to leave it. He brushed his thumb over her lower lip, and when she opened her eyes, he said, "I want to make you mine. I want to do everything with you. Things we haven't done with anyone else."

"Like what?" Her words whispered over his mouth.

Her tongue swept across her lower lip again, and he couldn't resist taking her in another kiss, drinking in the sweetness of her desire. He placed tender kisses over the bow of her upper lip, knowing from the way her body arched into him that she was craving more of him, just as he was going crazy for more of her. He wanted to stay right there, kissing her, loving her, until the sun came up.

"Tell me," she urged in a husky voice.

"Lizzie. You make me feel things I've never felt before." He captured her mouth again, breathing hard at the thought of sharing his dirty thoughts with her.

"Please, Blue. I want to be closer to you. Share your naughty thoughts with me."

His mouth moved across her cheek, along her jaw, and he latched on to her neck, sinking his teeth into her supple skin as she pressed her body to his. He couldn't resist lowering her to her back. His arms swept beneath her, holding her tight. They were fully dressed, and still their heat permeated his skin.

"I'm falling head over heels in love with you, and I don't know how to slow it down." He kissed her again, unable to believe he'd said the words that had burned inside him every time he was with her.

"Then don't slow it down. I'm falling for you, too. I want to be yours. Really yours."

His heart swelled to near bursting. His eyes blazed and his heart thundered as the words came out hot and fast and full of greed. "I want to make you mine in every way possible, and take you to heights you never imagined." He lifted her wrist to his lips and pressed a soft kiss to it. "To hold your hands at bay while I pleasure every inch of your body, until you're so impassioned, so lost in desire, that you can barely think, much less breathe." He kissed her again, harder, sealing in his confession.

"What else?" she said in another needful breath.

"Lizzie…" *She* was pushing him to places that were going to make him lose his last shred of control.

"Please, tell me?" Her brows knitted together, and that sexy pout slayed him.

He knew he'd never be able to deny her a single thing. "It might be too much for you," he nearly growled.

"If it's with you, it's not too much."

He searched her eyes and knew by the tantalizing seduction in their depths that it wasn't going to be too much. Nothing would be too much, but still, he didn't want to talk about all the things he wanted to do with her. He wanted to love her, here. Now. "Some things don't need to be put into words." He pressed his hands to her cheeks, brushing the pad of his thumb over her soft skin.

Her eyes went nearly black, and for a beat there were no words, no thoughts, just unbridled sexual tension about what would one day come. She pressed her hands to his cheeks and crashed her mouth to his in a savage kiss that nearly made him come undone.

"I'm yours," she said. "I want to explore everything with

you."

His breath rushed from his lungs as he tried to regain a modicum of self-control. "I love you so much." He kissed her again, their confessions taking root in his soul, their love spiraling around them, binding them together.

When they finally drew apart, he held her close, feeling the frantic beat of her heart. "Lizzie, love isn't a race. I want everything with you, when we're ready. When I no longer see a shadow of doubt in your eyes."

"There's no doubt," she said with too much conviction.

He smiled and pressed his mouth to hers again, tenderly this time.

"Not usually, but sometimes there's a hint of hesitation. My mother once said that love comes in stages, and if you rush them, you miss out on all the best parts. I want the best parts with you. I want every part. The anticipation, the laughter, the certainty of knowing that at the end of the day we'll be there for each other no matter what. That feeling that's burning through us right now will only grow hotter, and I promise you, by the time I take you there, you'll have no more doubt—and it'll make our love that much sweeter."

Chapter Fourteen

LIZZIE LAY IN Blue's arms beneath the stars, his body safely cocooning her. Guilt washed over her with every gust of wind off the sea. She'd come there to confess her secret, and instead she'd told him she loved him. She did love him, but that wasn't the secret she needed to tell him. How could she reveal the truth now and risk what they had when she loved him so much that she physically ached inside as she tried to weed through the guilt that was pulling her from his arms?

"Are you cold?" He reached for her shirt and helped her put it on.

"A little." She dressed quickly, struggling to figure out how she had allowed herself to get in so deep. When he'd been telling her how he felt, what he wanted to do with her, talking about a future, *their* future, she could picture it all. For a while, the webcast disappeared, like it had never existed. And she'd allowed herself to hang on to the fantasy and hang on to her love for him.

"Stay with me tonight," he said as he buttoned his jeans.

"I want to, but I can't." She felt on the verge of tears, needing to tell him the truth. She would never forgive herself if she went home without telling him, no matter how much it would kill her to do it.

"Blue, we need to talk."

He pulled his shirt over his head, and his eyes turned serious. "I shouldn't have said those things to you. It's too soon."

He reached for her, and she fell into the comfort of him. This was just like him, taking the blame without even knowing what she wanted to talk about. It would be so easy to quit the webcast and pretend it had never existed, but she couldn't do that to Maddy.

"It's not that. I'm on the exact same page with my feelings for you. I love you, more than I ever imagined possible." She hated hearing the fear in her voice. Her throat thickened, and she swallowed hard to try to regain her courage.

"Lizzie, what's wrong?" He lifted her chin, and tears sprang from her eyes. "Sweetheart?" He folded her in his arms and ran a soothing hand down her back. "You can talk to me. Whatever it is can't be that bad."

She pulled back, breathing hard. "I…" *I can't do this. I have to do this. Oh gosh. Why did I ever start the stupid webcast?*

Because I had no choice.

She swiped angrily at the tears streaming down her cheeks. She needed to do this. Blue deserved the truth.

"I need to tell you something, and I don't want to. I want to go home and pretend I never came over."

"This sounds serious." He released her, and she suddenly felt very alone.

"I think it is." *I wish it weren't.* She could barely concentrate past the fear rushing through her and the sound of her heartbeat in her ears. She was unwilling to meet his gaze and unable to turn away. She didn't know where to start. Should she tell him the whys of it all or start with the worst part and tell him what she did twice a week? Did it matter which she led with when the end result would be the same?

She could run to her car—drive away without saying another word. Then tomorrow she could try to pretend the whole thing had never happened—that she hadn't been meaning to tell him and chickened out. The pain of knowing what she was about to reveal nearly dropped her to her knees. What happened to the levelheaded woman she'd been? How could she have let her heart get so tied up in him when she knew she had a secret that wasn't fair to keep from the man she loved?

And she *did* love him, regardless of how fast it had happened. It was real and present and all around her, in the ache coursing through her and the worry rolling off of him in waves.

"Okay. I'm listening," he said, his devastatingly sexy and serious eyes locked on her.

"Before I tell you, I need you to know that my intent was not to deceive you."

BLUE'S GUT FISTED, and every nerve instantly caught fire. Nothing good could possibly follow those words. *Deceive* was a dangerous word, and not one he'd expected to hear from Lizzie. Despite the uncertainty he heard in her voice, he reached for her again, unable and unwilling to turn his feelings off based on one sentence.

"Come here, sweetheart. As I said, whatever it is, it can't be that bad." She went rigid beneath his touch, and when she finally met his gaze again, he knew that whatever it was, it was tearing her up inside.

"Oh, it might be," she said with a shaky voice. She inhaled

another ragged breath, and her eyes dampened again.

In an effort at self-preservation, he released her, trying to calm his own internal struggle of wanting to hope for the best but, taking in the confusion and sadness in her eyes, fearing the worst.

"I don't know where to start, so I'm just going to tell you."

"Okay." Every second felt interminable.

"I do a webcast every week, and I'm not proud of it, or maybe I am a little, but not really, but I do it anyway, and I should have told you." She paused, swallowing hard.

Blue hardly ever used the Internet, but he wasn't a novice. "A webcast? Is that like a podcast?" What the heck was she talking about, and why was this deceiving him?

"Sort of. It's basically a video show that I do twice a week."

"Okay. And?"

She fidgeted with a fraying thread on the blanket as she spoke in a low and serious voice. "It's a baking show, one I started in college."

He was totally confused. What was wrong with baking?

"I…um…earn money by monetizing the videos. You know, the longer people watch, the more money I earn from my partner programs."

"I don't know anything about video monetization, Lizzie, but how is this deceiving me? I don't care if you do baking videos. Is that why you leave me muffins and sweets in the mornings?" He reached for her hand.

She nodded, and a tear slipped down her cheek, ripping right through his heart. He gathered her in close again, pressing one hand to the back of her head. "I don't understand. Why are you so upset? So you make baking videos. What am I missing?"

She pushed back, and he could see she was holding her

breath.

"Breathe, baby." He squeezed her hand.

"I…I don't just make baking videos." She shifted her eyes away. "I'm the Naked Baker—" Sobs burst from her lungs, and she covered her face.

His mind reeled with confusion as he tried to wrap his head around what she'd said. "Naked Baker? You bake naked? Online? For money?" *Holy sh…*

She shook her head. Thank goodness he'd misunderstood.

"I wear an apron that covers my chest and down below. And heels." She wiped her eyes with her forearm, still looking away.

"An *apron?*" He couldn't even begin to process what she was saying. Too many emotions surged through him. "What else?" He was breathing hard, and his chest burned. *A measly apron and heels?*

"Nothing," she whispered.

"Nothing, as in you wear only an apron and heels?"

She barely nodded. If he hadn't been watching her so intently, he might have missed it. "Well, a flesh-colored thong."

"So, anyone who watches these videos can see your butt?" He didn't mean to bark at her, but he felt blindsided, like she'd taken his trust and stomped on it, just like Sarah Jane.

"They don't," she snapped. "I'm careful with the angles."

He paced. "You're *careful* with the angles? Come on, Lizzie, what does that mean? Why would you do this? You have a great floral business."

"I needed money when I was in college and—"

He felt sick to his stomach and held up his hand, silencing her. "You've been doing this since college and you never thought to mention it to me before? Before we made love? Before I opened my heart up to you?"

"Don't you see, Blue? That's why I kept turning you down when you asked me out, and telling you I wasn't good for you. I knew it wasn't fair of me to keep it from you, or to ask you to accept it."

He ran a hand through his hair, then fisted his hands, trying to squeeze the frustration from himself. "Don't tell me any more. Please."

He stared at her, trying to reconcile the things she'd told him to the woman he knew her to be. The look in her eyes was gut wrenching, the pain in his heart, unbearable. His mind reeled back a decade, to the night he'd walked in on Sarah Jane with that other guy.

He looked at Lizzie, unable to believe what she was saying. How could this possibly be? Did everyone in this crazy world lie?

Lizzie's tears stopped. Her chin rose, and she squared her shoulders, determination settling in her eyes. "I didn't mean to deceive you, Blue. It's not like I'm selling my body. I did what I had to do. If you'll just let me explain."

He narrowed his eyes, and when he spoke his voice was stone-cold, colder than he'd ever felt. "I can't listen to an explanation right now, Lizzie. I need time to process this. I love you, but you did deceive me, whether you meant to or not. That is what it is." He paused, trying to temper the acidic burn in his throat. The taste of the vile truth. "But the worst part is, you deceived yourself—and it sounds like you still are."

Chapter Fifteen

LIZZIE DROVE AROUND for an hour, vacillating between going back and trying to explain and patch things up with Blue and being too angry to see straight. How could he tell her that she was fooling herself? She knew just how low she felt about what she was doing every day, but she also knew how important it was to have a college degree these days. Not to mention that if she'd had to manage her school loans after college, she'd *still* be working in some crappy little flower shop for ten dollars an hour, destined to be doing so forever.

She'd been innovative, and she'd found a way to climb out from under her debt and help her sister avoid having to do the same. She should be proud of her accomplishments. That was what she'd told herself for all these years, but now none of that held the same weight, and the shame of it all was that she'd never meant to hurt anyone else. Least of all Blue. She never meant to fall in love with him, and she didn't mean to keep this from him, but it wasn't exactly something a person brought up on a date.

By the way, I'm the Naked Baker, just in case you were wondering what I did in my spare time. She'd bet that wouldn't have gone over very well.

She drove up and down the highway, berating herself and building herself up in equal measure, until she realized it was two in the morning and she still had a video to edit.

It was only after she'd edited the video and she'd fallen into bed alone, in her dark, silent bedroom that reality settled over her like a storm cloud, and her insides twisted until she could barely breathe.

She'd ruined them.

She'd lost the only man she'd ever loved.

Now it was six thirty in the morning and she had no idea if Blue was coming over to finish the renovations, or if he hated her and they'd never speak again. She felt his absence in the kitchen where he'd left heart prints, like fingerprints, in everything he did. She ran her hand over the counter, thinking of how many times she'd left him notes, expecting to come home and find them in the trash only to realize he'd taken them with him. How many times had the sound of his truck pulling up in the morning set her heart aflame? How many mornings had she hurried out before he arrived because she worried he'd see her attraction to him written all over her face?

She debated staying home to see if he came over, but the thought of seeing the hurt in his eyes again, hearing the venom in his voice, made her queasy. Even her skin stung with the painful memory. Not that she blamed Blue for his reaction. There was only one way that conversation could have gone down. She'd known that from their first date, hadn't she? Wasn't that why she hadn't accepted the dates in the first place? And once she had, wasn't that why she kept putting off telling him about the webcast? Because being with Blue felt so good and so incredibly right that the thought of ruining their relationship had made her sick to her stomach. Didn't she put it off so she could eke out as much time as she possibly could with him? To enjoy every kiss. To revel in the feel of his arms around her. To soak in his heartfelt words until she absolutely *had* to come clean?

She drove into town feeling selfish for having waited so long and fighting tears at every turn, her anguish almost overcoming her control. She parked and walked down the pier in the early-morning fog, a stab of guilt buried deep in her chest. Normally she loved this time of day, before shops opened and tourists filled the streets, but now it amplified her loneliness. She pulled the hood of her sweatshirt over her head and shoved her hands deep in her pockets, warding off the morning chill. Fishermen readied their boats beside the pier, and two older women walked down the beach, bundled up in jackets and hats. Strangers went about their business like normal, while Lizzie tried to hold on to the pieces of her broken heart.

She choked back tears, wishing Blue were with her and willing to talk things through. She could almost feel his hand on her back, see the mischievous glint in his eyes as he pulled her in close—he was always pulling her in close, as if he couldn't get enough of her. *Was.* She nearly choked on the word.

She needed to get a grip on herself. She had an entire day to get through and, she just remembered, a string garden class to teach tonight. When she reached the end of the dock, she sat down with her feet hanging over the water and her arms wrapped around her middle, bracing herself against the anguish that gripped her.

This was what it felt like to love someone so much she *had* to be honest with him. This is what it felt like to be honest— and to lose him. How would she ever go back to being who she was? Which brought her to a more troubling question. Who was she? Was she the good girl her parents had raised? The rebellious coed? The proud business owner? Or was she, really, the Naked Baker? A woman who dressed in nearly nothing for money? She knew who she wanted to be. A flower shop owner, big sister, and Blue's girlfriend. That was all she wanted.

But what she wanted didn't matter, and she'd accepted that when she'd committed to helping Maddy.

She buried her face in her hands as an even more treacherous thought hit her.

What would Blue think of her if—*when*—he watched the videos?

She pulled out her cell phone and sent him a text—*I'm sorry I hurt you*—and then she lay back on the rough, hard pier and stared up at the sky, praying he'd forgive her.

BLUE CLUTCHED HIS phone, staring at the text from Lizzie, remembering the way the color had drained from her face when he'd told her she'd deceived not only him, but she'd also deceived herself. He shoved his phone in his pocket, unable to deal with the roller coaster of emotions rattling through him.

He'd stayed up half the night watching the *Naked Baker* videos. There were so many of them that he'd been sick and angry watching one after another, feeling his heart chip away with each one. How many guys had watched her while they pleasured themselves? How many drunk college guys gathered around their computers laughing about all the things they'd like to do to her as she strutted around nearly naked? He had a good handle on the vast number of people who had done just that. He'd surfed message boards and forums for posts about the

Naked Baker and had been disgusted by what he'd found. Chat rooms filled with anonymous posts about her breasts and rear and all the dirty things guys would like to do to her. How on earth could he protect the woman he loved from those types of attacks?

He pushed from the chair on his back deck and paced, as he'd been doing all morning. How could she have demeaned herself like this?

Even after watching the videos, he couldn't reconcile the Lizzie he knew with the seductress on the videos. His Lizzie was seductive and sexy, but the woman on the videos brought it to a whole new level. Or maybe *brought it to a whole new low.* All those muffins and treats she'd left for him in the mornings were just leftovers from the dirty shows she'd taped the night before, made for the enjoyment of some other guys. And not just *some* other guys, but probably *thousands* of perverted guys.

How did she live with that? How could she uphold such a wholesome image in her daily life and slip into this other persona at night?

And why?

He still couldn't wrap his mind around the *why* of it. He should have let her explain, but he couldn't have listened to another word last night if his life had depended on it.

He stormed into the cabin and headed for the bedroom, stopping cold in the doorway. He couldn't look at the bed without seeing Lizzie lying with him, looking up at him like he was her everything. He gritted his teeth and forced himself to move across the floor to the dresser. Yanking open the top drawer, he took out the notes she'd left for him over the last few weeks and clenched his fist around them. He wanted to burn every last one of them, to rid himself of her memory. He strode into the kitchen and turned on the gas stove, clutching the notes over the flame. The heat seared his shaking fingers.

"Damn it!" He threw them on the kitchen floor and turned off the flame, unable to burn them. Burning them wouldn't change a thing. He loved her more than life itself, and he didn't want a stupid empty memory. He wanted Lizzie, but he had no idea how to deal with this mess.

His cell phone rang and he pulled it out. Trish's smiling face flashed on the screen. She was in Los Angeles. What was wrong that she'd call at this hour?

"Hey," he answered sharply.

"Whoa, B. Are you okay?" Trish asked.

"Yeah, sorry. What's up, sis? Something wrong?"

"No. I couldn't sleep. I was thinking about Jeremy and Susan. What did you get them as a gift?"

"You're thinking of gifts? What time is it there?"

She sighed, and he knew something was wrong. He rose to his feet, his protective urges surging forth.

"Trish? What's wrong?"

He hated that she lived so far away from him and his siblings.

"Nothing."

He exhaled loudly. "I suck at this figure-it-out stuff. You know that. Do I need to come out there and put some jerk in his place?"

She laughed. "No. Geez, B. I can do that myself."

"Then what's going on? And don't shrug, because you know I can't hear that." They both shrugged when they were on the phone and it drove their siblings crazy.

She laughed again. "I've been working on this film night and day and just realized that I haven't gotten them a gift, and I need to get them something."

"Well, I suck too, because I haven't gotten them anything either. Call Gage. He always gets stuff like this done. He can hook us both up."

"Oh, great idea. He'll figure something out for sure."

If only his problems were so easily solved.

"Duke told me that you're dating someone. Are you bringing her to the wedding?" She sounded more like herself now.

His chest tightened with the memory of asking Lizzie to go with him to the wedding. She had to have known how he would react once she revealed her secret. Why would she agree to go?

"I'm not sure."

As much as he enjoyed chatting with his sister, he wasn't in the mood for talking right now. In fact, he wasn't in the mood for anything, except maybe beating the living daylights out of something. But he had a commitment to fulfill, and he wasn't about to be the guy who blew off his commitments. He ended the call with Trish, took a cold shower to wake himself up after not sleeping all night, and drove over to Lizzie's. Maybe they could talk through this so he could better understand why she'd done it.

He arrived to an empty driveway again, and he was disappointed and relieved in equal measure. Walking into her house was unsettling. He realized, as he stood in her kitchen, that from the very first day he'd begun working on her renovations, he'd hoped they'd come together. How could everything feel so right between two people when one of them was hiding something so big?

How could they ever move past this? He wanted to. *Man*, how he wanted to. He loved her so much, but he was hurt. Stunned and hurt that she had waited to tell him.

He set his tools down and caught sight of the picture they'd painted together hanging on the wall in the living room. He crossed the room in a daze and stood in front of the painting. Though he was staring at the image they'd painted, he saw Lizzie's face, the light in her eyes when they'd gone to the festival, the way her smile radiated straight to his heart when they were dancing, and the raw sensuality she exuded when they were making out behind the stage. And then the image of her crying as she told him about her webcast and the devastation he'd heard in her voice. His heart shattered in his chest, but that wasn't the worst of it, as his thoughts turned to her sexy lists.

Did they stem from the same place as the *Naked Baker*? Had she shared those with the world, too?

Chapter Sixteen

LIZZIE CHECKED HER cell phone for the millionth time. She hadn't heard from Blue all day. He hadn't responded to the text she'd sent in the morning apologizing for hurting him, and she was left to think the worst. Not that she thought he would reach out to her, but that didn't stop her from jumping every time her cell phone rang or vibrated with a text—and it didn't stop her heart from shattering with every disappointment. She closed her shop at seven to prepare for the string garden class that she wished she could cancel, but she wasn't about to let down the three people who had signed up for it. It wasn't their fault she'd messed up her life.

She fired up her computer to check the email she hadn't taken the time to check last night. If she didn't check the *Naked Baker* emails often, they became too overwhelming to face. Not that she wanted to face them now. Even thinking about the program made her want to quit doing it. And that was a thought Maddy couldn't afford for her to have. Her eyes trailed down the list of senders. She froze when Sky knocked on the front door. She'd been avoiding Sky all day, knowing that her friend would see right through the mask of pleasantries she'd gotten away with in front of customers.

SEIZED BY LOVE AT SEASIDE

Hoping she'd go away, she returned her attention to the computer screen, as if she hadn't heard Sky knocking.

Sky knocked again. "Lizzie! Open the door!"

She reluctantly headed for the door, contemplating ways to get her friend to go away without being rude. She was afraid to talk with Sky for too long, knowing she'd likely break down and tell her the whole sordid mess. She had a class to run, and the last thing she needed was to do it with tears in her eyes. Plus, she knew how close Sky and Blue were, and if he'd already told Sky what had happened, then she'd have to deal with *that*, too.

She unlocked the door and immediately averted her gaze from Sky's to keep Sky from reading the emotions in her eyes.

"I've been trying to catch up with you all day," Sky complained. "You haven't answered my texts, and when I saw you walking back from the bakery, you must not have heard me calling you."

"I'm sorry." Lizzie headed back to her computer and focused on her email. "I've just been really swamped today." *Sidetracked by a broken heart.* She sifted through emails, and one caught her eye from the Food Channel Network, a cable television station. She clicked on it and skimmed the message, which asked for information about the legal owner of the show. Sky leaned uncomfortably close to the computer, and Lizzie closed the laptop, making a mental note to revisit the email after teaching her class.

"I was wondering if you and Blue wanted to join us for a barbecue over at Pete's tonight."

At least she had a good excuse not to go. "I wish I could, but I have a string garden class in a few minutes. Speaking of which, I'd better get ready." She walked to the front of the store, hoping Sky would take the hint and follow, which she did.

"Okay. Maybe this weekend we can get together for a double date?" she asked as Lizzie unlocked the door.

Not likely. Her heart ached with the thought. "I'm so swamped. I didn't get my inventory done the other night, so I'm not sure. Can we play it by ear?"

"Sure," Sky said as Lizzie opened the door.

"Thanks for the offer, but I better…" Lizzie pointed to the back of the store.

Sky pushed the door open. "Are you okay?" She lowered her voice. "Is Blue waiting in the back for you?"

I wish. "No, but I do have a class to get ready for. I'll stop by in the morning, okay?"

"You better. Are you sure you're okay? You look really tired."

"It's just been a long day." Lizzie thanked her for worrying about her and locked the door behind Sky, then leaned her back against the door, feeling the sting of fresh tears in her eyes. Clearly Blue hadn't told Sky anything yet. She had no idea if that was good or bad. She couldn't even begin to think clearly. How could anything be good right now?

She set out the supplies for her class moments before the three people who had signed up arrived. She pulled her shoulders back, thrust her chin up, and fixed a forced smile into place. One more hour—that's all she needed to get through—and then she could go home and bury her broken heart in a pound of chocolate.

Lizzie threw herself into the class, hoping it would help ease the ache of missing Blue. She loved making string gardens, and while she wasn't able to lose herself in making them as she'd hoped, answering questions and helping the others learn how to properly create the unique gardens was a good distraction.

She stood before Julie and Mike, the couple that had signed up earlier in the week, and Claudia, a twentysomething blonde, and said, "The first step is to knock the soil free from the roots of the plant." She had to admit that knocking the soil from the roots of the plants was sort of cathartic.

Claudia pulled her plant carefully from the pot and shook it. Julie and Mike did the same, while passing loving glances. Lizzie tried to ignore the jealousy spiking her adrenaline.

"Sometimes the roots wrap themselves into the pot, and if that's the case with yours, gently scrunch them and massage the soil loose." If only she could massage away the mess her life had become.

"Once you've freed the roots from most of the soil, dip them in the bucket of room-temperature water on the table." She watched Julie and Mike smile at each other as they dipped their plants in water, and she imagined doing that with Blue—sharing a smile. Would they ever smile at each other again? Or would he forever see her as a tramp that pranced around in an apron and heels for strangers?

"I think mine got too wet." Claudia held up her plant and frowned as the sopping-wet dirt plopped to the table.

"No worries. I always keep extras close by just in case." Lizzie helped her free the dirt and roots of a second plant, then showed her how to wet the roots without saturating them so much that they were unmanageable. There was something therapeutic about getting her hands dirty, and she realized as they laughed about the roots looking like worms that she was smiling after all.

"Now we're going to wrap the moss around the roots and squeeze out the excess water." She showed them how to wrap the moss around the dirt, remembering the first time she'd made a string garden and how she'd felt like she was creating a work of art. She'd been proud of her accomplishment, and as she watched her smiling students, she realized that they were probably feeling the same sense of accomplishment. Pride at being the one to have brought them that joy pushed some of the ache away, and she wondered...*Does anyone watch the* Naked Baker *and actually like to bake?* Maybe her entire audience wasn't made up of perverts after all.

Feeling a little jolt of hope at the thought, she turned her attention back to the class.

"Now we're going to tie the cotton thread around the roots. Mike, Julie, you can help each other and I'll help Claudia." She showed them how to wrap the string around the ball of soil and moss. "Eventually this thread will disintegrate and the roots would spread through the moss and into the soil."

"Like love." Julie smiled at Mike. Her long dark hair was tied back in a ponytail. Mike leaned over and gave it a gentle tug before kissing her, while Lizzie's heart broke anew.

"How is it like love?" Claudia asked as she wrapped more thread around the moss.

"Well, at first love needs your arms around each other." Julie wrapped her arms around Mike, then she turned to Claudia and said, "But eventually, even if you let go, the love has bound you together on a deeper level, and you know the person you love is always there." She released Mike, and their bodies remained pressed together.

Or you reveal that you're not who the other person thinks you are and you crack right down the middle.

Claudia sighed. "I sure hope I find that someday."

Lizzie felt her throat thickening and tried to quickly get the class back on track. "Okay, let's get this finished so we don't run too late."

She cleared her throat to regain control of her voice, which was trembling with sadness she hoped no one else could hear.

"Now we're going to take the bonsai and peat moss mixture and shape it into a ball, like this." She focused on the ball of soil and moss and rounded it out to the size of a small grapefruit. The others did the same.

"Now that we've created this wonderful, bonded ball of dirt and moss." She smiled at Julie. "The ball of *love...*" *Gah! Love. Stupid love. Stupid me.* "Now we tear it in half and sandwich the roots between the two halves, reshaping the ball around the roots." Her soil and roots fell apart. *Of course they did, like everything else in my life.*

"When it falls apart—because just like love, it's tenuous at best..." She lifted her gaze and saw a horrified look on Julie's face. She quickly added, "Kidding. I'm kidding. Like love, all you have to do is take a little care and add more of the mixture to bind it together." She grabbed more soil and patted it into a perfect ball. "See? Now we'll use the twine I set out beside the sheep moss. This part is tricky. It takes a bit of finesse to hold this part together. We're going to cover the ball with your sheep moss and secure it with the twine to keep it from falling apart."

"See? Like love, it takes finesse," Julie said with a concerned look in her eyes, as if she knew exactly what Lizzie was thinking. "Nothing happens easily. Nothing worth having, anyway—right, Mike?"

"Right, Jules." He leaned in and kissed her again. "Twine me," he said, holding up the ball of soil.

Lizzie watched them work together to create a perfectly bonded string garden, and she found herself wishing life could be that easy. In less than an hour they had created a perfect blend of soil, moss, plant, and string—and last night it had taken her only minutes to tear apart the heart of the man she loved.

She forced herself to wrap up the class. "These are pretty simple to keep alive," she said. "Just fill a bucket with a few cups of water and soak them for ten to fifteen minutes once a week."

"Won't it drip all over?" Claudia asked.

Lizzie smiled. "It can get messy, so I don't suggest that you do this in your kitchen sink. But after you soak it, let the string garden drain in a utility sink until it absorbs all of the water and stops dripping."

Julie stared at Lizzie as she said, "Just like love, once again. You have to flesh out all the excess baggage to get the good stuff to stick."

"Are you a marriage counselor?" Lizzie asked as she gathered the buckets.

"No. I'm a high school guidance counselor. Kind of the same thing, only the marriages in high school tend to last about a week and end in tears." Julie reached for Mike's hand. "The few that last longer are the ones with the messiest sinks."

AFTER WORKING ON Lizzie's kitchen, Blue drove out to his cottage and worked for a few more hours, hoping to get some of his frustrations out of his system. When that didn't even make a dent, he drove out to Cahoon Hollow and parked at the edge of the parking lot, thinking about Lizzie and how important she'd become to him. Not a minute passed when he wasn't thinking of her, wondering what she was doing, how she was feeling. Just last night he'd been imagining a future with her—and he still couldn't imagine one without her. He'd told her there was nothing he couldn't handle, and darn if that weren't true. But this situation was proving to be a monster that wasn't easily eliminated.

Even though this was different from what he'd experienced with Sarah Jane, it felt painfully similar. Both women had broken his trust.

Why did this hurt a million times more than when he'd caught Sarah Jane with another man? Not only was Lizzie not touching another man, but he'd watched the videos. No one would ever put the bespectacled blond woman together with sweet brunette Lizzie Barber. She'd done a great job of keeping her identity a secret. Blue had even checked Who Is, a website that provides data on the owners of domains, and she'd made all of that information private, too.

He told himself that it shouldn't matter if she'd kept her identity private or not; she'd still broken his trust. But he knew that was a lie. *Everything* mattered. Lizzie mattered, and even though he was hurt and confused, it was Lizzie that still filled his heart and his mind—and it was Lizzie he was worried about now.

He pulled out of the parking lot, and a few minutes later he pulled up in front of Lizzie's dark and empty house, wondering where she could be this late. Her class had ended more than an hour ago. Maybe she was with Sky. Sky had called him twice this afternoon, but he hadn't had it in him to answer the calls. She was so excited about them finally dating that he didn't want to go through the *Don't worry; it'll all work out* speech that girls always had at the ready. He was also upset with Sky for not warning him about this whole mess.

His phone vibrated with a text and his heart hoped it was from Lizzie—although he couldn't imagine why she'd text him, especially after he hadn't returned her text from earlier that morning. He looked at his phone, and the disappointment at seeing his sister's name hurt way too much for him to admit, even to himself. He shoved his phone into his pocket without reading Trish's text and drove away.

Chapter Seventeen

AFTER ANOTHER SLEEPNESS night, Blue was showered and dressed before dawn. He needed to see Lizzie, to make sure she was okay and to apologize for reacting like a jackass. He wanted to understand why she would put herself in that situation. *If* she'd even talk to him after the way he'd shut her down when she'd tried to explain. Not that he could have helped how he'd reacted. To say that this had been a blow would be putting it mildly. Hearing that Lizzie was the Naked Baker had completely snowed him under.

The ache of not being with Lizzie was equally as unbearable as the pain of feeling duped. Unwilling to go another day without talking to her, he drove over to her house at six o'clock, parked out front, and waited for her dark house to come to life.

When the lights turned on, he headed around to the kitchen door. He lifted his hand to knock and hesitated, drinking her in for a minute as she stood in the center of the kitchen, her gaze hovering over the sink. He wondered what she was thinking and whether she was thinking of him the way he was thinking of her. She turned, and their eyes connected. Heat stroked down his spine, and a second later, when he must have come into focus through the window on the door, her eyes filled with sadness. His stomach knotted and his heart ached anew.

A hundred unanswered questions settled between them. A full minute later, Lizzie rolled back her shoulders and lifted her chin. He wondered how often she'd had to ready herself like that. Was it hard for her to don the apron and heels and perform in front of the camera? Or did she enjoy it?

Blue's heart pounded faster with every step she took toward the door, making it hard for him to breathe.

He heard the locks turn, and then the door swung open. She was right there, her sad eyes puffy, as if she'd been crying all night, her sweet lips, which usually appeared to be smiling, were downturned at the edges, and it nearly killed him.

"Hi," he managed.

"Hi."

"I'm sorry to show up without warning."

She stepped aside to let him in. "It's okay. You can work. I'll be out of here in a minute."

He stepped in close, fighting the urge to reach out to her, to hold her until the sadness left them both. To kiss her until they forgot why they were upset in the first place. She closed the door behind him, and the need to be closer was too strong to resist. He touched her shoulder as she took a step away.

She turned, blinking up at him through those impossibly long lashes of hers, drawing him in closer.

"Can we talk?" He shoved his hands in his pockets to keep from holding her so she couldn't walk away. It would be so easy to take her in his arms, love her, and forget the rest for a while, but he'd messed up as much as she had, and he didn't want to force her into talking with him.

She nodded and pressed her lips into a thin line.

"I watched the videos," he admitted, feeling ashamed, as if

he'd done something dirty, and that shame quickly began changing into anger again. He worked hard to push it down deep. He didn't want to get angry. He wanted to talk.

"Oh." She dropped her eyes, and the heartache in that one word slayed him again.

He couldn't stand not touching her and reached for her hand. He wanted to comfort her as much as himself. He needed the connection, if only for a second. "Lizzie, I know I didn't give you a chance to explain the other night, and I'm sorry. It was a lot to deal with, and honestly, I'm not sure I've even begun to scratch the surface, but I need to understand it. I want to understand it."

"What do you want to know?" she asked softly.

How you can be so close to me and make me feel so loved while you're doing that for other guys to see? He shifted his eyes away and pushed his selfish thoughts to the side to focus on more important questions.

"How did you get started in all this, and why, when you have so much?"

She nodded again, narrowing her eyes as if she was remembering something painful. "Honestly, Blue, I don't think any of what I have to say will make a difference if you've already decided that you don't want to be with me." She turned away.

"I haven't made any decisions. How could I? I don't have any information other than that you make these videos." *And I love you, and love doesn't turn off like a light switch.*

"Yes, I make videos." She spun around with renewed energy—negative energy, aimed directly at him. "I make baking videos wearing nothing but an apron. I did it to make money because when I was in college my father got ill and my parents had to close down the inn for about six months, so we had no money. But I wanted to get my degree, because that's what you do after high school. You go to college and do all the right things so you can have a good life." She paced, her voice escalating. "I've always done the right thing. Always."

"Lizzie, I didn't mean—"

"No, Blue. You asked. Now let me explain, please." She crossed her arms over her chest, her eyes glistening with unshed tears. "I took out loans and did all the things college students do, okay? But it wasn't enough for me. I didn't want to start my adult life strapped with loans and then spend the rest of my life working them off for ten bucks an hour. I wanted to own my own flower shop. Maybe that was selfish of me. I don't know."

"So you turned to making half-naked videos?" He hated that he couldn't keep the distaste from his voice.

"Yes," she said defiantly, arms crossed, eyes shooting daggers. "At first it was a joke. A girlfriend said we should do it and see if we could earn money that way. She said her brother made videos about gaming, walk-throughs or something, and he was earning a ton of money. I said no, but...I don't know what happened. It was the end of the semester, and I had no idea how I was going to get money for next semester's books and tuition. I was working in this rinky-dink flower shop on weekends and two evenings a week and barely making enough money for groceries. I've never eaten so many ramen noodles in my life." She paced the kitchen. "But you wouldn't know about that, Blue. You come from a wealthy family. You had your life mapped out for you. College was paid for, books, food. You've never had to figure that stuff out."

"That's not true." Even as he said the words he knew every bit of what she'd said *was* true. He'd worked through college, but if he hadn't, his parents would still have had enough money to send him and his siblings to college—to any school they'd wanted. "Okay, fine, that's true, but that doesn't mean I can't understand where you're coming from."

She rolled her eyes and scoffed. "Oh, yes, it does. You've never looked into your future and wondered how you were going to make ends meet, or stared at a paper that said you owed fifty-seven thousand dollars for an education you got only to please your family."

"Okay. I understand *what* you're saying, why you needed money. But why this particular thing? I'm sure your friend's brother didn't wear nearly nothing on his videos. Why *this*? Why not just baking, or flower stuff, fully dressed?"

"Like that would earn any money? Come on, Blue. You're not stupid. You know why."

He blew out a frustrated breath. What did he want? To hear that it was all made up? That she didn't do it? She couldn't take it back. He didn't know exactly what he wanted, or what he needed, but he knew he needed Lizzie.

"Am I the only one in the dark about this? I trusted you, Lizzie. I thought you were being honest with me. Honesty is all I ever asked for. What I can't figure out is how you got Sky to keep it from me." He crossed his arms over his chest, a barrier between him and the awful feeling of being made a fool of.

She leaned against the counter and her shoulders rounded forward. "I didn't."

"Right. You expect me to believe that Sky kept it from me on her own? You know perfectly well she would never do that. She tells me everything. Everything, Lizzie. I knew about Sawyer before you did." He closed his eyes for a beat, absorbing the sting of his words. "I'm sorry. I didn't mean—"

She held up her hand to silence him. "No. You're right. You

are closer to Sky than I am, and I'm sure she would have told you if she'd known."

"She doesn't know?" He watched her eyes, looking for the truth, and it was staring right back at him.

Without a word, she shook her head.

"What do your parents think about it?"

She lifted damp eyes to him. "They don't know either. They're the reason, well, one of the reasons, that no one knows. You're the only one I've told."

He felt like he'd been punched in the gut. "You lied to everyone? For all these years? Your sister? Your parents? Your best friend?" Anger simmered inside him again.

"I couldn't tell my sister or Sky. It might have slipped out around my parents."

He stepped in closer, unable to quell the anger and disappointment bubbling up and spewing out of his mouth. "You lied to everyone you knew? Don't you feel any sense of loyalty? An ounce of trust? No," he said as he paced. "I guess you wouldn't. You cared about paying off your school loans and opening your business, and the heck with everyone who trusts you."

Her eyes blazed as she closed the distance between them. "How dare you judge me so unfairly. Don't you think I'm ashamed of what I've done? Do you think I'm proud? Wait— maybe I am a little, for finding a way out of debt, but how dare you think I take this lightly or that I don't care about my family and friends. I care about everyone, which is *why* I didn't tell them. This would kill my parents! And if Sky knew, or Maddy knew, and it slipped out around my parents, then my parents would be as angry with them as they would be with me."

"And what about your self-respect, Lizzie? Didn't that come

into play at all during these years of half-naked baking for strange men who probably jerked off a zillion times to you?" He couldn't stop the anger from tumbling from his lips, despite the tears rolling down her cheeks and the acidic burn in his gut.

Her voice lowered to an icy calm, and her gaze followed. "*I* don't matter. How can you not understand that? Maddy matters. I might have started doing this for myself, but now? Now I'm doing it so Maddy doesn't have to. And you know what, Blue? I'd do it all over again. I'm an adult. I've made my bed. I've made my mistakes. And I'll live with them for the rest of my life, but Maddy won't have to. She'll get the education she deserves and she can be proud of, and she'll come out without loans looming over her head. She needed a shot at having a future that included more than a minimum-wage job, and I gave her that opportunity."

Shaking his head was all Blue could do as her rationalization ricocheted in his mind. "You've got this all figured out, don't you? No matter what the cost?"

She crossed trembling arms over her chest and thrust her chin out. "This is what I have to do."

"No, Lizzie. You don't have to do anything you don't want to do. There are other ways to make money."

"Not for me there aren't. Not for Maddy, either. Don't you think if I earned enough from my shop, I would stop doing the videos in a heartbeat?"

"I don't know. Would you? Will you ever walk away from it? Will anything ever mean enough to you to leave it all behind? Or will money always be your driving factor?"

"That's unfair." She held his gaze. "It's not like I want millions of dollars or like I live an extravagant lifestyle. If I hadn't had a flood and insurance hadn't paid for the repairs, I would never have renovated my kitchen. And…" She turned away, and when she finally turned back, she blew out a long breath and fell silent, as if she had no fight left in her.

"You know what, Blue? Obviously my judgment is off. I was falling in love with you. I thought we had a real connection, but you don't know me at all. Not really. Not the parts of me that matter, because if you did, this wouldn't mean a thing."

He reached out to her, but she pulled away.

"How can you say that, Lizzie? You're hiding behind all of this. Is it sexy? Yes, it would be if you were acting it out for me—*for us*—in the privacy of our own home. But you're rationalizing your way in and out of this whole mess."

She drew in a deep breath, shoulders shaking so badly she reached for the counter. "I'm proud of finding a way out of debt. And I'm proud of what I've done for Maddy."

It was hard not to admire her determination, almost as hard as it was to deal with the betrayal.

"How can you put yourself out there the way you do and say you're falling in love with me? If you loved me, then you wouldn't be able to fathom stripping down twice a week and seducing a bunch of strangers for money."

"You told me to trust you, Blue. You said you wanted to be the man I shared my secrets with, but I guess you wanted to handpick those secrets."

He strode to the door, feeling low and lost and like the mess he was, but he was too brokenhearted to do anything else. With one hand on the doorknob and his back to Lizzie, he said, "I'm a man of my word. I'll finish your renovations, and I'll try to stay out of your way. But open your eyes, Lizzie. Someone who's proud of what they're doing doesn't lie about it to the people who love them."

Chapter Eighteen

LIZZIE WAS SHAKING so badly after Blue left that it had taken her an hour just to leave the kitchen. So much of what he'd said had been true—she *was* rationalizing, and if her family and friends knew what she was doing, they would be hurt, ashamed, and embarrassed by it, too. But, right or not, she stood firm in her convictions. Not everyone had it easy or made preferable choices in life. Not that she thought of herself as being underprivileged or forced into doing what she'd done, but if she had to do it again, she would. There were things she'd do differently, like tell Blue about it *before* they got in so deep, but she still would have taken the same path. It was an embarrassing thing to do, but it was a means to an end.

She sat on the floor in the living room staring up at the painting they'd made the other night, futilely trying to weed through her tangled emotions. Was she being stubborn? Should she stop doing the show and plead for Blue to come back to her? She felt empty, depleted of all the goodness they'd shared. The hole he'd left when he'd walked out the door might never heal. How could love hurt so much?

She always did the right thing. *Always.*

Didn't she?

Blue's words sailed painfully through her mind. *Someone who's proud of what they're doing doesn't lie about it to the people who love them.*

He was one hundred percent right, and she hated that. She forced herself to her feet and went into her bathroom to get a grip on herself. Why was it that when a woman cried it affected every ounce of her being? Her eyes and nose were pink and puffy, and her hair was all over the place, as if she'd been out in a windstorm. She brushed her hair and washed her face, forgoing any makeup, because she was sure she wasn't done crying.

She packed up her laptop and headed out to the car, determined to fix the things Blue was right about. She had been rationalizing, saving herself embarrassment, by not telling Sky about what she was doing. Of all people, Sky would understand. She was not only her closest friend, but she hadn't grown up with a silver spoon in her mouth.

Lizzie started her car as Blue's truck pulled up to the curb. She closed her eyes and breathed deeply, not at all ready for another confrontation. She pushed her broken heart out of her throat, got out of her car, and stomped over to him, determined to stand strong.

"What else could you possibly have to say?" she asked with a stoic stare.

"I promised to finish the work. I'm here to do that." He got out of the truck, and the sadness in his eyes made her heart ache. He reached for her, and she bristled.

"Lizzie, please. This is hard for both of us."

She didn't even try to respond, knowing she'd cry if she did, and when he tugged her in close and wrapped his strong arms around her, the urge to melt into him was overwhelming. There was no stopping the tears that fell from her eyes. Blue's comfort felt too good.

"I love you too much to walk away from us," he said with such tenderness to his voice that it tugged at her to tell him the same. "I don't want to be the kind of couple who ends things in a fury, Lizzie. That's not us. We just need to talk, so we can both come to grips with our feelings and figure out where we go from here."

He felt too safe, but he wasn't safe, not the kind of safe she needed.

"You once told me that you'd never get enough of kissing me, and I told you that I'd never regret being close to you." She forced herself to meet his apologetic gaze. His lips were so close, and she knew if she went up on her toes and pressed her mouth to his, he'd kiss her back, despite his misgivings, despite what happened between them. She wanted that kiss so badly she could taste it, but that wasn't good enough, and she knew in her heart it wouldn't solve a thing.

"I'm sorry, Blue, but right at this second, I do regret it. It hurts. Every time I look in your eyes, every time you touch me, it brings back the things you said to me." She paused, biting back the urge to cry. She pushed from his chest on shaky legs.

"Lizzie, I have so much more to say. Can we please just talk about this?"

"No. I can't talk about it, not right now. I know that you feel like I did this to you, but despite what it looks like, I didn't do this *to* you. Maybe I should have told you sooner, but that wouldn't have changed what I've done or what I will continue to do for Maddy." Before she broke down in tears, she said, "I have to go."

She ran to her car, holding her breath the whole way, and

sped down the street and around the corner, where she pulled over and slammed the car into park—and finally let go in an endless stream of gulps and sobs. She cried for having kept her secret for so long and for the look in Blue's eyes when she'd told him, and she cried for the parents she wished she'd had and for the reality that no matter how much she wished her life could be different, this was the hand she was dealt.

An hour later she stood at the back door of Sky's tattoo shop clutching her laptop and feeling like a drowned rat. If she hadn't known she looked like death, the look in Sky's eyes as they rolled over her would have been a dead giveaway.

"Holy cow. What happened to you?" Sky pulled her into a comforting embrace, and for a moment Lizzie allowed herself to soak in that comfort.

After the way Sky had reacted to finding out about Blue asking her out, she didn't expect a warm welcome of any kind once she revealed what else she'd kept from her. But there was no way she'd let anyone think she was doing the wrong thing.

Sky tried to usher her inside. "Come sit down with me."

Lizzie shook her head. "Can we talk for a minute?"

"Yeah, sure." Sky held her by the shoulders and searched her eyes. "Are you okay by yourself for a minute while I lock the front door?"

Lizzie nodded and waited nervously for Sky to return. When she did, they sat in silence on the back stoop. The afternoon sun beat down on them but did nothing to quell the chill running through Lizzie's heart.

"Sky, I think Blue and I broke up."

Sky folded her into her arms. "Oh, no. Lizzie, no wonder you look like hell. What happened?"

"It's my fault." Tears sprang from her eyes as she pulled out of Sky's arms. "I didn't tell him about something I should have."

Sky reached for Lizzie's hand. "Tell me what happened. I'm sure whatever it is, you guys will get through this."

Lizzie shook her head. "I'm not so sure. And I'm not sure you'll forgive me either."

"Forgive you?" She let out a little laugh. "What do you mean? You didn't cheat on Blue, did you? Because you're right; I might not forgive you for that. He's my friend, too."

She shook her head again. "I haven't been with anyone else." This was much harder than she'd thought it would be. Her chest tightened up as she tried to figure out what to say.

"Then what could I ever *not* forgive you for?"

She opened her mouth to blurt it out, but no words came. Fresh tears rolled down her cheeks. "Shoot. This is so hard."

Sky gathered her in close again. "Lizzie, you can tell me anything."

"No. No, I can't. People say that, but they don't really mean it. It's like when someone says they'll love you forever, and you think they really will. Only you don't think through all the conditions that go along with that love."

"Okay, slow down." Sky held her by the shoulders again. "Slow down and clue me in, because you're not making sense and you're scaring me a little."

Lizzie inhaled deeply and blew it out slowly. "Remember when you asked about how I started my business, and I said I took out loans?"

"Sure."

"I didn't exactly take out loans." She nibbled on her lower lip, folding and unfolding her hands. "I had enough money to open it outright."

"Okay."

She averted her eyes, looking at the ground, at her hands, anywhere but at Sky. "I do a webcast that I've monetized, and that's how I paid for my shop and my school loans. And Maddy's tuition and books."

"A webcast? Well, that's good, right? I mean if you're earning enough to do all those things, why didn't you just tell me? Were you worried I'd be jealous?"

She lifted her eyes to Sky's. "No. I knew you'd never be jealous, but I've been ashamed by the type of show it is."

"Are we talking *porn?*" Sky's eyes widened with the possibility.

Lizzie shook her head. "No. I've got clothes on. Just not many." She opened her laptop and laid it on Sky's lap. She'd already queued up one of the *Naked Baker* videos.

"The *Naked Baker?*" Sky's jaw gaped. "Holy cow, Lizzie."

Lizzie buried her face in her hands. "I'm not naked. Just watch five minutes of it—you'll get the idea." She turned away as Sky clicked play. When her voice sounded, it felt foreign to her. She could clearly hear the difference between the put-on sensuality on the video and the real emotions that accompanied the things she'd said to Blue when they were intimate—the things that came straight from her heart.

A minute later Sky closed the laptop. "I can't watch any more," she said softly.

Lizzie waited for Sky to give her a hard time, and when she said nothing, and gently placed a hand on Lizzie's shoulder, it pulled more tears from her eyes.

"Did Blue see these?"

Lizzie nodded without turning to face her.

Sky wrapped her arms around her from behind and rested

her cheek against her back. "It's gonna be okay."

It was all Lizzie could do to shake her head as more tears fell.

"It really will be okay," Sky reassured her.

Lizzie turned in to Sky's embrace, and she cried on her friend's shoulder. She was at no loss for reasons for her tears. She cried for keeping the truth hidden from everyone she loved, she cried for the demeaning things she'd done to earn money, and she cried for the man she'd never meant to hurt. And then, when she thought she'd cried all the tears she could possibly shed, she leaned back and looked into Sky's eyes and she cried for the friendship she truly, desperately needed and the woman she hadn't been fair to.

"You don't hate me?" she asked.

"Hate you? You didn't do anything to me, other than not trust me with your sexy little secret. No, I don't hate you." She wiped Lizzie's tears away and smiled. "In fact, I think I love you even more knowing you're not the Goody Two-shoes you appear to be."

They both laughed at that. Lizzie swiped at her tears, thankful that she hadn't lost her best friend, too. "I'm sorry, Sky. I'm sorry I lied to you about everything, including Blue asking me out. I'm so sorry."

"Shh. It's okay." She pressed her hand to the laptop. "So Blue saw the videos? How many are there?"

Lizzie closed her eyes as she answered. "Two per week since my sophomore year of college." She opened her eyes, and Sky's hand was covering her mouth.

"Oh, Lizzie. And he...what? What happened?"

She filled Sky in on what happened with Blue and felt the weight of the world fall from her shoulders. She hadn't realized how much effort it took to keep her secret.

"I'm going to tell my family this weekend when I see them."

Sky touched her hand. "I don't know if I'd do that. Your parents definitely won't be cool with this."

"I know, but Blue's right. I'm hiding this from the people I love most, and while I'm embarrassed by it, I don't really believe they'd turn me away because of it." She wasn't as confident as she sounded, given her staunch upbringing, but saying aloud that they wouldn't gave her a kernel of hope.

"Lizzie, Blue doesn't know your parents like I do. I think he's wrong to push you to do that, and I think you know that."

"He didn't push me. He just opened my eyes." She reached for her laptop. "I want to show you something else." She pulled up the email she'd read the other night before leaving the shop and opened the query from the Food Channel Network, then turned the computer so Sky could read it.

"It sounds like they want to turn it into a cable show," Sky said excitedly. "The *Naked Baker* on television? Oh my gosh! What are you going to do?"

She shrugged. "There isn't exactly anything *to do* yet. It's an inquiry, probably just a form letter or something. I haven't even had time to think about it. Besides, it's not really a possibility. I mean, a webcast is one thing, but doing that as a full-time job? Giving up my shop? Moving away from the Cape to wherever they'd want to film it? No way. That was never my plan. It's one email. Who knows what they really want, but if they do want to make it into a show, I can't see how it's something I could even consider." With all of her relationships being put to the test, that email was the least of her concerns.

"Does Blue know?"

"No. It would just add pressure to an already untenable

situation." Not to mention that she'd told him that she regretted being with him, which wasn't really true. She regretted *not* being with him, but hurt had twisted her thoughts.

"Lizzie, he'll come around. This is a lot for a guy to come to grips with. Guys are possessive. I know Sawyer would have a hard time with it, and can you just imagine what my brothers would do if they found out I was doing something like that? I'd be banished to a high tower under lock and key. Not that there's anything wrong with it, but guys are funny about that stuff."

Lizzie's shoulders slumped. "Is it really that much to come to grips with? I mean, obviously I knew in my heart that no guy would want to date a girl who did this, but I thought what Blue and I had was stronger. I thought it was different, and real, and could weather anything."

"You're my two best friends in the world, and I would bet anything that you'll figure this out." Sky shook her head. "But I still wouldn't tell your parents."

"You know what? I kind of want a clean slate. If I've already lost Blue, what else really matters? I think I'm going to tell my parents, just to get it all out in the open, and I might as well talk to the Food Channel Network. At least then I'm doing something other than thinking about all the ways I ruined the best thing that's ever happened to me."

Chapter Nineteen

BLUE DID A week's worth of work in one day in Lizzie's kitchen. He loved her so much. How could he have thought that he could work around her things all day, smell her perfume, walk the same floors she walked, without that love blooming bigger, digging deeper? He had to get past his issues with this *Naked Baker* thing, because nothing was worth losing Lizzie.

Hadn't he lied to her, too, when he'd said he wanted to be the man she trusted with her secrets? Obviously he'd done a lousy job of being a stand-up boyfriend. She'd opened herself up to him with courage and conviction. She'd trusted him—and only him—the same way she had on their date when she'd told him that she needed him to be strong, because she knew she couldn't be. And he'd been too wrapped up in anger and hurt to see her confession for what it was.

Now, as he finished leveling the oven, he realized what else he'd been too blinded by his own emotions to recognize. She'd been going through all this alone this whole time. She'd worked at night to pay off her debts and help Maddy without any support from anyone. She'd kept it a secret, and while that might have been wrong in *his* eyes, who was he to judge her?

She was stronger than anyone he knew. She'd needed a solution, and she'd done just what she'd said. She'd figured it out. *Alone.* Without the support of friends or family. Or him.

He'd acted like a jackass, and they had a lot to work through. *He* had a lot to work through. He still wasn't sure he could deal with knowing strangers watched her in those sexy videos. He wasn't even sure if he could handle his family and friends finding out she made them. He was jealous, and that realization made him feel even more like a jerk. *He* didn't matter now. What mattered was apologizing to Lizzie and letting her know that she wasn't alone anymore—something he should have done the moment she'd told him. But he was only human.

Blue was gathering his tools when Lizzie came through the kitchen door later that evening. Her jeans were torn at the knee, and she had dirt all over her hands and streaked across her cheeks. His heart squeezed at the sight of her, and his protective urges sent him rushing to her side.

"What happened?" He wanted to take her in his arms and kiss away the pain and loneliness he saw in her eyes, but knew he shouldn't. Instead, he ran a dish towel under warm water to clean her up.

"I slipped on the hill at the cemetery when I was dropping off flowers." She toed off her dirty shoes and dropped her flower tote to the floor.

He tried to concentrate on wiping the dirt from her cheek instead of on the sadness in her eyes, but his heart was aching too badly after everything they'd said to each other. He felt sick over their situation and all the hurtful things he'd said and the way she'd so forcefully told him that she regretted being close to him. Now, standing so near, cupping her cheek in one hand as he cleaned her face and saw all the emotions he'd been wondering if she still felt, he could barely hold his feelings back. He wanted to drop to his knees and apologize a hundred times over, but she obviously needed help right now.

"Are you hurt?"

"No, just annoyed." She reached for the towel and rested her hand over his. "You don't have to…"

"I want to." Their eyes held, heat filling the space between them, despite the harshness of their earlier argument. She was already too big a part of him to let the fissure between them grow any bigger. But for the first time in his life, Blue felt unprepared. He had no idea how to get from this terrible place they'd landed back to where they belonged. He finished wiping her face and knelt to check out her knee, taking a moment to regroup.

"Your jeans are torn pretty badly."

"They're old. It's okay."

"You're bleeding." He held her calf, wishing desperately he could take back the hurtful things he'd said and they could start over and deal with this before they started dating. Maybe then it wouldn't feel like such a betrayal. But even that didn't matter anymore. All that mattered was taking care of Lizzie, and if by some miracle, she'd forgive him for his reaction, then he'd make sure she never felt alone again.

He wiped the blood from her knee, and tried to gain control of his emotions as desire to hold her filled him again. He finally rose to his feet and met her gaze.

"You should change so we can clean up your cut."

Her lips parted as if she was going to say something, but he had so many things he wanted to say first that he cut her off.

"Lizzie." He couldn't resist touching her cheek, brushing his thumb over her jaw. "I'm sorry I said all those things to you. I had no right to judge you or to make you feel bad for what you're doing. I love you so much, and you trusted me, but I was too blind to see it." Her lower lip trembled, and he stepped in closer. "I don't know where we go from here, but I miss you. I love you. I can't stop thinking about you."

She dropped her eyes. "Blue—"

He lifted her chin. "We don't have to talk about it right now. We'll just end up arguing, and I don't want that. I just need this. I need to be close to you. Even if only for a few minutes. I need you to know I love you and to know how truly sorry I am for everything I said."

She pressed her lips together and nodded, as if she needed him, too. And when she walked into his open arms, it felt like she'd come home.

"You smell so good, Lizzie." He slid his hand to the nape of her neck and gazed into her eyes. "You feel like you're still mine, and I know I have no right to even think that way."

She lifted one shoulder.

"I hate myself so much for overreacting. I was hurt, but I understand now, and I feel like I betrayed you by saying I would be here for you and then wasn't." He cringed inwardly as that last bit of truth left his lips. "I'm so sorry, sweetheart."

He touched his forehead to hers and closed his eyes, breathing her in, hoping, praying she'd give him another chance. "Can you ever trust me again? Do you miss me at all, or did I ruin us?" he whispered.

"I..." Her whisper faded, and her hands clutched his waist. "Blue." Her fingers dug into his skin through the fabric of his shirt, and she had that wanting look in her eyes, as if she, too, knew that their being close wouldn't help, but she needed it as badly as he did.

"I know it won't fix anything, but I so desperately want to kiss you."

She nodded, the slightest of movements. She went up on her toes, as she'd done so many times before, and he lowered his lips to hers. The first touch sent a shock of awareness through him—chased by a wave of guilt. Her mouth was warm and tender, and when she pushed away, confusion in her eyes, he feared he'd made things worse.

"Blue," she said sharply, covering her mouth with a shaky hand. "We can't. You can't kiss me. We'll never make sense of this."

"I'm sorry. I thought you wanted it, too. I can't help it. I just feel so much for you." He took a step away, rubbing a knot at the back of his neck. "I'm confused by everything."

"So am I, but *this* isn't going to help." She took a step back.

Her words, her actions, told him to stay back, but the look in her eyes had him closing the distance between them again. He couldn't talk, couldn't think, could only feel, and there was no way he could let her walk away.

She stared up at him with defiance in her eyes. When *she* grabbed his shirt and tugged him into a savage kiss, his thoughts reeled away. Their bodies smoldered together like melted metal. His emotions soared and skidded, spiraling out of control as his hands moved roughly over her hips.

"You said no," he said between kisses.

"I didn't mean it. I need you, too." She sealed her mouth over his. "Touch me. Kiss me."

Lizzie grasped at his chest, his arms, seeking purchase anywhere she could as he lifted her into his arms. She angled her mouth, allowing his to slant over hers and deepen the kiss.

Setting her on the counter, he stood before her, searching her beautiful face for regret—but there was only love and desire looking back at him.

"I love you, Blue, and I'm so sorry," she said breathlessly.

Her eyes turned dark and lustful and she crashed her mouth to his in another possessive, fierce kiss.

"I want you more than I want to breathe," he admitted in a heated growl. "But if *any* part of you thinks this might not be right, tell me no. Tell me you don't want me, Lizzie, and I'll step back."

"I want you, Blue." She answered so fast it took him a second to realize he hadn't dreamed it.

He scooped her into his arms again, devouring her mouth as he carried her into the bedroom, telling himself he could do this. He could love her and make love to her and still give them both space to figure everything out.

INSIDE LIZZIE'S HEAD a war was taking place, a battle between her undeniable love for Blue and her unwillingness to give up her convictions. She knew she shouldn't have made love to him, knew it wouldn't solve anything, but she'd needed to be in his arms again. And now, as a sated smile graced his beautiful mouth, she didn't regret their lovemaking one bit.

"Lizzie," he whispered. "I can't stay away from you."

Her entire body relaxed. She hadn't lost him forever. *Thank heavens.* Did he know that everything he did and said had the power to slay or elate her? Did he realize that as badly as what he had said to her hurt it had also opened her eyes? Did he know she loved him more than she thought possible? That she couldn't stay away from him, either? She should tell him all those things, but she didn't want to talk, couldn't afford to have another blowup about what she was doing with her life. She wanted—*needed*—to revel in their closeness for a while longer.

"Can we pretend, for just five minutes, that this is our life? That this is where we are?" she pleaded.

His eyes closed, and she thought he was going to plunk her down on her feet and tell her she needed to grow up, but he tightened his arms around her, silently holding her and not asking for a darn thing.

"Let me draw you a bath," he said sweetly.

A nagging reminder sounded off in the recesses of her mind. She needed to film her show tonight.

That could wait.

A bath sounded lovely.

Being with Blue was lovely.

I just want to pretend we're okay for a little while longer.

Blue led her into the bathroom, where he lit the candles that she kept on the windowsill and filled the bath with heavenly smelling bubbles. He touched her shoulder as he moved from one task to the next, smiling lovingly, as he helped her into the tub.

"Be careful. Your knee might sting."

He was still so caring, despite how hurt and upset he was, and that touched her deeply. She knew Sky was right, that despite her convictions, the webcast was a lot for a guy to accept. She held on to his hand and sank beneath the bubbles. When he stepped away, she tightened her grip. "Please stay?"

He sat on the edge of the tub and reached for a washcloth.

"With me." She shifted her eyes to the tub. "Please?" She scooted forward, and he stepped in behind her, placing a leg on either side of her as she settled her back against his chest.

She'd never felt anything as luxurious as being loved by Blue.

"Lizzie," he whispered against her ear, and then, as if he was at a loss for words, he kissed her shoulder.

Her heart tugged at the emotions winding around them.

He soaped the washcloth and gently bathed her arms. With one arm around her waist, he washed her shoulders, her breastbone, tending to her carefully, whispering about how much he loved her and how sorry he was. He trailed kisses along her shoulder, and when he stopped washing her and wrapped both arms around her waist, resting his head against her cheek, she heard him breathing deeply, as if he were so thankful for this time together.

She had the feeling neither of them knew where to go from here, and she didn't want to break the spell of this closeness. She needed this, needed *him*. Gosh, how long had she needed him? A year was a long time to fight her feelings, and she knew, as he turned her in his arms and gathered her in close, her knees pressed to her chest as he wrapped his arms around her, that she'd been doing just that. She had no fight left in her. It was exhausting to defend herself and exhausting trying not to feel and not to love. Almost as exhausting as living a lie.

"I'm so sorry, Lizzie. I know we don't want to talk about it, but I hate what I said to you. I can't claim that I've come to grips with what you do, but I will never again say anything hurtful. I want so badly to be part of your life. I just need to figure out how to get past all of this."

She wanted to beg him to try, but she'd done enough of that already. He was being as honest as a person could be. Hadn't he always been honest with her even before they'd started dating? Blue hid nothing from her. He gave, and gave, and gave some more.

"It's okay," she finally managed, feeling anything but okay. She didn't know how to do this either. She'd never felt so much for anyone, and if there was one thing she was sure of, it was that she didn't want those feelings to go away.

He kissed her temple and tightened his hold. "No, it's not okay. My heart aches because of what I've said and how I've acted. I want to be a man who can step back and let everything roll off my back, but that's just not who I am. But I'm willing to try. I *want* to try. I love you so much. For you I'd do anything."

"I don't want you to be that man, Blue. I want you to be who you are, not someone who ignores his true feelings." She rested her head on his shoulder and wrapped her arms around him. "We're at a crossroads, and I'm not sure which way to go."

He held her until the water chilled and the bubbles dissipated; then he wrapped her in a towel and carefully dried her off before tending to himself. They dressed in silence, and then Blue reached for her again like it was the most natural thing in the world, despite the sadness that welled in his eyes. Lizzie didn't want him to leave, and she knew what she was about to ask might be met with anger, but she had to try. He was obviously trying. He was trying so darn hard.

Within the safety of his arms, she said, "I have to tape my show tonight."

She felt him hold his breath.

"Stay with me?" she asked, knowing he probably wouldn't.

He drew back and gazed into her eyes with confusion and discomfort, and, miraculously, with undeniable love. "I don't think I can. I'm not there yet."

She nodded, feeling the sting of rejection all the way to her toes.

Chapter Twenty

LIZZIE LEFT BLUE in the kitchen packing up his things and went down to the basement to tape her show. She stood at the bottom of the steps, eyes closed, arms wrapped around her middle, and contemplated running back upstairs—*Stay with me. I'll stop making the videos. Just love me, Blue. Love me and let me love you.*

She opened her eyes and turned, catching a glimpse of Madison's picture hanging on the wall. Her eyes shifted back to the stairs. *Two years, Blue. It's only two more years.* A night was too hard for him. Two years would be impossible. She had to let him go. She was used to putting herself and her feelings last. This was just another thing she needed to do. She pulled her shoulders back despite the tears slipping down her cheeks and headed for the bathroom.

Fifteen minutes later, dressed in a pair of heels and her trusty apron, blond wig in place, thick frames perched on her nose, she stood in front of the computer and tried to fake a smile—and failed. With a groan, she tried again, pacing, trying to work off the nervous energy that was turning every nerve to ice. She didn't feel sexy or seductive. She felt like she'd hurt the only man on earth who mattered. Forcing herself to look at

Maddy's picture again, she cleared her throat, pulled her shoulders back for the millionth time, and told herself that she could do anything for forty-five minutes or an hour.

One minute at a time.

She turned on the camera and did her best to turn the heat up in her voice.

"Have you missed your Naked Baker? Because I sure have missed you." *I can do this. I can do this.*

She waved a hand over the baking supplies. "Today I have a special surprise just for you. We're going to make nipple cupcakes." She narrowed her eyes and winked at the camera, feeling sick to her stomach. "That's right, just the right amount of frosting for you to settle that dirty little mouth of yours over and enjoy."

Over the next few minutes she struggled to push the hurt and stress of the day to the side, to push past the love she and Blue had shared, the tenderness of his touch as he bathed her, the look in his eyes when she'd said she had to tape her show— *This is for Maddy. I can do this. I have to do this*—and she concentrated on doing what she'd been doing twice a week for what felt like forever. For better or for worse, this was her life.

BLUE STOOD AT the top of the stairs unable to tear himself away from the seductive voice traveling up from below. Even here, standing in Lizzie's home and knowing that she was downstairs dressed in an apron, filming the show, he couldn't reconcile that feigned seductive voice with the woman he loved. He didn't know what drove him down the stairs—morbid curiosity or jealousy—but he walked down quietly, stopping when she came into view. He'd seen her on the video wearing the blonde wig and thick dark glasses, but it still shocked him to see her in the getup right there in person. The apron she wore outlined the swell of her breasts, wrapped around her hips, and barely covered her private parts. His gut clenched when she turned and he saw she was wearing a skin-colored thong that covered absolutely nothing.

He watched her in silence, taking in everything she said as she moved around the kitchen, removing one tray from the oven as she put another in, all the while narrating each step and dropping seductive lines like teaspoons of sugar. Blue couldn't help but be mesmerized by her, because he wasn't seeing the blond beauty everyone else saw, the woman who was working meticulously to perfect frosting on cupcakes. No, the woman he saw was the one who was hiding beneath the costume. The woman he held in his arms, and in his heart, who'd taken the time again tonight, when she was upset and worn out, to go to the cemetery to pay homage to people she didn't know. The woman who, despite the way her life had been upended, despite the fact that it was almost midnight and she had to be exhausted, still came down here to film a show so her sister wouldn't have student loans.

The woman he loved, admired, and worried about, in equal measure.

A part of him still felt the videos were demeaning. She was a strong, intelligent businesswoman, with radiance that lit up a room and a heart of gold. She was the woman who was making him question all the things he believed to be true about people and trust, loyalty and lies. All the things he believed to be true about himself. She was the woman he loved, and he wished there were some way he could help her achieve her financial

SEIZED BY LOVE AT SEASIDE

goals without putting her in such a compromising position. But what he realized was that while he worried the videos were demeaning, she'd obviously been able to overcome that aspect for Maddy's sake.

Didn't he feel like a fool? He'd never known anyone who put others first the way she did.

Blue quietly retreated upstairs, not wanting to disrupt her. He gathered his things and drove home, trying to figure out how to reconcile the situation in his mind with the one in his heart.

Chapter Twenty-One

FRIDAY WAS A blur. After getting up early and redecorating the cupcakes she'd made the night before so they no longer looked like giant nipples, Lizzie dropped them off at the homeless shelter before finally arriving at work late, nearly missing her supplier. She'd been too busy all afternoon to answer Blue's calls, and if she were honest with herself, she also wasn't ready to speak to him. She really *did* understand why he hadn't stayed last night, even if she wished he wasn't bothered by the webcast.

She was living a contradiction that she didn't know how to remedy. Knowing she was doing something that he didn't readily accept, something she felt ashamed of—even if thinly rimmed with pride for being able to take care of her own finances, and Maddy's as well—warred with her unwillingness to refrain from doing it. And the whole situation left her feeling empty and lost.

But last night when she was in Blue's arms, she'd felt full again. She'd felt *found*. She tried not to analyze the precarious position she'd put herself in, or the fact that she felt trapped by her own desires—teetering between the man she loved and the need to help her sister. She thought about calling Blue, but she knew she'd be too emotional to drive and talk, and it was already after four. She'd promised her parents she and Maddy would be there by six thirty, and she needed to haul her butt down to Harborside University if they had any hopes of making it on time. She grabbed her purse and locked up the shop.

"Taking off?"

She was startled by the sound of Blue's voice, and her hand flew to her heart. Blue stood a few feet away, devilishly handsome, his eyes wavering between confident and tenuous. *I did that to him. I stole his confidence in us.* Her heart sank with the realization.

She let out a fast breath, unable to fall down that hole at the moment. "I have to get Maddy. I'm late."

"I've been calling you all day." His tone was thoughtful, not vengeful or upset, as he followed her out back to her car.

He was here, and last night, he'd been with her. It wasn't his desire that was wavering, she realized. It was probably his trust, and that cut her even deeper.

"I know. I'm sorry. It's been a crazy day, and it's going to be crazy until I get Maddy dropped back at school tonight. She called earlier and said she can't stay for the weekend after all because of some talent event at her friends' bar or something."

"Bar? She's nineteen."

Surprised by his concern, she tossed her purse in her car, noticing a sheen of purpose hovering in his eyes. "Yeah. I know. It's a bar and restaurant. The Taproom, I think it's called. They're not serving drinks. She's going just for the event itself."

He touched her lower back, and his gaze turned thoughtful. "I was hoping we could talk. I'm sorry I didn't stay last night."

"It's okay. I understand." She tried to smile, but couldn't muster it, even though she was already so much happier than she had been just a day ago. She was rushing and confused, and wanted so desperately to stay there and talk things through so they could move forward together and get back to that magical place they'd shared—but she was scared to death they might never get that far.

"Thank you for the sweet note this morning," he said with a warm smile that stole her breath, "but I missed my sugary treat."

"I wasn't sure you'd want them now that you know why I bake so often." She'd left a clean coffee mug beside a fresh pot of coffee for him, along with a note thanking him for being understanding the night before, but she'd been too conflicted to leave a cupcake.

"Lizzie, there's so much we need to talk about."

"I know you need time to figure out if you want to be with me, and I get that."

"I want to be with you, Lizzie." His voice went serious and soft at the same time, something she was sure only he could pull off. "*Want* isn't the issue. You have to know that. And I didn't mean to upset you last night by leaving."

"I'm not upset that you didn't stay. It just hurt, and I don't know where we stand—"

"Where we stand is that I want to try to make this work. We have a lot to talk through, but I know we can get past this."

"You…you do?"

"I do, Lizzie."

The sincerity in his voice tugged at her heart. But she didn't have time to talk through things now. She had to get Maddy, but she did want to tell him what she'd wanted to say last night.

"I didn't get to thank you last night for convincing me to tell Sky. I didn't get to say much of anything, because my heart was going crazy and my mind was in tatters—in the very best kind of tatters, of course." She felt her cheeks flush.

He stepped in closer, holding her gaze, and placed his hands on her hips. His voice was smooth, rich, comforting. "I wasn't trying to convince you of anything, and I'm sorry I overreacted."

She knew she should react to his apology, but she still hadn't decided if he'd overreacted or not. What she did know was that she had to tell him what was circling around in her head.

"I know you weren't, but I told Sky about the webcast, and it was like crawling out from under a dark cloud. I never knew my secret was weighing so heavily on me, but you were right. I was rationalizing in order to continue. I'm planning to tell Madison and my parents tonight. As difficult as it was to come clean, Blue, it was also freeing, and I'm thankful that you opened my eyes to what my life had become."

"You told Sky?"

She saw the surprise in his eyes, and as he drew her closer, the rest of what she'd been holding back tumbled out.

"I did, and Blue, being with you is everything. I never knew that I could miss you so much after only one day. But when we were apart, a piece of me was missing. I haven't been able to think straight all day, and I just feel empty. Being close to you again made me think about what I really wanted and what I needed. I want to be with you, Blue."

He breathed a relieved sigh and embraced her. "Thank goodness, because I can't go another day without you."

She forced herself to push back, unwilling to fool herself or him. "I care for you a great deal, and I know that you still care for me, and that gives me hope for us. But after giving it probably way too much thought, I'm certain that I need to continue with the webcast, for Maddy's sake."

His brows knitted together in confusion.

"I made a commitment to her education, and that's a commitment I won't back down from. It's only two more years, which I know must feel like a lifetime to you." Needing the connection and for him to realize how strongly she meant what she was about to say, she pressed her hand to his chest, surprised to feel how fast his heart was beating. "When you've been doing this as long as I have, you realize that two years will go fast. I still can't believe that you had been asking me out for a year before I finally came to my senses. A year went quickly, Blue, didn't it?" *Please say yes. Please, please say yes.*

"That was the longest year of my life," he answered with a hint of exasperation *and* a smile. "You infiltrated my dreams and lingered in my mind every minute of every day. Two years is a ridiculously long time. This is all new for me, so I don't really know what I'm dealing with, but I know what I want, Lizzie, and I want to be with you."

She held her breath for a *but...*

He swallowed hard, sending his Adam's apple bouncing up his neck. "I saw you taping last night. I only watched for a minute, but—"

"You watched me?" *Oh no. That's the kiss of death.*

"I couldn't help it. I was getting ready to leave and I heard you talking, and...I'm sorry. I went down and watched from the stairs for just a few minutes." He reached up and touched her cheek. "But what I saw was a woman who was acting, not *my* Lizzie. On some level I've understood that the whole time, but on a deeper, more intimate level, there was still a twinge of something gnawing at me."

She dropped her gaze, unable to take much more. She was already standing on a precipice and was afraid that one strong gust of wind would send her over the edge.

He lifted her chin and gazed into her eyes. "I realized that I haven't felt the claws of jealousy for so long, I didn't recognize them."

She fisted her hands in his shirt, stifling a laugh of relief, because it would be wrong to laugh at something like this, but she'd been so scared about what he might say that laughing was about all she could manage.

"Jealousy? Over guys I don't know or care about?"

"What can I say? I'm jealous over my girl." His lips quirked up, and in that split second, the tide changed between them. "When I first started working at your house, I was your friend, but I was hoping to become more. And every note, every sugary treat, every flash of your adorable dimples, made me want to cross that line even more. And then suddenly, there you were, and you were *mine*. And I was the happiest man on earth. Then I found out that while you were mine, you were seducing other guys with the same sugary treats and seductive voice. I'm not judging you. This part isn't about you. It's about *me*. I can't help it if I'm jealous, and I admit it. I am as jealous as the day is long."

"No, I guess you can't help it." She was still clinging to his shirt, trying to remain stable on this roller-coaster ride of emotions. As relieved as she was, and as much as she knew they needed to talk this out even more, she was painfully aware of the time and of her impending confession to Maddy and her parents hovering over her, making her even more anxious.

"I have to go get Maddy, but we both need to be sure about all of this. I know two years is a long time in your eyes, but I've been doing this for so long that I finally see a light at the end of the tunnel. I hope that when I get there, you'll be waiting for me."

Chapter Twenty-Two

MADDY HADN'T STOPPED chatting since they left the university grounds, and Lizzie couldn't get a word in edgewise. She hardly had the heart to interrupt her sister's rant about the trials and tribulations of college life; after all, she agreed with them.

"I mean really, Lizzie. Where do these guys get off thinking that just because a girl goes to a party that she wants to sleep with someone? I like parties, but that doesn't mean I'm there looking for a guy to hook up with." Maddy shoved a Twizzler into her mouth and pushed her long, honey-colored hair from her shoulders. "All I want is to get my education, have fun with my girlfriends, and *maybe* meet a nice guy. Don't get me wrong. I'm not opposed to sex in general, but…Are there nice guys out there? Are there guys who aren't busy drinking and sleeping with every girl in sight?"

Lizzie laughed, but inside she was thinking, *Yeah, there are. And I hope I haven't lost the best of them.*

"There are, Mad, but they may be hard to come by in college. Think of a hundred kids raised like us—no dating, nine-thirty curfew—all set free for the first time ever. Of course they're going to be all over everything they possibly can get their hands on. They're rebelling, and experiencing, and living life the way they haven't been allowed to. But that doesn't make them bad people."

"Just horny people," Maddy said with a laugh. "Geez, I've been talking this whole time. I'm sorry. I'm just so sick of it all, and the girls are just as bad, but I won't go there." Her eyes rolled over Lizzie like she could see the discomfort prickling her skin. "What's up with you lately? How's the shop?"

"The shop is great, but I do need to talk to you about something."

"If it's about my books, I got a job at the bookstore next semester. I'll get a discount, and I hope to earn enough to pay for them myself." Pride radiated from her sister's hazel eyes. "See? You taught me well. I'm trying to pay my own way so Mom and Dad don't have to stress about it and so you don't have to keep shoveling your hard-earned money my way."

"That's kind of what I need to talk to you about. You know I don't mind paying, right? And that Mom and Dad would if they could."

Maddy grabbed another Twizzler from her purse and waved a dismissive hand, then pointed the long red candy at Lizzie. "I know you don't *mind*, but I still feel bad."

"Well, don't." Lizzie pulled off the highway at the exit for Brewster and drove toward their parents' house. "Mad, I haven't exactly been honest with you about where the money for your college is coming from."

Maddy offered a Twizzler to Lizzie.

"No, thanks. Mom's making dinner," Lizzie said.

Maddy pulled a Snickers from her purse and waved it in front of Lizzie. "You know you want it." She tore open the wrapper and handed the delicious chocolate to Lizzie.

"Gosh, I love you." Lizzie bit off a hunk while Maddy nibbled at her licorice. "Did you hear what I said, Mad? I lied to you."

"Uh-huh. But you never lie. You're even more straitlaced than me."

"Not really. It just seems that way." She pulled over in the parking lot of their old elementary school and parked the car so she could give Maddy her full attention.

"Oh no, what are you going to tell me?" Maddy's hands fell to her lap, a look of worry riddling her beautiful young face.

"It's not that bad. Well, it is, maybe, but…here goes. When I was in college and Dad got sick, I had to pay my own way, too, and I ended up with loads of school loans. I saw myself working for minimum wage for the rest of my life and never realizing my dreams because of it, and so I found a way out. And that way out paid for my school loans, my flower shop, and now for your school, too."

"Just tell me what it is, Lizzie. You sound like Mom when she's dancing around something she doesn't want to talk about."

"I do a video webcast called the *Naked Baker*—but I'm not naked; I wear an apron—and it's all monetized. I earn money from it to pay for your school."

Maddy's lips pressed into a firm line, and then she burst into laughter. She laughed so hard her head tipped back. "Oh my gosh, you had me there for a second. You? The *Naked Baker*? More like the *Proper Baker*."

Her laughter was contagious, but it also irked Lizzie to know that everyone saw her as such a good girl. "Madison, I'm telling you the truth."

Maddy whipped her head in Lizzie's direction. "No, you're

definitely messing with me."

Lizzie leveled her most serious big-sister stare at her.

Maddie gasped. "For real? Why? I thought you made enough money with the flower shop to help."

Lizzie shook her head, shame burning her cheeks. She told Maddy the whole sordid story, and when she was done, they sat in silence for so long Lizzie felt sick to her stomach.

"Do you hate me?" she finally asked.

"Hate you? No. I just can't believe you would do that. Not that there's something wrong with it, but there kinda is." Maddy's gaze softened apologetically. "Do Mom and Dad know?"

Lizzie shook her head.

"Please don't tell them. They can't take this, Lizzie. I guess I've always known that you would do anything for me, and now that the initial shock has worn off, I get it. But *they* won't be okay with this. Gosh, I can't even picture you doing something like this. Mom and Dad will have a stroke."

"Hey, I make a great blonde, and my legs aren't bad."

Maddy rolled her eyes. "You're gorgeous all over, but..." She reached for Lizzie's hand. "Thank you for doing all that, but maybe you shouldn't do it anymore. I feel responsible. I *am* responsible. Oh no. This is my fault. I've turned my sister into an online ho!"

"Wow, Mad, don't soften the blow or anything." Lizzie looked out the window, caught between laughter and dismay.

"I didn't mean that. I just...Lizzie, now that I know what you're doing, I can't keep taking your money."

"You can and you will." Lizzie started the car. "And I have to tell Mom and Dad. I can't keep lying to everyone."

"They won't understand, and then I'll be to blame for that,

too."

"Mad, I'm a grown-up. This has nothing to do with you and everything to do with me and my choices. No matter how Mom and Dad take it, it's not your fault."

An hour later, Lizzie wished she'd listened to Maddy's advice. Her parents sat at either side of their dining room table with pained looks on their faces. Her mother's trembling hand covered her mouth; her thin brows were pinched together, and her father scowled, his eyes flaming with disappointment.

"Dad, say something. Anything," Lizzie pleaded.

"You're not the girl I raised." Vernon Barber pushed from the table, avoiding eye contact with Lizzie. He bent and kissed the top of Maddy's head. "Madison, thank you for coming home for dinner."

It might have been the condescending way he made the proclamation about her or the emotions of the last few days getting the better of her. Lizzie wasn't sure what tipped her over the edge, but she threw her napkin on the table and pushed to her feet.

"I'm paying for the education you couldn't afford. How about saying something like, *Thank you. We may not think it's the best way to go about it, but good job.*"

"Lizzie!" Maddy snapped.

Lizzie had never raised her voice to their father before, and she knew she was skirting a dangerous line, but she was too angry to stop.

Her father waited until she was done, then silently left the room.

"Vernon," their mother said in a harsh whisper. Margaret Barber watched her husband walk upstairs; then she picked up her fork and, without looking at Lizzie or Maddy, said, "Shall we finish our meal?"

Maddy gave Lizzie a stern look that clearly said, *I told you so!*

"Mom, I want to talk about this. I'm sorry I didn't tell you and Dad sooner." Lizzie's stomach ached, but it wasn't sadness that had her pushing her mother to talk. It was anger. Anger at feeling like she'd needed to keep the whole darn thing a secret in the first place, anger for putting herself in this position. Anger at her father for walking away.

When her mother didn't respond, she pushed harder. "Talk to me, please?" Lizzie pleaded.

Her mother placed her fork beside her plate and folded her hands in her lap. Her eyes were sad and confused at once, but there was no mistaking the sheen of love hovering above the other emotions. "Elizabeth, I know you did this for your sister. And before that, for yourself, but that doesn't make it right."

"It doesn't make it wrong, either," Madison said, surprising them all.

Their mother exhaled a long breath. "This will take your father some time to get over."

"And you?" Lizzie asked, bracing herself with the table to keep from running from the room.

"You're my daughter, and I love you." Her mother reached for Lizzie's hand and gave it a gentle squeeze. "We all make mistakes. Some are just bigger than others."

They finished dinner in silence, and before Lizzie and Madison left, their mother embraced them both and said, "This will just take some time," to Lizzie.

When Lizzie dropped Maddy off at her dorm, Maddy hugged her tightly and said, "You're the best sister I could ever have, and I love you and appreciate your ability to be a ho in private."

Maddy had always been able to cheer Lizzie up, and after their tense dinner with their mother and being shunned by their father, she needed to remember why she was doing the show in the first place. And when it came to Maddy, she still felt like no concession was too big.

Chapter Twenty-Three

BLUE WORRIED ALL evening about Lizzie telling her family about the webcast. As proud as he was of Lizzie for wanting to finally tell her family the truth, the more he thought about it, the more concerned he became. He'd had hours to be introspective about Lizzie's webcast, and among other things, he realized that while complete honesty was vital to him, that didn't mean it was right for everyone else. He didn't want her to come home to an empty house if the evening didn't go well, so he'd driven to her house a half hour ago and had been waiting for her on her porch ever since.

When his cell phone rang, he hoped it was Lizzie, but wasn't surprised to see Sky's name on the screen. He answered the call knowing he hadn't been fair to Sky either. "I'm sorry I didn't return your calls."

"I hope you have redeemed yourself. What the heck, Blue?"

"Don't you think this whole thing was a freaking blow to me?" He paced the yard. "First, she completely steals my heart, then she reveals that she walks around in an apron and heels for strangers. It's not like she's on *Rachael Ray*, fully dressed."

"She's not naked, Blue. I watched a video. I think she looks hot as a blonde."

"She'd look hot bald." He smiled, thinking about how true that was. "That's not the point. She owns me, Sky. Heart and soul, and now…"

"She owns you? And this is the first I'm hearing of that? Now who's blown who away?"

He smiled. If anyone knew how much it meant for Blue to fall for a woman, it was Sky. She'd been there every step of the way over the past few years, and she knew he rarely dated, much less opened up to anyone but family.

"I should have been in touch. I'm sorry. It's been a crazy week, and now we've got this to deal with. But, Sky, make no mistake about it. I love her, and I admire her—I just have to learn to deal with this other stuff."

"Oh, Blue." Sky sighed, and her voice turned stern again. "When I first met Sawyer and had a hard time with his boxing, you told me that boxing wasn't who he was; it was what he did. So where do you come off holding this over Lizzie's head?"

He pictured the scowl on her face as she challenged him. "That's just it. I'm *not* holding it over her head. I'm trying to deal with my own jealousy—and you know me, Sky. I don't get jealous. Besides, this is different. You opposed *what* he did, not…"

He walked around to the side yard and headed out back, away from the lights of the porch, which made him feel exposed. His gut burned as he bit back what he really wanted to say. *I love her so much it hurts, and I can't protect Lizzie and her reputation from all the things they say about her online.*

"Not what?" Sky pushed.

"You were opposed to Sawyer's fighting, but—and don't you dare think for a second that *I* believe this—but it wasn't like he was out doing something where people could think that he was slutty. Women weren't watching him seduce the camera like a pro."

"So what? So she's good at seduction. That's a feather in her cap. You're being a jackass. I hope you know that."

"Didn't you hear me? I told you that *I* don't feel that way. I've read the things people write online about the *Naked Baker*, and it makes me want to kill someone." Renewed anger simmered inside him. He wished he had the answers and the wherewithal to be able to ignore the things he'd read online about Lizzie, but it made him want to hurt the people who wrote it.

Sky sighed. "So, what are you going to do?"

"The very best I can. I'm trying to work through my own issues. That's our biggest hurdle. And you know she's doing this for Maddy, right? For her *sister*. She's just so incredible. Who else would do that?"

"SOMEONE WHO PUTS family first." The anger in Lizzie's voice resonated through her with a vehemence she had no idea she possessed. "Of all people, I thought you'd get that."

Blue spun around, and the phone dropped to his side. He hadn't even heard her car pull up. "Lizzie!"

"Stupid me. I got your messages and rushed home after dropping Maddy off. I thought you really wanted to talk, but this—"

"It's Sky!" He held the phone out toward her. "She called to give me a hard time."

Lizzie stormed past him toward her kitchen door. She heard him tell Sky he had to go as she went inside and stalked into the living room. Seconds later he grabbed her arm from behind.

"Let go, Blue." She was too mad to talk rationally. "I'm just *slutty, seducing the camera like a pro.*"

"You heard that out of context." He reached for her, and she shrugged him off. "Come on, Lizzie. You heard part of what was said, but it wasn't meant the way you're making it sound. Do you really think *I* think you're slutty? If you heard that, then you heard me say I read the stuff online about you and I wanted to kill the people who wrote it. I'm defending you, Lizzie, *not* demeaning you."

She sank down to the edge of the couch, unable to remain standing any longer. "I don't know what to think. Or what to feel anymore." She wiped angry tears from her eyes. She was so sick of crying she could scream.

Blue crouched in front of her and lowered his voice. "I would never call you that. I was telling Sky the difference between her not agreeing with Sawyer's boxing and me having issues with your video stuff. I worry about what people might think about you." He gasped a breath. "Damn it. That sounds messed up, too."

Lizzie scowled. She knew exactly what he was trying to say because that was one of the main reasons she hadn't told people about it. But it still hurt to hear it from him.

He placed his hands on her thighs, and when she looked away, he touched her chin, bringing her gaze back to his. "Lizzie, sweetheart, what you heard was my own frustration. I care about you so much. How am I supposed to protect you from anonymous viewers posting lewd crap about you online? How can I protect your reputation?"

"I don't need you to protect me or my reputation. Don't you get that?" She'd spent years protecting it just fine by keeping it hidden.

"But I'm a guy, and I love you. It's the same as not letting you go into a bad area alone at night, or keeping you warm when it's cold."

His voice was sincere, and the look in his eyes was so apologetic that it cut right to her heart.

"That's not *too* sexist of a remark, is it?" She crossed her arms over her chest and turned away. He moved in closer and wrapped his arms around her waist, bringing them so close she could practically taste the mint on his breath.

"Don't you see? That's what I was trying to say to Sky. Not that *you* were slutty, but Lizzie, you have to know that there's stuff all over message boards on the Internet about the Naked Baker and what guys want to do to her. And how am I supposed to feel about that? They say all this sex stuff, and I can't pound the tar out of them because they're hiding behind electronics. They're anonymous trolls."

"Anonymous trolls who are paying for Maddy's college— and who paid for mine and for my flower shop. I don't read that stuff. I made a decision when I first started this that I would never read any of that because it's too upsetting."

"Right. Exactly."

"So? Can't you just not read it?" She knew by the look in his eyes that it wasn't even a fair question to ask.

"Seriously? It wouldn't change the fact that I know what they're saying. Anonymous or not. Just tell me this. Do you still *want* to be with me?" The hope and love in his eyes washed over her like a caress, drawing the truth she didn't want to hold back.

"More than anything." She breathed deeply, trying to get ahold of her emotions.

"Then we'll figure this out together. This *all* scares me. I wish I could just tell you it's sexy and watch you tape your shows, and go on with life as it was. I'm trying, Lizzie. I'm trying to get past my own issues. If this is what you want to do, then maybe we can come to a compromise that we both can live with, because I know I don't want to live without you."

"I can't really compromise with Maddy's future, and I'm not going to let *you* pay for her college."

He laughed. "You saw me going there, huh?"

"Weren't you?"

He took her hand in his and brought it to his lips, pressing a kiss to her knuckles. "Babe, there isn't anything I wouldn't do for you, but if I've learned one thing in the time we've spent together, it's that you have too much pride for me to step in and take over. This is *your* thing, your commitment. I just want to find a way to make it something we can both live with, and maybe that makes me selfish for not just accepting it for what it is, but my heart is too wrapped up in you to just blindly accept seeing you put yourself in a position where other people can write unsavory things about you."

"I know. I get it, but I don't know what the answer is."

"I honestly don't either. Maybe if I make sure I'm not around when you're filming the shows. I can always set up an electric shock on my laptop to zap me when I try to surf the message boards to see what's being written about you. My cousin's friend, Dex Remington, is a computer guy. I bet he can rig something up." The tease in his smile warmed her heart.

"Aw, you'd shock yourself for me? Now, that's true love." Lizzie bit her lower lip, mustering up the courage to tell him the rest of her news, so they would have no more secrets between them. "There's more."

"More?"

"Yes. My father isn't speaking to me, and my mother is doing I have no idea what." She tried to stave off tears at the realization of her father turning his back on her.

"My father said I'm not the girl he raised, like I'm some kind of delinquent." She drew in a deep breath as Blue gathered her in his arms, holding her tight. "At least my mother ate dinner with us, even though she was clearly upset. But my dad…"

"It's going to be okay. He's your father *and* he's a man, so you have a double whammy, but you also have the bonus of unconditional love on your side. He'll come around."

She scoffed. "I don't think my father knows what unconditional love is." She pulled back and wiped her eyes. "He wouldn't even look at me."

Blue's eyes filled with remorse. "This is my fault. I shouldn't have said any of those things about not telling your family. I'm so sorry, Lizzie. I wish I could take it back."

"No. I'm still glad you said what you did. It's hard to live a secret life, and even though this is hard right now, it somehow also feels a little better. At least Maddy doesn't hate me for it. For a minute I thought I was going to lose everyone." She drew in a sharp breath and blew it out slowly. "I have other news, but I don't know if it's good or not."

"Lay it on me, because at this point, there isn't much that we can't handle."

"The Food Channel Network wants to talk to me about the possibility of making the webcast into a cable show." She bit her lower lip to keep pride from slipping out in a smile.

"The Food Channel Network? FCN? Really? That's impressive. You must have something they think they can make a fortune off of."

"Well, I'm up to more than half a million views per show, so I guess so."

His eyes widened. "You have more than half a million views per show?"

She nodded. "Sometimes more, sometimes less."

"That's a lot of dudes looking at you." The side of his mouth quirked up playfully. He must have noticed how the comment pierced her heart, because he followed it up with, "Baby, it was a bad joke. I'm sorry. I don't know much about online statistics, but that number sounds pretty amazing. I guess the real question is, do you want to keep doing the show, or if there was a way to earn the same money but not do it, would you want to do that?"

She could see the gears of his mind churning. "That's not even an option. Come with me."

They went to the basement, where she retrieved the ledgers she kept for the webcast and tossed them onto the counter.

"Look at the numbers. It's all in there. I earn a lot from the show. I'd have to take on a second career to earn that much." She felt weird knowing that he was going to see how closely she tracked all of the information. At first she'd tracked the views and income just to see if there was a pattern, but then she'd begun picking apart the shows and sort of obsessing over it, tweaking each episode to the point where she could expect a little bump with each one. She worried that he might think she cared about it for the wrong reasons. The show had become such a big part of her life that she *did* care about it doing well. *For Maddy.* It was all for Maddy. "I'm going to wait upstairs."

She left him poring over the ledgers. He came up a short while later with the ledgers under one arm and sat beside her on the couch. He laced their fingers together and brought hers to his lips for another tender kiss.

"May I sit with you while I finish? If we're going to be in this together, I have a few questions."

She nodded, hoping the questions weren't going to be too painful. He leafed through the ledgers, asking questions about statistics and how she'd come up with a few of the ideas she'd had to boost views. He went through the books for a long while, and when he finally set them aside, he rubbed the back of his neck with a serious look in his eyes.

"Lizzie, you've created a viable business, not just a webcast," he said with a look of incredulity.

"Enough to help Maddy, at least." She leaned back and pulled her legs up on the couch beside her.

He picked up the financial and stats ledgers and set them on his lap again, motioning for her to come closer.

"You've tracked and evaluated everything, from the best times to broadcast to the types of things that increase your ratings—facial expressions, comments, and hand movements." He flipped through a few pages and pointed to one of the graphs she'd created. "You've stripped down your shows minute by minute, evaluating every last thing and equating it to dollars and cents."

She felt her cheeks flush. "I'm a little anal. I guess my business and marketing degree paid off after all, huh?"

"Babe, you're brilliant." He flashed a flirty grin that made her heart soar.

She gave him a playful shove, and he laughed, pulling her into a hug that filled her with relief. Maybe they really would get through this together.

"I don't know for sure, but I'd bet you could sell the rights to your show for more than you can make over the next two years by continuing to do it yourself."

"No way." She laughed. "Talk about a pipe dream. It's a rinky-dink little webcast."

"No, it's not a rinky-dink little anything. If it is an option, would you want to consider it? If you could get the money you need for Maddy? It would obviously give me peace of mind, knowing Maddy was taken care of and you weren't putting yourself out there nearly naked, but I don't want you to walk away from this because of me." He searched her eyes, and she knew he'd see the hope she felt swelling in her heart.

"You're serious? If that's really an option, I would do it in a heartbeat. Every time I do a show, I hope it's the one that will make enough money for me to stop. Do you really think it's worth a shot?"

"I think it's worth taking it to Duke, who knows more about valuing businesses than anyone I know. If anyone can figure this out, he can. And he can clue us in on behind-the-scenes stuff that we'd—*you'd*—need to consider."

She squeezed his hand. "*We.* I like *we* better." Inhaling a breath full of renewed hope for more things than she cared to take stock of for fear of jinxing them, she said, "But what if it doesn't work? I can't lose you twice, Blue. That would be too hard. I need to know that if we can't figure this out, then you'll still want to be with me even if I continue doing the webcast, because I'm not going to stop if this doesn't work. Otherwise—"

He tugged her in close, and she felt the beat of his heart, sure and steady, against her own. "I'm not losing you again, Lizzie. I may not like knowing half a million guys are ogling you, but that's *my* issue. And it's something I'll work on. Make no mistake about how much I want to be with you. I adore you. This is just a test of strength, for both of us. I'll support whatever you decide, one hundred percent."

He pulled back, and his eyes turned serious. "What I care most about is that from here forward, there are no secrets between us. Because when you first told me, I felt like I'd been betrayed, like I was reliving Sarah Jane all over again."

His confession stung, but she understood his feeling of betrayal and pushed past her own pain to explain. "I never meant to hurt you. I wanted to tell you, but selfishly, I wanted more time with you before I did."

"I know, babe. Don't you see? It really was—is—my issue, and I understand that now. Yes, you probably should have told me sooner, but either way, my pride got in the way. I'm sorry I reacted so harshly, and I know you could never be that type of person. You're an incredibly unselfish woman who does for others at her own expense. I was a little slow on the uptake. Not only do I see things more clearly now, but I'm in awe of you and the selfless things you do."

Lizzie dropped her eyes, feeling unworthy of such a compliment. Blue lifted her chin as he'd done so many times before, his eyes boring into her.

"I've honestly never met a person who does so much for others, and I'm sure I've only witnessed a small part of your generosity. This whole thing might have started as something you did to dig yourself out of debt, but how much of yourself have you put into this for Maddy? How much of your life have you put on hold in order to do it? That's inspiring, regardless of what you're wearing—or *not* wearing," he said with another teasing smile.

When his lips touched hers, the defenses she'd been clinging to for so long subsided, and a powerful sense of relief swept through her. She clung to that relief, and to Blue, as they kissed their differences away and he loved the doubt right out of her.

Chapter Twenty-Four

SUN STREAKED THROUGH the curtains in Lizzie's bedroom, casting a hint of warmth across Blue's legs. Even with all the turmoil of the last two days, he had no doubt about his feelings for Lizzie. They were both learning, trying, and yes, it was painful and difficult. The situation between them tested everything Blue had always believed about love and loyalty. But it also made perfectly clear how deeply he loved her and that he would do anything and everything to prove to her that he was with her for the long haul.

The sadness in Lizzie's eyes last night had destroyed him, and he'd wanted to drive straight to her parents' house and shake some sense into her father—but Lizzie needed him more than her father needed a swift eye opener. Lizzie was the same person he'd raised—all the morals and ethics he'd taught her were soundly ingrained, which was precisely why she was doing the webcast. Hopefully her father would figure out how incredible his daughter was and come around quickly.

He turned onto his side and wrapped an arm around her, tugging her in closer.

"How's my girl?" He kissed her cheek.

"Mm, better now." She turned to face him. Her half-lidded

eyes were sleepy and sexy, with an undercurrent of worry. "Are we okay? I mean, really okay?"

"We are." He pressed his lips to hers. "We hit a rough patch, but we made it through."

A sweet smile spread across her lips as the worry slipped away. "*A rough patch* that kinda sucked."

"It more than sucked, but we're not going there anymore."

She pressed her lips to the center of his chest, sending a shock of arousal through him. "I like the sound of that."

Her hands played over his chest, and the sensual look of seduction in her eyes awakened every inch of his body.

"Wish I had whipped cream," she said in a husky voice.

As she lifted her eyes to his, the world fell away, and he made sweet love to her.

Afterward, as she nestled against him, he'd never felt so alive, so in love, and he knew that all he ever wanted—all he ever needed—was right here in his arms.

EVEN WITH BLUE holding her, all his muscles glistening with their deliciously earned sweat, a gratified smile on his lips, and the look of love in his gorgeous blue eyes, Lizzie still wanted more. More of his strength, more of his love, more of *him*.

She still had a few minutes before she had to get ready for the day, and as he brought his lips to hers, she could think of no better way to spend it than making love with him again. Then reality clawed its way into her head and she realized she'd forgotten to edit the webcast that was supposed to run today.

Her eyes flew open. "Oh no," she said into his mouth.

"That's not exactly the reaction I was hoping for."

"I forgot to edit today's video, and I have to be at work in forty minutes to meet the supplier." She wiggled away from him. "I'm so sorry. I want to make love with you again and again, but..." She pushed to the edge of the bed, and he wrapped an arm around her from behind.

"Blue, this isn't funny. It takes me over an hour to edit each video." She tried to stand, and he held her in place.

"I said I'd be here for you, and I meant it. Tell me what to do with your supplier, and I'll go meet him."

Her heart nearly stopped. She whipped her head around and was met with a genuine warm smile that reached all the way to Blue's eyes.

"But you have your cottage to work on."

"And I have a cabin to live in. There's no rush. I told you I'm here for you, and I meant it. Tell me what to do." He sat up next to her.

His body heat seeped into her skin from shoulder to hip. She wanted to be close to him again, not edit a stupid video. She smiled at the thought of climbing on top of him.

He tipped her chin up with his finger, his smile turned sinful, his eyes filled with desire.

"You keep looking at me like that and neither of the things you need to get done are going to be accomplished."

The way his eyes traveled over her sent heat snaking through her and tangled her thoughts into a very naughty web. But it was the deeper emotions in his eyes that brought her lips to his, and the way those emotions took hold when they kissed, and touched, and *loved*, that claimed her heart.

Chapter Twenty-Five

AFTER MEETING WITH Lizzie's supplier Saturday morning, Blue returned to Lizzie's house and found her finishing up the edits for that evening's webcast. Every time he saw her she was doing something for someone else. He didn't know how she kept going each day with such a positive outlook, especially when her father was completely shunning her *and* she was maintaining two businesses.

Sunday greeted them with an uncommonly warm fall morning. Lizzie called her father, but he wouldn't even come to the phone. Blue wanted to drive down to Brewster and give him a piece of his mind, but again, he knew Lizzie needed him there with her.

He spent a few hours finishing up the renovations in her kitchen and then called his brother Gage to confirm that he'd taken care of a gift for Jeremy and Susan and called Trish to touch base and make sure she wasn't upset that he'd rushed off the phone the other night. She was so excited to hear about Lizzie coming to the wedding that she asked him a dozen questions, all of which he was happy to answer. After Trish gave him the third degree, he and Lizzie prepared to call Duke.

Lizzie fidgeted as they sat down together in the living room.

"The Food Channel Network returned my email—on a weekend, if you can believe that," she said. "They asked if I was open to discussing acquisition offers, so I told them I'd be interested in hearing their ideas."

"Wow, that's incredible. I guess their execs really are interested in your show. The ball's in their court, and it gives you time to get your ducks in a row, but only if you're sure you want to do this."

"If this works, I swear I'll be the happiest person on earth. I have the best boyfriend in the world, *and* this would finally get me out from under the exhausting cycle my life has become."

He heard relief in her voice but still needed to fully believe that she wasn't considering selling the rights just for him.

As if she'd read his thoughts, she touched his hand and her lips curved up in a sincere, loving smile. "Blue, I want this. I want this with all my heart. As proud as I am for finding my way without any help, I've always been ashamed of doing the show, too. Like it's my dirty little secret. I don't want to worry that a customer might come into the flower shop and recognize me from the webcast. Or that I'll take my kids to school one day and someone's husband will recognize me. Or a teacher. Can you imagine how embarrassing that would be?"

It seemed to Blue that relief had swept through him so many times in the last twenty-four hours that he should be floating on a cloud by now. He and Lizzie were definitely on the same page, and her mention of children made him wonder if they were on the same page with that, too.

"That might be embarrassing, but as long as I'm by your side, no one will dare say a derogatory word. If they do, I'll take care of them." He pressed a kiss to her temple as he opened the laptop and felt her bristle.

"All my worst fears are coming true." She stared at the computer screen as she spoke. "My father won't even speak to me, and people I know are finding out what I do in my off hours."

He knew Lizzie was nervous about speaking with Duke, but Blue also knew it wasn't the discussion about statistics and revenue that had her tied in knots. It was the thought of Duke watching the videos, which he would inevitably have to do.

Lizzie's gaze—and voice—turned thoughtful. "I don't know why, but this made me remember something that happened with Maddy. When she was sixteen, she went to a party. Of course my parents didn't know, but when I went to pick her up, she was totally not herself. She finally told me that she'd almost slept with a boy."

Blue's jaw clenched tight at the thought of her sweet sister sleeping with a guy at such a young age.

"I always thought I'd be a really cool big sister when it came to those things. You know, pat her on the back, tell her that she was smart enough to make good decisions, and that as long as she was safe, it was her body and her choice. I trusted her." Lizzie gazed into his eyes. "But I didn't act that way. I got pissed and said a bunch of stuff I shouldn't have, because I was scared for her. I couldn't protect her, and I knew that if she'd done it and other kids had found out, well, you know how cruel high school kids can be."

He reached for her hand and gave it a gentle squeeze. "I'm sure she understood."

"She didn't, not until she went away to college. After her first semester she finally forgave me and things returned to normal. Not that we weren't speaking or anything like that, but she was more careful with what she shared with me. I haven't thought about that night until now, and I think it's kind of the same thing as what happened between us. You're worried about what other people say or think, and you can't fix that."

"I was a jealous jackass, too. Let's not forget that." He pulled her in close and kissed her. "I love you, and I love that you cared enough for Maddy to want to protect her."

"I've always wanted to protect her, but that's not where I'm going with this. That night taught me that one day I'd have to deal with her giving herself to a guy and I'd have to trust her judgment." She paused again, her eyes drifting over his face, then holding his gaze. "I guess I want to thank you, Blue, for trusting my judgment enough to be here with me."

"Lizzie, you don't have to thank me. I definitely don't feel like I deserve to be thanked after the way I reacted. And I hope you know that you don't have to talk to Duke, and you don't have to go through with talking with the network people, either. You can continue with what you're doing, and I promise, I will stand by you."

She wrapped her arms around his neck and kissed him. "I know you will. Now call your brother before I chicken out about revealing the Naked Baker side of your girlfriend to your family."

Blue chuckled as he called Duke.

"Hey, B. What's going on?" Duke answered with his weekend voice, which was more effervescent than his professional voice.

"Hi, Duke. I was hoping to pick your brain about acquisitions."

Lizzie paced nervously.

"Sure, what are you considering?"

"It's not actually for me. It's for Lizzie. She's puts on a webcast and she's making pretty good money from it, and now the Food Channel Network is knocking on her door."

"That's a big deal. FCN is a major player. What's the webcast?" Duke asked.

Blue explained about the *Naked Baker* while Lizzie turned a pretty shade of crimson. He reached out to her, but she covered her face and pulled away, as if Duke could see her through the phone.

"Dude, those types of shows are hot right now. Did FCN tell her what they're thinking? Did they talk numbers?"

Blue was relieved that Duke's reaction was positive and that he didn't say something negative about the type of show she was doing. Then again, if he wasn't Lizzie's boyfriend, he might not have reacted the way he had, either. "Not yet." He smiled at Lizzie and mouthed, *It's all fine. Relax.*

She nibbled on her lower lip, and it made him want to draw her in close and reassure her, but he had to focus on the conversation with Duke first.

"Well, if she's really thinking about selling out, send me the financials and her business plan and let me look it over. We'll make sure she's got the best proposal she could possibly have before she walks in the door. FCN is here in Manhattan. I know one of their acquisition execs, Carly Christianson. She's a hard negotiator."

"Great, something to look forward to," he said sarcastically. "We're putting the proposal together, so we'll send you everything by the end of the week."

"These types of negotiations can be a bear. Make sure Lizzie's mentally prepared for it. Networks are known for trying to swoop into the little guys' houses and take advantage quicker than they can say *thank you.*"

Blue glanced at Lizzie, who was standing by the window

nibbling on her lower lip. He knew that when push came to shove, that tenuous persona would go out the window. "My girl can handle anything." He blew Lizzie a kiss, and she grabbed the air like she caught it and pressed her hand to her cheek. That small act of love warmed him all over.

"I'll do some research, pick a few industry brains, and look into comparable transactions and metrics." Duke was speaking fast. Clearly he'd gone into investor mode. "They'll look at precedent transactions and cash-flow analysis, although I can't imagine there's much analysis to do in that regard unless she's using proxies and doing a boatload of marketing. Online investors usually gravitate toward earnings multiples for business valuation because of its simplicity in the face of scarce comparable data, but I'll dig into all of that. You get me her financials for the last three years, projections for the next two, and stats: views, length of time spent on site, et cetera, and I'll handle the rest."

"Thanks, man. We'll get it all together." As he listened to his brother clicking away on his computer keyboard, he imagined Duke watching Lizzie in her apron and heels, purring into the camera, and jealousy scraped up his spine.

One look at Lizzie, and he slayed that green-eyed monster before it had a chance to do any damage. He ended the call with Duke and folded her into his arms.

"Well?" she asked in a quiet voice.

"Get ready for the ride of your life, sweetheart. The Ryder boys have got your back."

Chapter Twenty-Six

OVER THE NEXT week and a half Lizzie and Blue fell into a routine as naturally as they'd come together on their first date. Blue spent the days working at his cottage on the bluff, sending Lizzie sweet texts to let her know he was thinking of her while she was working at the flower shop. Sometimes he stopped by midafternoon to bring her lunch and see how she was doing. She knew he worried about her being upset over her father not speaking to her, and his love was comforting and a reminder that when you love someone, any hurdle could be overcome. If only her father would learn to jump.

The Food Channel Network had contacted her again and scheduled a meeting in New York for Friday. She was excited beyond belief and more nervous than she ever thought possible.

She and Blue had worked tirelessly through the evenings, combing through ledgers, collecting graphs and figures, preparing the strongest proposal they could for the network, and sent the information to Duke. Lizzie fought the urge to call and thank her father for pushing her to earn her degree, which she realized had helped her tremendously over the years. Thanking a man who wouldn't speak to her would be not only difficult, but heartbreaking.

Blue still wasn't quite ready to watch her film an episode. She could tell that he was still fighting jealousy, but she also knew how hard he was trying to push past it and support her. She was actually relieved that he didn't want to watch her film, because the idea of Blue watching her made her nervous. She worried she'd either fall into full seduce-Blue mode or look like she was trying too hard and totally flub up the episode.

Even though he wasn't comfortable watching, tonight he wanted to help her edit the show she'd taped the night before to get a better understanding of her process. *Baby steps.*

They sat before the laptop, waiting for the video to queue up. It was one thing to talk about the videos or for Blue to watch them without her in the room, but even though her heart told her that their relationship was strong enough to handle it, she worried that watching a *Naked Baker* video together could reignite Blue's discomfort.

Lizzie looked up from the laptop where they were working and stole a glance at the man who had relentlessly pursued her, challenged her, and had, remarkably, remained by her side. She'd never met a man like Blue before, blatantly honest about everything, even his insecurities. She didn't know a single man who would readily admit that jealousy stood between him and what he wanted, or that his need to protect her, and her reputation, was causing him conflict. She'd always considered herself an honest person, but she was quickly learning that her idea of honesty wasn't nearly as clearly defined as his. He'd shown her more about unconditional love than her own father had, and it made her love him even more.

He lifted his eyes, caught her watching him, and reached for her hand. She loved his tender touches as much as she loved his heated ones.

"Why don't you try calling your dad before we get started?" He smoothed his hand down her back. He always seemed to know what she needed.

She had called her father every day since they'd had dinner, and he still refused to come to the phone, which just about killed her. Her mother was trying to act normal, but Lizzie heard tension in her voice and felt the strain of their relationship every time they spoke. Lizzie hated feeling like a disappointment to them, but she'd come this far. She wasn't about to back down.

"I'm too nervous about you watching the video to call tonight."

His eyes warmed as he drew her into his arms. He was always drawing her into his arms, even more often now than before he'd found out about her secret. She used to pop out of bed in the mornings, but waking up in Blue's arms had changed everything. She was in no rush to leave the house, because nothing outside could possibly feel better than being held by the man she loved.

"I told you I'm ready for this," he insisted. "I'm not going to let you down, and once you see I can watch it, you'll be less worried about my family finding out."

"What if your family reacts like my father did?" She had almost begged off attending his cousin's wedding because she worried about how his family would react, but she knew that wouldn't be fair to Blue, especially since he was going to such great lengths to overcome his issues with the webcast and to support her decisions.

"Then I'll be right here by your side setting them straight, but they won't react that way. Duke is a businessman. He's so impressed with what you've done that he commends you every chance he gets. And all my brothers have a thing for hot women, so they'll think it's sexy." He touched his forehead to hers. "Fair warning...You should prepare to see the jealous boyfriend in me come out if they hit on you."

"They wouldn't do that." She laughed at the thought, even though Jake had flirted with her and every other woman in his path last summer. She'd seen the way Jake and Blue stood up for each other, and she knew that now that Jake was aware that they were dating, he'd never cross that line.

"Not if they know what's good for them. Call your dad, and then we'll get started. He has to come to his senses at some point." He pressed his lips to hers. "Remember, sweetheart, I'm proud of you, Maddy's proud of you, Sky is proud of you, and your father will be too. He just needs to get over himself first."

"You don't know my father." She pulled out her cell phone and walked to the other side of the room while she made the call. Her mother answered on the third ring.

"Hi, Mom."

"Hi, honey. How are you?" Her mother spoke quietly, and Lizzie knew her father must be nearby. It made her sick knowing that she'd put her mother in this position—and equally as ill knowing that her father could so easily turn his back on her.

"I'm okay. I'd be better if Dad would talk to me. Is he there?"

"He is. Hold on."

She heard her mother cover the phone, but the conversation between her parents was too muffled for her to decipher. When her mother returned to the phone, her sigh told Lizzie everything she needed to know before she said a word.

"I'm sorry, honey," her mother said.

"It's okay." Lizzie closed her eyes against the sting of her father's rejection. But as she opened her eyes, something inside her snapped. She wasn't a little girl making bad decisions. She was an adult, and she'd stood by her decisions to everyone else. Why was she practically begging for her father's approval?

"You know what, Mom? This isn't okay. I hate to do this to you, but since he won't talk to me, can you please put me on speakerphone?"

"Honey, I don't think that's a good idea."

She felt Blue's hand on her shoulder, and when she gazed up at him, the pride in his eyes drove her on.

"Please, Mom?"

A moment later her mother's voice echoed through the line. "Okay, you're on speakerphone."

"Is Dad in the room?" She knew better than to ask *him* to answer.

"Yes, honey," her mother answered.

Blue crossed his arms over his chest, his biceps twitched, his eyes narrowed, and she had a feeling that if he could climb through that phone and shake her father into submission, he would. She drew from his strength and held her chin high.

"Dad, I hope you'll stay in the room long enough to hear me out. My whole life you've taught me to do the right thing. You taught me that regardless of what I had, to always make sure I gave to others. When I wanted to skip going to college and try to make a go of a flower shop, you said that college would teach me things I never realized I needed to know." She expected to hear her father storm out of the room any second, but she had to say what was in her heart, regardless of what he did or didn't do.

"And you were right. I learned all about business, and it's

helped me tremendously with my flower shop. And it's helped me analyze and strategize and provide for Maddy's education with my webcast. I know you don't approve of what I'm doing, but I'm still your daughter." Tears of anger and hurt welled in her eyes as Blue's arm circled her. "I hope one day that you'll see I *am* the same girl you raised, only I'm stronger now and more capable of making good decisions. Decisions that have helped me and Maddy."

She gulped a breath, ignoring the bite of her father's silence.

"I love you, Dad, and all I'm asking is that you take a step back and see me for who I am, not whatever misconception you have about who you think I've become." Her trembling hand dropped to her side as she ended the call, and she buried her face in Blue's chest.

BLUE WISHED HE could walk out the door and pay her father a visit to knock some sense into him, but Lizzie needed him right now. He'd made the mistake once of walking away when she needed him, and he wasn't going to do that again. Her father could wait. Blue was so proud of her for taking a stand. He couldn't imagine any father ignoring such a heartfelt plea. But if her father remained distant, there was no way Blue would sit back and let the woman he loved be hurt again.

"Are you okay?"

She inhaled sharply, and when she pushed away, her eyes were full of determination.

"Yes. I am finally more than okay." She swiped at her damp eyes, and her lips curved into a smile.

Her strength floored him, but he'd known all along how

strong Lizzie was. She hadn't backed down for him. Why would she back down for anyone else?

"I realized as I was talking *at* my father that he's the one who taught me to be this way, so who is he to judge me?" She took a step away, waving her hand angrily. "I mean, he might not agree with me wearing nothing but an apron, but he taught me to give, to help others, and that's what I do every day of my life. And I'm hardly wearing any less than my bathing suit. That *has* to count for something."

Before he could say anything, she added, "And you know what else pisses me off? I'm not the only one who put my mother in this position. That's mostly his doing."

"Hopefully you finally got through to him. If he doesn't come around, then it speaks volumes of him as a person."

"He's not a bad guy, Blue." She crossed her arms protectively over her chest.

He loved her innate desire to protect her father despite how upset she was.

"I'm sure he's not. He's just a father watching out for his daughter. All I'm saying is that hopefully he'll see what an incredible woman you are and come to his senses soon. I hate to see you suffer over this. I never should have suggested that you shouldn't hide from the people who love you."

"Oh, yes, you should have. You opened my eyes to everything, most importantly, the difference between unconditional love, like ours, and whatever it is my father has for me." She took his hand and led him to the computer. "Let's get this sucker edited so we can move past the nerve-racking part of the night and into the fun part."

"Ah, the fun part." He kissed her lips. "Like maybe your Naughty-Love list?"

"I was thinking more about the other list." She raised her brows in quick succession.

"You're not going to make it easy for me to concentrate, are you?"

"That's the plan…"

They took the computer upstairs and set it on the table between them. They'd spent the last three days working through every statistic Lizzie had ever kept, analyzing them from every possible angle. He'd quickly learned that Lizzie was not just a beautiful, talented florist and bright businesswoman, but she had a brilliant analytical and strategic mind. She'd created a business that was continually climbing up the ranks of things he'd never known existed, like Alexa rankings—rankings of websites based on hits and length of time spent on the site— and surpassing partner income thresholds one after another. It was no wonder the Food Channel Network was courting her. If she did this full-time, she could easily earn hundreds of thousands of dollars. She obviously wasn't putting herself out there to achieve her own fame and fortune, or she'd be making more videos and forgoing her flower shop altogether, which was just another thing to admire about her.

Blue readied himself for an uncomfortable ride as they be-gan the editing process. Every muscle in his body tensed as he watched the woman who had stolen his heart seduce the camera, and he felt the claws of jealousy prickling his skin again. He pressed his hands to his thighs, telling himself to focus on the show, not on the sexy look in his girlfriend's eyes or the way she moved like a cat on the prowl, graceful yet powerful.

As the video rolled on and Lizzie began pointing out angles that were problematic and the way she tweaked scenes by removing a second or two of video, lighting issues that made her want to retape certain sections of the show, and about a dozen other nuances he'd never imagined her dealing with, Blue became engrossed in the process. She was incredible, the way she analyzed everything from the tone of her voice, the looks she flashed, and even the way she moved. She gave as much attention to detail and to every aspect of the show as Blue did to his carpentry work.

Blue found himself analyzing the video completely from a business standpoint, sans the jealousy that had initially plagued him. By the time they finished, Lizzie had two full pages of notes about what she liked and disliked about the video, things she needed to tweak, and differences between this video and her last, so she could compare the outcomes. She was so focused on making the video perfect that it was easy to understand how she was able to put herself out there in this fashion while carrying on her daily life and while falling in love with him. She'd separated herself from the *Naked Baker*. This was obviously a business venture that she took very seriously. Regardless of whether she was seducing a camera or creating a beautiful bouquet of flowers, she clearly gave it her all.

Lizzie closed the laptop, tension knitting her brows.

"We survived," he said as he brought her hand to his lips and pressed a kiss to it. The tension in her face slipped away.

"Yeah, we did." Her brow wrinkled again. "You're not feeling weird about me? What did you think?"

"Not even a little. I think you're even more incredible than I did before we watched it." He lifted her onto his lap. He didn't want her to worry about anything, least of all that his feelings for her would ever change. He could no sooner walk away from Lizzie than he could turn away from family. He tucked her hair behind her ear, and her lips curved up in a relieved smile.

"When you first told me about this, I couldn't imagine how you separated who you were in the video from who you are on a day-to-day basis. But when we were working just now, and for the past few days as you've brought me into your webcast world, I've come to realize that you put your heart and soul into making this a success, the same way that you do with your flower shop. The same way that you do with Maddy, with me." Blue pressed his lips to hers. "I think your father should edit a video with you."

She laughed. "Yeah, right."

"I'm kidding. Sort of. If you took him through these steps and he understood all the aspects of this incredible business you've created, it would put it into clearer perspective for him. I really believe that if your father could disregard the fact that his daughter is walking around in nothing but an apron and see your incredible business efforts for what they are, he would come around."

"I doubt that," she said as she ran her finger along his skin, just above his shirt collar, making it hard for him to concentrate.

"I also think you've got your work cut out for you where FCN is concerned."

She twined her arms around his neck. "Do you really think I'm doing the right thing? What if they say no?"

"Then you're in no worse shape than you are right now. But you do realize this is a no-brainer for them, right? If they can make a seamless transition to another actress using the momentum you've already put in place, then you're golden."

Her brow furrowed, and he touched his lips to hers, knowing exactly what was worrying her.

"And if they don't, I know you plan on continuing to host

the show until Maddy graduates, and I'll be right here by your side." He shifted her onto her back on the couch and came down over her, smiling as he pressed his lips to hers. "Or maybe I'd rather be right *here*, on top of you."

"Or maybe…" She glanced at the front door. "You'd rather be in your truck lying on top of me at White Crest Beach."

He blinked in surprise. "In my truck?"

"I added it to my Naughty-Places list," she said with feigned innocence.

He wanted to kiss that innocence out of her. "You did, did you? When did you do that?"

Her cheeks flushed. "About ten months ago."

"Ten months? When you were turning me down every chance you got?"

Desire filled her eyes. *So long, innocence.*

He rose to his feet and scooped her into his arms as she giggled and wrapped her legs around his waist.

"Heck, yeah," he said as he carried her toward the front door. "Let's go knock number one off your Naughty-Places list."

"Number ten," she corrected him.

He stopped cold, wondering what the first *nine* places on the list were. "Ten?"

She nodded again. "We already checked off number one. The beach."

"That's not fair. I had no idea we were working on your list. I could have made it more memorable." He walked outside and pulled the door closed behind them.

"That made it even more fun, and whether we're working on a list or just having fun, being close to you is always memorable. Besides, I added an eleventh place to the list." She leaned up and whispered, "The lighthouse."

Chapter Twenty-Seven

THE BREWSTER INN was a modest, pleasant-looking inn, located on the corner of a residential and commercial street in the heart of Brewster. Wednesday afternoon, Blue walked through the white picket fence, and he followed a slate path through beautiful gardens toward the front door of the inn. He had no doubt that Lizzie had had her experienced hands on the pretty plantings. He sensed her creative style in the varying heights and variety of flowers and shrubs. Thinking of Lizzie renewed his determination to set things right between her and her father. He'd never met the man, but all night he'd thought about what Lizzie had been handling alone for so long. It was time she got the support she deserved, and if there was a shred of a chance that talking to her father would help, then he'd make the effort.

He knocked on the door, thinking about how this probably wasn't the best way to get to know his girlfriend's parents, but so be it. He wasn't about to watch her suffer for one more second. She wasn't alone in this endeavor, no matter how her father decided to handle the situation, and he wanted her to know that every step of the way—though Lizzie had no idea he was making this visit.

A slim woman who couldn't have been more than five feet tall, with silky dark hair and the same upturned lips as Lizzie, answered the door. She smiled, and deep dimples appeared in her cheeks.

"Hello," she said with a curious look in her hazel eyes.

Blue saw Lizzie in twenty years in the woman's face, heard the same sweet tone in her voice, and his chest tightened knowing that Lizzie's mother was pitted between her daughter and her husband.

"Hi, Mrs. Barber?"

"Yes."

"I'm Blue Ryder, Lizzie's boyfriend. I was wondering if I could have a moment of your time. Actually, I was hoping to speak with both you and your husband."

"Lizzie's boyfriend?" Her smile widened as she stepped toward the porch and lowered her voice. "I'm sorry, I didn't know she had a boyfriend."

It didn't surprise Blue that Lizzie hadn't mentioned their relationship, given what was going on between her and her father and her parents' conservative nature. But that didn't mean the omission didn't sting. That fueled a different type of fire in Blue, who came from a more open and accepting family. He wished that no matter what was going on in her life, she had the support of her family, the way he always had.

"That's not surprising," he admitted. "You can call her if you'd like. I'll be happy to wait here."

Her eyes traveled over his face for a moment, as if she was deciding if he was trustworthy. She smiled and stepped back, indicating for him to come inside. "That's not necessary."

She led him into a parlor that reminded Blue of his grandmother's house. An Oriental rug covered dark hardwood floors, and the furniture looked as if it had been there for thirty years, though it was not frayed or marred in any way, simply dated. The sofa was covered with a burgundy and cream striped fabric, and the cranberry-colored wing chairs were patterned with diamonds. An antique china cabinet stood in the corner of the room, and an old-fashioned wooden desk sat between two large windows on the far wall.

"I'll go get my husband. Please excuse me for a moment." Mrs. Barber walked down the hall, and he heard her ascending the wooden stairs he'd seen from the foyer.

Blue noted the literature on the coffee table, *Inns of Cape Cod* and *Gardens of New England*. He tried to imagine Lizzie growing up in this house and what it might have been like for her. His house had always been loud and busy, a stark contrast to the silence of the inn. Then again, there weren't six children running around the inn. His parents' home tended to be quieter now, too, although their house still vibrated with the energy of the rambunctious Ryder family even when they weren't all there.

He turned at the sound of heavy footsteps approaching. At six three, Blue had about an inch on Lizzie's father. Wearing a blue and white striped button-down and tie, with cropped brown hair that was graying around the temples, Mr. Barber looked more like a city businessman than a man who ran a cozy inn. Nonetheless, the middle-aged man had a commanding presence, with perfect posture, wide, square shoulders, a thick barrel chest, and dark eyes.

"I'm Vernon Barber. My wife tells me that you're Lizzie's boyfriend?" He lifted his chin and looked down his nose at Blue. The vee between his brows was so deeply set, Blue thought it might be ever present and not simply caused by his surprise visit. His stern lines contrasted with his wife's softer presence in her jeans and a pretty knit top.

"Yes, sir. Blue Ryder. It's a pleasure to meet you, and thank you for taking the time to speak with me." Blue shook his hand, not at all surprised by the firmness of the man's grip.

Vernon motioned toward a chair. "Please, have a seat."

"Can I get you something to drink?" his wife asked.

"No, thank you, Mrs. Barber. This will only take a few minutes." Blue sat in a wing chair as they settled into the sofa across from him.

"Margaret and Vernon, please," she said with a kind smile.

Blue's eyes caught on the bookshelves behind the sofa, and he realized that he hadn't seen a single family photo. His family had photos on nearly every wall. He reminded himself this was their place of business as well as their residence, which gave him a mild sense of understanding even though his father and siblings had plenty of family photos even at their offices.

"How is my daughter?" Vernon crossed one ankle over his knee and leaned back with his hands folded neatly in his lap.

His use of *my daughter* rubbed Blue the wrong way. It felt like he was distancing himself from her.

"Lizzie is doing well, despite the issues between the two of you." Blue paused, waiting for a reaction, knowing he was plowing in like a bulldozer, but he had a feeling that was what this man needed. "She's one of the strongest women I know."

Margaret smiled and sat up a little straighter. Vernon's facial expression remained unchanged as he nodded in acknowledgment.

"Lizzie has always been very strong-willed," Margaret said.

Maybe that shouldn't bother him, but it did. *Strong-willed* was different from *strong*. He was beginning to understand what

Lizzie had grown up with and what she was currently up against, and it only endeared her toward him more. She was even stronger than he'd imagined.

"I realize that you don't know me, and maybe it's not my place to speak for Lizzie, but I am in love with her, and I'm hoping we can find a way to bridge the gap that's come between you." Blue hadn't planned on going there with this conversation. He'd planned on simply trying to make peace with her father and to get him to understand what a generous person and skilled businesswoman his daughter was, and that she didn't deserve to be dismissed by him. But Blue didn't work that way. He'd always been led by his heart, and this was no different.

"Blue, I don't think this is a conversation I want to have with you." Vernon rose to his feet and looked down at his wife, who pressed her lips together and remained seated. "Margaret?"

"I want to hear what he has to say," she said as she reached for his hand. "And I wish you would, too."

Vernon crossed his arms over his chest as Blue rose to his feet and met the formidable man eye to eye.

"Thank you, Margaret," Blue said gently before turning his full attention to Vernon. "Sir, I don't have a daughter and can't claim to know what it would feel like to know that my daughter hosted a show like the one Lizzie does." He felt the need to say the name of the show, to show her father that he wasn't bothered or embarrassed by it. "But my girlfriend, your daughter, a woman whom I adore, a woman whom I never imagined would do something like this, is in fact the Naked Baker."

"And you apparently have no issues with that." Vernon's voice was dead calm and clearly meant to be intimidating. "You're probably one of those guys who watches that show, along with a dozen of other pornographic shows on the Internet."

Blue's eyes never wavered from his. "I see your ability to misjudge is not restricted to family members." He wasn't about to defend himself to this man. He had tunnel vision—*clear the way for a reconciliation for Lizzie*—and it was obviously going to be an uphill battle. But Blue wasn't one to give up. He had to believe that if Margaret had stayed with this man all these years, he must have some redeeming qualities as a father and as a husband, and Blue hoped to unearth at least some of them.

When her father didn't react to his comment, Blue continued speaking. "I wonder, Vernon, are you aware of what your daughter does besides this webcast?"

"She's a florist," he said with an air of boredom.

"And?" Blue cocked a brow at his brief, cold answer. He could tell by the way Margaret was fidgeting in the same fashion Lizzie did when she was nervous that she was biting back a response. Or maybe suppressing the desire to nudge her husband into saying more.

"Let me share with you what I've learned about Lizzie," Blue said proudly. "Did you know that after working a ten-to-twelve-hour day at the flower shop—the flower shop that she managed to open and run successfully on her own—she takes flowers to the cemetery and leaves them on the headstones of people whose graves go untended?" He noted the quizzical look in her father's eyes and softened his tone. "Sometimes she takes them to the assisted-living facility, or the firehouse, or the police station. She's also been known to hand flowers out to strangers as they pass by the shop after hours."

Blue shifted his eyes to her mother. "And did you know that the things she bakes for her show go to the homeless shelter?

That's right, at six thirty in the morning, with a full day ahead of her, she takes it upon herself to deliver the freshly baked goods to those who need them."

"I didn't know that," her mother said wistfully.

When her father still didn't respond, Blue said, "And the show she's created? She works on that late at night most days, after she's gone to the homeless shelter, worked a long day at her flower shop, and delivered flowers to whomever she thinks needs them the most." In an instant, Blue decided not to try to explain to Lizzie's parents how successful her webcast had become or that she was in talks with a major network to sell the rights. He didn't get the sense that her success made a difference one way or another, and who Lizzie was had nothing to do with her success. If her father couldn't see how caring, how selfless, and how incredibly generous his daughter was, it was his loss.

To his surprise, Vernon's shoulders dropped a hair. If Blue hadn't been watching for clues of the man softening, he might have missed it.

"Lizzie is a savvy businesswoman, but more importantly, she's the most generous person I know." Blue slid his hands casually into his pockets and shrugged.

"I just thought you should know, and I'm sure you already know that the money she earns from the webcast goes directly to Maddy's school expenses. She doesn't keep a penny for herself, even though that means she pays a higher tax rate on her earnings from the flower shop."

He held a hand out to shake Vernon's, and Vernon's mouth opened, as if he was going to say something, but as Blue shook his hand, the man remained silent.

This conversation is nowhere near over.

Blue kept his thoughts to himself as he took Margaret's

hand between his and thanked her for taking the time to speak with him. He took a step toward the door, unsure if he'd made a difference or not, and before walking into the foyer he said, "Thank you for raising such an amazing daughter. She was so determined to put her own social life aside in order to fully concentrate on earning enough for Maddy's education that she refused to go out with me for an entire year—what she didn't know was that I would have waited ten, if that's what she needed to feel safe."

Chapter Twenty-Eight

SKY WHOOSHED THROUGH the front doors of P-town Petals carrying bags from Wild Rice, a clothing shop at the west end of Commercial Street. It was a pricey shop, with dressier clothing than Sky typically wore, and as Lizzie came around the counter to greet her, she wondered where Sky was going to need to wear something so special.

"Dinner with Sawyer's parents?" she guessed.

"Ha! Hardly. These are for you, girlfriend." Sky plopped the bags on the counter and began rummaging through them. "I knew you wouldn't have time to shop for an appropriate outfit before going to your big meeting in New York. And let's face it"—Sky ran her eyes down Lizzie's P-town Petals T-shirt and jeans—"Cape Cod attire is not exactly big-city appropriate."

Sky pulled out the prettiest navy blue skirt and white blouse Lizzie had ever seen. It looked more professional than anything she had ever owned.

"You didn't have to do that." Lizzie couldn't help running her fingers over the silk blouse.

Sky put it in her hands and then withdrew a pair of nude-colored heels and a cute pair of earrings to top it all off.

"I don't know what to say." Lizzie was completely befuddled. No one had bought her clothes in years. Sky had lived in New York before returning to the Cape a few years ago. If anyone could pick out the perfect outfit for a meeting this important, it was Sky. Her style was more relaxed, like Lizzie's, but she'd struck the perfect balance between professional and casual. Lizzie knew she'd feel like a million bucks in the outfit.

"Don't say anything. Just try it all on." Sky ushered her toward the bathroom in the back of the shop and waited outside the door. "I'll watch the store while you tell me how things are going with Blue. I talked to him this morning, and he had that fully sated sound to him."

Lizzy laughed. "He's definitely satiating," she said through the door as she admired the outfit in the mirror. "This is so pretty, but, Sky?" She opened the door and turned so Sky could assess the outfit. "Do I look as much like a fish out of water as I feel?"

"Girl, you look like the *only* fish in the water. Gorgeous. You'll knock 'em dead."

"You really think so? I feel like I'm playing dress up. I'd much rather go wearing my jeans and Petals shirt—not that that's an option, but still."

Sky turned her by the shoulders so she was facing the mirror. "Repeat after me."

Lizzie put on a serious face. "Okay. This is good. I need to practice, because I'm wicked nervous."

Sky smiled at her in the mirror. "Okay, ready?" When Lizzie nodded, Sky said, "Hi. I'm Lizzie Barber, the queen of naked baking."

Laughter burst from Lizzie's lips. "Totally not helping. But the outfit? Sheer perfection. You can still hold on to your best friend nomination."

Lizzie changed back into her jeans as Sky filled her in on what to expect in New York: how busy the subways were, how to flag down a taxi, the fast pace of the city. Lizzie hadn't given much thought to those things. She was nervous enough about the idea of talking about her show to people she didn't know.

"Blue said he's going with you, so you'll be fine."

"He is, but not to the meeting, just to New York. I really want to do this alone. Even though he is totally supportive, I think I'd be more nervous with him in the room, and besides, it'll give him a chance to catch up with his family. We're actually staying with his parents Friday night, then coming back Saturday morning."

"He's so proud of you, Lizzie. He's sure you're going to sew this up and get an offer. How do you feel about it?" Lizzie hung the outfit on the coatrack, and Sky followed her through the store as Lizzie rearranged a few plants.

She smiled as she turned to face her friend. "I can hardly believe that I might actually be able to have a normal life again. It's been so many years since I've had evenings free that I'm not sure what I'll do with the time. But I'm already imagining walks along the beach with Blue, bonfires with you and everyone else." She bit her lower lip to trap in her excitement.

"Blue said you work almost every night on the show. I had no idea it was so consuming, and I *really* have no idea how you bounce around here all day with endless energy when you're doing so much."

"My schedule is crazy, but I'm used to it. I do everything for the show at night. I film twice a week, then edit twice a week. When the shows air for the first time, I watch the beginning to make sure there aren't any glitches, and then I take Sundays off."

Sky followed her back to the refrigerated section, where Lizzie took out the wilting flowers that she'd give away this evening.

"No wonder you hardly ever go out with me when I ask. This will be life changing if it comes through." Sky watched her putting the flowers in her tote.

"I know. I can hardly stand it, I'm so excited. And I'm also really nervous about meeting his parents, so it's going to be a nerve-racking few days."

"You'll love his family. I've only met his brothers, but they're all so down-to-earth. I'm sure his parents are wonderful, too."

"I'm a little nervous about them finding out about the show. Look at how my dad reacted." Lizzie leaned against the counter. She'd been trying not to think about how much it hurt that her father could push her aside so easily, but sometimes, like now, the ache was inescapable.

Sky embraced her. "Don't worry. Your father loves you too much not to come around." She pulled back and said, "That's why he's acting like this, you know. That's why he's always been so protective of you and Maddy. He loves you two so much he doesn't know what else to do. Sort of like the way my brothers have always been so overprotective of me."

"I hope you're right, because if this deal doesn't come through, I have two more years as the Naked Baker, and I'm not going to leave Maddy hanging just to appease my father—no matter how much I love him."

"Speaking of love…" Sky smiled and arched a brow.

Lizzie grinned.

Sky squealed. "I knew it! I'm so happy for you!" She threw her arms around Lizzie, and they both laughed.

"Blue's already changed my life in so many ways, and even though he was jealous at first, I kind of like knowing that. I think it would have been weird if he didn't feel funny about me doing the show. I definitely wouldn't want him prancing around in nearly nothing for women—online or offline." Lizzie sighed. "I can't imagine my life without him, and to be honest, I can't even imagine a night without him anymore."

Chapter Twenty-Nine

THERE WAS SO much adrenaline coursing through Lizzie Friday morning when she arrived in New York City that she was surprised she hadn't bounced out of her seat on the airplane. She'd practiced what she was going to say in the meeting at least a hundred times, and by the time the cab pulled up in front of the Food Channel Network's building in Manhattan, Lizzie's stomach was doing somersaults.

How could she have thought she could handle this? The conversation with Duke last night had made her more anxious, even though he'd confirmed that she had all her ducks in a row and the proposal looked perfect. What he'd said about Carly Christianson, the woman heading up the acquisition department for FCN, wasn't nearly as comforting. *She's a hard negotiator. Be ready to negotiate as if your life depends on it. She'll try to lowball you, and if she does that, very politely thank her for her time, tell her the meeting is over, and get up and walk out without looking back.*

How on earth was she supposed to do that? She had a feeling she'd be fighting to remember how to breathe.

Blue stood protectively between Lizzie and the passersby as she stepped from the cab onto the busy sidewalk. She'd never been to New York, and she was amazed at the sheer number of people on the sidewalks and the constant honking of car horns. When she looked up, the height of the buildings made her dizzy. She clung to Blue with one hand, clutching the strap of her messenger bag with the other.

"You look gorgeous, and your proposal is perfect. You're going to do great," Blue reassured her.

"You're sure I won't look too out of place? Like a beach girl trying to be a city girl?"

Blue's eyes heated as he stepped in closer, and that made her stomach quiver in a better way. "You'll always be *my* beach girl, but I think you've proven that it doesn't matter what clothes you wear. You have a brain that's sharper than anyone's in that building. You've created two businesses by yourself. Don't you forget that, babe. No matter what they say, this is all you. You make the decisions. If they play around, take Duke's advice and get out with your chin held up high. They need you more than you need them."

Lizzie wrapped her arms around Blue's waist, loving the way her heels brought their mouths closer to the same height. Not that she was close enough, but she'd take every inch she could get. "I need you more than I need anything else in this world, Blue. I'm so glad you're with me."

"You don't need me, sweetheart. But I'm glad you *want* me." He pressed his lips to her cheek, and she knew he was being careful not to mess up the lipstick she wasn't used to wearing. "Now get in there and be your amazing self. Are you sure you don't want me to go with you?"

Her nerves nearly silenced her voice, but she managed, "I'm sure."

"Okay. Text me when you're done and I'll meet you right

here. Good luck."

She felt Blue's eyes on her long after she walked through the glass doors of the intimidating building. His strength stayed with her as she rode the elevator up to the tenth floor, where she followed a prim-looking woman into an empty conference room that was bigger than her flower shop and overlooked the city. His supportive gaze and comforting words carried her through as her heart slammed so hard against her ribs she feared she might pop a button on her blouse.

The conference room door opened, and a dark-haired woman with almond-shaped eyes entered the room wearing a fitted white suit that did nothing to hide her curvaceous body. Her pin-straight posture and cool, professional gaze made Lizzie's skin prickle. She had perfectly styled brown hair and a mole on her left cheek. The woman could win an Eva Mendes look-alike contest hands-down.

"Lizzie, such a pleasure to meet you." She extended a lithe arm and—*thank goodness*—a genuine smile that softened her perfection just enough to take away the prickliness. "I'm Carly Christianson, and I'm so glad you could make it out to meet with us."

Carly moved with the grace of a feline and an air of precision as she swept into her seat at the head of the table.

"Thank you. It's a pleasure meeting you as well." Thankful that her voice actually worked, Lizzie started to believe that she could do this. Carly didn't seem as harsh as Duke had said. Maybe he'd been preparing her for the worst.

Lizzie spread her files out on the table and drew her shoulders back, preparing to embark on the spiel she'd practiced on the plane ride from the Cape, when the door behind Carly swung open and three men in suits filed in with serious faces and curious glances. Behind them, two well-put-together women entered the room, bringing with them a whirlwind of anxiety that landed dead center in Lizzie's chest.

"Let me introduce our team," Carly said. "Kerry Michaels, head of marketing, Bradley Manion, chief financial officer…"

She spoke fast, each word meticulously pronounced, and Lizzie tried to concentrate on the names and positions that went with each face. But the blood was rushing through her ears so loudly that she found it difficult to process. How would she make it through her sales pitch if she couldn't even concentrate through the introductions?

"We're very impressed with your program, and we'd like to hear about how it came to be. There is very little about it online, and you've done an excellent job of masking your identity. We scoured the Internet and have not been able to find a single connection between Lizzie Barber and the *Naked Baker*."

"Yes, that's done by design." Lizzie was shocked that the answer came so easily. She went on to explain how she'd learned about proxy servers in college from a friend, and from there she took them on a tour of her journey from *Cooking with Coeds* to the *Naked Baker*. She was surprised at how confident she sounded and was even more pleased to realize she'd been able to make eye contact with each of the members of the FCN team without faltering in her explanation.

One of the intimidating bunch, a blond female with angular features and a sharp gaze, said, "We'd like to see your tax returns to verify the figures you've provided."

"Yes, of course." *Holy cow, tax returns?* They must be serious. "I can have them to you by Monday."

One of the handsome men sitting across the table asked,

"Have you at any time had a business partner?"

"No. From the inception of the program I have been the only person working on the show."

They fired off questions from all sides for the next forty-five minutes, and Lizzie hoped she was handling her answers well. She was being honest, and she couldn't do much more than that.

Carly cleared her throat and lifted her chin. All eyes shifted to her, and she looked even more regal than she had when she'd come in. With respect shining in the eyes of the others, the intimidation Lizzie had sought to avoid suddenly settled in.

"Lizzie, you've proposed a sale of the rights to the program, but you do realize that you *are* the program, don't you?"

Lizzie's mouth opened, and her brain scrambled to find an answer. She and Blue had talked about this. Duke had given her tips on what to say, but her brain had gone completely blank. Her pulse sped up, and she felt her cheeks flush. She was in for a full-on panic attack if she didn't get a grip on herself soon.

She dug deep, remembering what Duke and Blue had told her. *She's a hard negotiator. Be ready to negotiate as if your life depends on it.* Blue's words came next. *You make the decisions. They need you more than you need them.*

In their advice, she found her voice—and her answer. "Yes, up until this point the show has been all my doing, from planning to taping, editing, and analyzing. But I wear a blond wig and thick dark glasses, and as you pointed out, my identity has been kept secret. If you hire the right actress to play the part, so the sensual side of the program remains essentially the same, viewers will never connect the dots. Furthermore, I only have the ability to tape the shows twice a week, because I do have another business to run, but another person might be able to film seven days a week, generating even more income."

"Seven days a week is the plan," Carly said with a sophisticated tone and a wry smile.

"I'm also willing to consult on a limited basis, with meetings
handled at such times that they will not negatively impact my
other business." She had no idea where that came from, but it
sounded well thought out and that was a feather in her cap.
They began ping-ponging questions at her again, and as she
volleyed answers, surprising herself with her abilities, she
realized that if she had the confidence to do the *Naked Baker*
program, she could sit at this table with sophisticated city
people and handle herself just fine.

NIGHTCAPS BAR WAS a favorite gathering spot among
Blue's brothers and their friends. It was owned by Dylan Bad, a
guy who knew how to make anyone feel welcome, and because
of that, the place was always jammed. This afternoon was no
different. Blue had been sitting at a booth with his brothers
Cash and Duke since he'd dropped off Lizzie, and there hadn't
been a quiet moment since they'd arrived.

Normally crowds and noise wouldn't bother Blue, but his
attention was already stretched thin, as he was worried about
how Lizzie's meeting was going with the FCN executives.

"B, your leg has been jumping up and down a mile a minute
since you got here. Would you relax? She'll do great." Duke
sipped his beer and checked out a brunette at the bar. He'd
come from the office, still dressed in his suit and tie. Duke was
the sharpest dresser of the Ryder men, and Blue had come to
realize that it didn't matter if Duke was working or not. He was

always dressed nicely, preferring polo shirts to T-shirts and slacks to jeans.

"I'm not worried about how she'll do," Blue said honestly, knowing she'd do just fine. "I'm nervous because I know *she's* nervous about how she'll do."

Cash ran a hand through his dirty-blond hair. His eyes held Blue's with an assessing gaze. "Holy mackerel."

"What?" Blue shot a questioning look at Duke, who shrugged.

"You've fallen for her." A knowing smile spread across Cash's face.

Blue couldn't hide the grin pushing at his cheeks. "I'm not even going to try to deny that."

"The first Ryder man to get tied down." Cash slapped him on the back.

"First you buy the property we were supposed to share, and now you're in love with the woman I was going to ask out?" The raising of Duke's brows told Blue his oldest brother was just giving him a hard time.

"You're too slow, too old, and not quite as handsome as me," Blue teased as he checked his phone for at least the tenth time since they arrived.

"Please. I am in no way, shape, or form looking for love. You enjoy that monogamy nightmare." Duke lifted his chin toward the woman he was eyeing at the bar. "Plenty of fish in the sea."

"You're missing out, man. There's nothing like having that one special person to share your life with." Blue sucked back his beer. "Speaking of which, I can't sit around here waiting for her to text. I want to be there when she comes out of the building. I'm going to head over now. Meet you at Mom and Dad's?" He tossed money on the table and waved to Dylan behind the bar.

"Wait up," Cash said as he and Duke joined him, as he'd known they would. "You're only here for a few hours. Do you really think we're going to go our separate ways? Duke's going to drive us over to Mom's. Let me just text Jeremy. He and Susan wanted to meet up with us since Mom's been helping them plan the wedding. Where's Lizzie's meeting?"

Blue gave him the address, and Cash texted Jeremy on the way outside. They walked the few blocks to where Lizzie's meeting was being held, and on the way Blue stopped to pick up a Snickers bar and a bouquet of roses.

"Snickers?" Cash laughed. "What is it with girls and chocolate?"

"The Snickers is in case it didn't go well. Roses are in case it did." They passed a jewelry store and Blue stopped to look in the window, which took not only him by surprise, but his brothers, too. As he stared in the glass at the sparkling engagement rings, he had no doubt that a lifetime was exactly what he wanted with Lizzie. But buying one of these glitzy rings was not.

"Seriously, dude?" Duke slung an arm over Blue's shoulder. "Look at you, all grown up. Wow. I'm impressed."

Blue slid him a shut-up look.

"Go on in. See how you feel." Cash nudged him toward the door.

"Nah. I just wanted to look. I'm cool." Blue began walking again, and his brothers fell into step beside him. Boy, he'd missed being around them, seeing their smart-aleck smiles, and even just feeling their energy as they talked. It had been hard not to tell them about Lizzie's webcast, but although Duke knew, he was professional enough to keep her business to himself, as he would any proprietary information. Blue knew

Lizzie was nervous about the rest of his family finding out, and although she'd never asked him not to tell them what type of show she hosted, he respected her enough not to bring it up—even though he had complete faith in his family not to give her a hard time about it.

Just as they arrived at the building to meet Lizzie, Jeremy stepped out of a cab. He had come from the office, and looked professional in his slacks and tailored shirt as he helped Susan from the cab. She looked as gorgeous as ever in a pair of skinny jeans, high heels, and an oversized knit shirt. She was a top fashion blogger, but she was so down-to-earth and family oriented that she never flaunted it.

"Thanks, babe," she said to Jeremy as she wrapped her arms around him and they kissed like almost newlyweds should. Then she turned her crystal-blue eyes on Blue and hugged him, too. "I've missed you so much! And I'm so happy you're bringing your girlfriend to the wedding!"

"Thanks, Susan. Me too."

Susan stepped back and hugged Duke. "You're looking as dapper as ever."

"And you're quite beautiful. Sure you want to marry this guy?" Duke teased, just as Lizzie walked out of the building behind him.

Her head was down, her hair covering her face, as she dug through her purse.

"Lizzie," Blue called to her as he closed the distance between them. She lifted sad eyes to him, and his chest tightened. He took her in his arms and whispered, "It's okay. Whatever happened, it's all okay."

Chapter Thirty

LIZZIE TRIED NOT to let the fact that she'd just walked out on what was probably the most important meeting she'd ever have ruin the afternoon, despite the disappointment she felt settling into her bones.

"What happened?" Blue asked quietly.

"They said that there was no show without me, so I took Duke's advice, thanked them, and walked out with my head held high." She swallowed past the itch of regret crawling up her throat.

"Aw, babe. I'm so sorry, but you know what? Forget them." Blue pulled her into another hug. "That's right. You're awesome on your own. You don't need them to do a darn thing for you."

Duke pulled her into a warm embrace. "He's right, Lizzie. You did the right thing. You left with your dignity intact, and believe it or not, you have a leg up. They're probably sitting up there wondering what they did wrong."

"Hey, isn't someone going to introduce us?" Cash asked.

From the photos in Blue's house, Lizzie recognized the strappingly handsome dirty-blond haired man as Blue's brother Cash, and there was no mistaking Jeremy as a Ryder with the same strong features as the others. She'd seen Susan's blog, but heck if she wasn't twice as beautiful in person. The entire group—the three Ryder men and Susan—were all warm smiles and open arms, making them even more attractive.

"Men." Susan embraced Lizzie. "I'm Susan, and I'm so glad to meet you. It's about time another Ryder man gets off the bachelor roster."

"What is it about everyone wanting us to settle down? Just because Jeremy bit the bullet doesn't mean the rest of us have to," Duke said with a smile that told Lizzie he was teasing. "Why don't you give Jeremy's siblings a hard time?"

"Because Trey, Drew, and Isabel are so busy, they have no plans of settling down anytime soon," Jeremy explained. "Hi, Lizzie. I'm Jeremy." He embraced Lizzie and said, "Blue's a great guy. I'm happy for you both."

That took the edge off a little.

"Welcome to the chaos," Cash said as he drew Lizzie into a warm hug. His brothers and Susan were so friendly and welcoming that she was instantly comfortable among the close-knit group. "I take it your meeting didn't go as well as you'd hoped?"

Lizzie's eyes shot to Blue, wondering if Cash, Jeremy, or Susan knew about her webcast. Blue shook his head, and she was thankful that they were so in tune with each other that he knew exactly what was worrying her.

"Not exactly, but it's not a big deal." As the words left her lips and Blue laced his fingers with hers, she felt another wave of disappointment wash over her. She hadn't realized how badly she'd wanted this deal to go through. She'd already been dreaming of the extra time she and Blue would have together without the stress of filming, editing, and managing the entire *Naked Baker* program.

Thankfully, Susan looped her arm in Lizzie's and stuck to her like glue, asking a host of questions about her and Blue and taking the subject off the failed meeting. The drive to Blue's parents' house was full of laughter as the men talked about work and volleyed teasing barbs at one another, while Susan and Lizzie became fast friends, talking about Jeremy and Blue and what it was like to live in New York.

Blue's parents lived just outside the city on several wooded acres. By the time they reached their house, Lizzie knew all about Susan and Jeremy's families and their impending wedding. She also learned that Jeremy had lost his mother to cancer when he was a teenager, and Blue's mom had been stepping in to help ever since, which was why she had helped plan the wedding.

"It's kismet," Susan said as they walked up the sidewalk toward Blue's parents' two-story colonial. "You and Blue are supposed to be together, and we were all supposed to meet."

Jeremy leaned down and kissed the top of Susan's head. "That's my fiancée. The social connector."

Blue draped an arm over Lizzie's shoulder as his parents came out the front door. He whispered to Lizzie, "Are you sure you're okay? Do you want to go somewhere to talk before hanging out with everyone?"

She loved that he was so thoughtful, but after chatting with Susan and being surrounded by such happy banter, she already felt much better. "You really do care about me, don't you? You're seeing your family for the first time in months and I'm still the first thing on your mind."

"Did you ever doubt it?" He pressed his lips to hers, and the heat their kisses always brought filled her from head to toe.

"Not for one second," she said. "Everyone has been so nice

and easy to talk to. I think the distraction is helping, but thank you for offering." Her stomach fluttered nervously at the sight of his parents, although as they stepped from the porch hand in hand, their friendly smiles had a calming effect.

His mother's shoulder-length hair was the same dirty-blond shade as Cash's, and behind her amber-framed glasses, Lizzie noticed that she shared his warm brown eyes, too. His father, also wearing glasses, had dark hair like Blue, peppered with gray, and surprisingly, he sported a silver soul patch, which gave him a younger, edgier look than Lizzie had expected. He was a big man, like his sons, well over six feet tall, with a broad chest, and she noticed as he made a beeline for Blue and pulled him into a hug that he also shared his sons' confident gait and warm blue eyes.

"I've missed you, son." His father's voice was deeper than Blue's and filled with emotion as he hugged his son longer than Lizzie had ever been hugged in her entire life by her own father.

"Baby," Blue's mother said. "Oh, honey, I have missed you so much." She held his shoulders as she searched his eyes with an inquisitive gaze. "You look happy."

Blue smiled at Lizzie. "More than happy, Mom. And it's all thanks to Lizzie. Lizzie, this is my mom, Andrea, and my dad, Ned."

"Hi. It's nice to meet you," Lizzie said.

"We greet with hugs," Andrea said, opening her arms. Lizzie stepped in and was surprised how comfortable and natural it felt to be in his mother's arms and how different his parents' greeting was from that of her own parents. "Welcome to our home."

"Step on in here, young lady," Ned said, arms open wide. He hugged her with a firm embrace, just like Cash and Duke had.

Blue stayed close to her, keeping one hand on her lower back, as their parents hugged each of the others and then they went inside. If *love* and *family* had a scent, it enveloped her the moment she walked into their house. The house was decorated in earthy tones, and not only were family photos hung on nearly every wall they passed, but she could feel the importance of family all around her. Jackets were hung on hooks in the foyer rather than neatly tucked away. A pair of slippers was tucked on the first riser of the staircase, giving the house a lived-in feel, which she found herself wondering over. What would it be like to be part of this warm and inviting family?

There was a framed picture of Susan at a big blogger event, and she wasn't even officially part of the family yet. Photos of Blue standing before his house at the Cape, the landscaping out front newly planted and a proud grin on his lips, were hung beside pictures of Ned and Andrea and Blue's other siblings.

As they walked into the living room, Lizzie noticed more pictures of the boys caught midlaugh or wrestling in the yard. Pictures of Trish gazing adoringly up at Blue and Duke, or arm in arm with her father or mother. In one photo Cash had his younger brother Jake in a headlock and was grinning ear to ear. There was so much love in their eyes, and the way they touched and held each other, the laughter that was evident in so many of the pictures, made it easy to feel the positive energy of the family radiating from every single picture.

"Let's sit in the living room and chat a bit," his mother said.

Blue's parents sat beside each other on the couch, and the minute they sat down Ned reached for Andrea's hand. Lizzie loved that they were so openly affectionate, which was so different from her own parents. Even in the short while she'd been in their presence, it underscored what she already knew in her heart. She wanted to have that kind of relationship and she wanted to have the same kind of welcoming home that they did. She glanced at Blue, who was laughing about something Cash had said, and her heart felt full. She wanted those things with Blue.

Jeremy and Susan settled onto a love seat, and Susan tucked her feet up beside her, resting her head lovingly on Jeremy's shoulder. Duke sat on the arm of the couch where his parents and Cash were sitting, and Lizzie and Blue sat together on another sofa. A thick shag throw rug covered hardwood floors, and though the room was large, with a high ceiling, built-in bookcases, and a set of French doors overlooking a gorgeous yard, it felt cozy. She knew that had nothing to do with the size of the room and everything to do with the people in it.

They talked about the flight from the Cape and her flower business, and Lizzie noticed that Jeremy and Susan were touching and whispering the whole time. Every so often Lizzie caught Blue's mother smiling at the sight of them, and when she did, Ned squeezed her hand with a loving look in his eyes.

She couldn't imagine her father being nearly as comfortable—if at all—if she and Blue were to be so openly affectionate. Because of that, she was keeping a little distance between them—and Blue was doing his best to keep her from doing so, drawing her closer every time she inched away.

"Lizzie, I understand that you were here for a business meeting. I hope it went well," Andrea said as Duke took a seat beside his father. Ned reached an arm across the back of the couch, and Duke moved closer to him.

Lizzie couldn't look away from the two men with their heads leaned toward each other as they talked quietly, Ned's grown son tucked safely beneath his arm. She longed for the closeness Blue's family clearly came by naturally. In this house, with love in every corner, somehow the failed meeting no longer felt very important.

She realized that Andrea was waiting for her answer and finally said, "It didn't go as well as I'd hoped, but that's okay. It was a pipe dream."

Blue kissed her temple. "You didn't need them, babe."

"Was it a meeting for your flower business? Are you thinking of branching out?" Ned asked.

Lizzie's stomach clenched. She really didn't want to lie to his parents, but after coming clean to her parents and dealing with the aftermath of her father's reaction, she didn't want to take the chance of inciting the same type of reaction the first time she met Blue's family, even though they seemed so accepting.

Blue came to her rescue. "It was for a baking show she has online."

He always knew just what to say or do. His answer sounded simple enough without being a lie, but now she felt like she was making him cover for her, and that didn't feel good either.

"Well, I'm sorry it didn't go well, but I'm glad you came to New York. The wedding will be so busy, I wouldn't have time to get to know you there." His mother stood, and Ned held on to her hand. "Would anyone like a drink? I'm going to get some lemonade from the kitchen."

"Susan?" Jeremy asked.

"I am kind of thirsty, but I'll get it." Susan rose to her feet, and Jeremy pulled her down for a quick kiss. Again, Andrea's smile warmed at the sight. "Do you want one, Jer?"

"No thanks," he answered. "I'll grab a beer with the guys in a little bit."

"Babe?" Blue asked Lizzie.

"I think I'll join your mom and get a drink." Blue smiled as Lizzie rose to her feet. "Would you like something?"

"Just you." He stood and nuzzled against her neck. She felt her cheeks flush, and his mother laughed softly.

"Oh, it is nice to see my son so happy." Andrea glanced at Duke. "Now, if we could only find the right woman for our eldest bachelor."

Duke scoffed. "You have four other children you can harass, Mom."

"Oh, please. One day Gage will open himself up to a real relationship again." She leaned down and kissed Duke's forehead. "You know Trish is planning on taking some time off soon. I think she's starting to think about settling down. Cash is so busy, I have no idea how, or if, he finds time for women, and Jake? Well, a mother can always hope, but that boy is always looking for the next adventure. I don't know if he's ever going to truly settle down."

"And that's okay, too," his father added. "Not everyone has to get married, even if *we* think there's no greater happiness than finding the one person who makes every day brighter and more meaningful."

Lizzie could hardly believe the conversation unraveling before her. Her father zipped up at the thought of his daughters having boyfriends.

Susan looped her arm in Lizzie's, then she took Andrea's hand and said, "Girl time. Yay. I wish Trish and Isabel were here."

They went into the kitchen, and Lizzie felt warm and fuzzy inside as she helped fill glasses with lemonade.

Andrea touched her shoulder. "I'm glad you came in to chat with us."

"The guys will talk about sports and work," Susan added. "*Lemonade* is our code for girl talk."

"Oh, I like the way you think." Lizzie followed them out to the back porch, where they each sank into rocking chairs overlooking the yard. The house sat on the top of a gentle slope, giving them a beautiful view of acres of woods and the sun setting just beyond. The air was crisp and woodsy, with an undercurrent of pine and happiness.

"Are you nervous about your wedding?" Lizzie asked.

Susan laughed. "I wish. That would make me more normal, wouldn't it? But while I have a knack for fashion, I am so bad at preparing for anything that I don't really get nervous about events anymore. With blogging, things that come spur-of-the moment always come across the most natural, and if I worry about what I'm writing, I almost always mess up. Besides, *thankfully*, Jeremy and Andrea planned almost the whole wedding, with my mom, of course." She reached out and squeezed Andrea's hand. "As long as I know I'm marrying the man I love, that's all I care about. I know the wedding will be beautiful."

"You didn't mind?" The words slipped out before she could stop them. "No offense, Andrea, but doesn't every bride want to plan her own wedding?"

"Not our Susan. She was glad to hand everything over other than her dress and the bridesmaid gowns. She even let Jeremy decide what colors he wanted for the suit. And Jeremy, well, he's such a planner. He always has been, like my Cash. Those boys have always been prepared for anything.

"He would have driven me crazy watching over my shoulder

anyway," Susan added with a raise of her brows. "We make a perfect pair. He's prepared and I need him to be. But enough about our wedding. I want to hear about you and Blue. Are you two serious?"

Lizzie was surprised that such a successful fashion blogger wouldn't be more worried about her wedding. But then again, Susan was so laid-back that she wasn't having an extravagant wedding. They were having a small wedding with just family and close friends at one of Duke's hotels.

She felt the urge to gush about Blue, to tell them how much she loved him and how he'd stuck by her without being afraid to tell her his true feelings about the *Naked Baker*, but that would mean she'd have to come totally clean with them about the program. And the thought of that made her stomach hurt.

Instead, she said, "Yes, we're pretty serious."

Andrea sipped her lemonade and ran her finger around the rim of her glass as she spoke. "Let me tell you about my Blue. You know how some kids are always on the go? Jake was like that. He was always taking off into the woods or with friends. Trish was a social butterfly, the only girl, you know. Duke, Gage, and Cash have always been more serious, but Blue? Blue was the boy who brought home stray dogs to take care of, and birds, and bunnies. He's always been guided by his heart, and part of that has always been taking care of those he loved. He built a fort for Jake over spring break one year when he was in middle school. Got up every morning and spent hours in the woods. We didn't really know what he was up to, but he'd march out there with his toolbox at the break of day and come back at dinnertime, dirty and grinning like he'd just stolen the cookie jar. He told us afterward that he worried that if Jake got caught in the rain, he might need shelter." She smiled at Lizzie.

"Little did he know that Jake would grow up to be one of the best search and rescue guys on the East Coast—and a heck of a survivalist. But that was Blue. He put his heart and soul into everything he did, and usually it was for others. He'd work with his dad in the yard or help him fix the car or the roof. He always wanted to have his hands on something. When Trish was upset over some boy, he'd distract her, take her out, cheer her up." She lifted her eyes to Lizzie again. "It's wonderful to see him open up to you, Lizzie. He's such a giver, and, well, he'd closed his heart off for so long that I worried about him. I wasn't sure if he'd ever really let anyone in again."

Lizzie couldn't help but say, "He's the most generous and loving man I know." In that moment of opening up, she realized that she wanted to be completely honest with them. She and Blue were in love, and she allowed herself to imagine a future with him, a family, a life without the *Naked Baker*, even if that was two years away. She didn't want to have any more secrets in their closets. She tried to push her insecurities aside, but she wasn't quite there yet. Instead she said, "I've never met a man who is so open with his feelings."

"Oh, that's a Ryder thing. It took some time with Jeremy," Susan said with a shake of her head, "but he came around. Jeremy had this harsh professional edge when I met him, but underneath, he was soft and squishy."

Andrea laughed. "I don't think anyone else in the world would call Jeremy soft and squishy."

Lizzie's heart was beating so fast she almost backed down from exposing her secret, but she felt close with these women already, and if she had any hopes of a future with Blue and a good relationship with his family, she knew she had to be honest.

"I have something I want to share with you, but it's a little embarrassing. I won't be upset if it makes you think less of me, but I want to be honest with the two of you. With your whole family, really, but…"

Andrea's brows knitted together. She reached for Lizzie's hand. "Honey, you look like whatever this is, it's really weighing heavily on you. We aren't a judgmental bunch, but if you aren't comfortable sharing, then please don't feel pressure to."

Lizzie was thankful for her understanding, but she'd hidden enough, and now she was causing Blue to hide something from his family. She knew Duke was keeping her secret, too, and she didn't want that.

"Thank you, but I want to tell you." She told them about the *Naked Baker* program, explained how it had come about and all the way up to her father's reaction and the meeting with FCN. When she was done, she felt free. Free and ashamed, and she lowered her eyes to her lap and waited for judgment to claim her, because really, how could they not judge her?

She was nearly drawn to tears when Susan walked over and hugged her. "You have one lucky little sister, and shame on your father. I think Andrea and I should have a talk with him."

"You *are* a resourceful woman, aren't you," Andrea said. "Why on earth would that embarrass you?"

Lizzie blinked up at them, trying to swallow past the lump in her throat. "Did I not mention that I wear an apron and heels and act seductive?" She was sure she'd mentioned every detail, but now she wondered if she'd only said it in her head.

"Sure you did," Andrea answered. "But you also said that the viewers can't see your private parts, so what's the harm in that?"

"I sometimes wear lingerie for my blog," Susan said with a

smile. "It's all the same. I seduce the camera no matter what I'm wearing, and Jeremy had a heck of a time with that at first. Hey, it's all part of the job. How did Blue react?"

With his mother's eyes on her, Lizzie answered honestly. "He was a little hurt that I didn't tell him before we became close, and he doesn't love the idea of men watching me, but he came around pretty quickly. I don't blame him, though. I should have told him before we got too close, and I know it's a lot for a guy to accept."

"All guys are like that," Susan said, lowering her voice. "Jeremy wanted to know who was taking the lingerie pictures of me for my site." She smiled. "He was so cute."

"Lizzie, I'm sorry about your father's reaction. Have you tried talking to him one-on-one?"

Lizzie couldn't believe that Andrea was more concerned over her father's reaction than the videos themselves. "He won't speak to me."

"That's a shame, that he'd let something like this come between himself and someone he loves. I can't imagine how hurt you must be." She embraced Lizzie, and then a smile formed on her lips. "Don't you worry, honey. Love is stronger than pride. Of that I am one hundred percent certain. Your father is probably having a little crisis of his own over this that has very little to do with you. Once your father realizes that this isn't about him, he'll come around."

"I'm not sure I understand."

"As parents, it's very difficult not to evaluate everything your children do and wonder what other people will think or how it will reflect on you as the parent. That could be what your father is experiencing."

"My father had a hard time with me posting scantily clad

pictures at first," Susan said. "He came around, though, so I'm sure yours will, too."

"Really? That makes me feel a little better."

"Give him time, honey," Andrea said. "Stripping ourselves of our egos is a difficult thing to do."

"Who's stripping what?" Blue asked as he stepped out on the porch with his father and brothers in tow.

As Blue reached for Lizzie's hand, she felt even more accepted and loved. No one would ever fill the space her father held, but between Blue's love and the support of the others, she didn't feel nearly as devastated as she had when she'd left her parents' house.

"Miss me?" Blue whispered against her ear.

"How could I?" She already felt like part of his family's inner circle. "I love you so much, even when you're not here, you're still with me."

Chapter Thirty-One

LATER THAT EVENING, in Blue's childhood bedroom, Lizzie lay across the bed in a pair of lacy panties and one of Blue's tank tops, which hung off her shoulder, with her laptop open, moonlight streaming through the curtains.

"Aren't you tired?" Blue lay beside her in his boxer briefs and rubbed his hand over her thigh.

"Yeah, but the show airs tomorrow. I have to finish editing it."

He wrapped his arm around her and kissed her shoulder. "How about if you do it in the morning before we head back to the Cape?"

"I can't take a chance of not getting it done." She tilted her head, looking way too sexy for her own good. "That meeting with the network just drove home the reality that I have to keep doing this—only I am going to show them. I'll find a way to make the ratings even better."

"I know you will. I'm sorry that the meeting didn't turn out the way we'd hoped, but, Lizzie, I'm not going anywhere. I'm here to stay."

"I know. I just didn't realize how much I was counting on having more time with you and having a more normal life. I had visions of us spending nights out at your cottage and not worrying about taping, editing, and tracking views to a show that has already sucked up so many hours of my life."

The sadness in her voice cut through Blue's chest. He slid his hand beneath the back of her shirt, over her warm skin, and shifted his thigh over the back of hers, wanting to be closer, to comfort her.

"My favorite person in the world told me that two years was nothing. That it would pass by quickly. I wasn't so sure, but I realize now that as long as we're together we can get through anything. Two years, two decades. A lifetime." He brought his lips to her spine and kissed his way up to her neck as she tried to concentrate on editing the video.

She closed her eyes for a second, and he felt tension seep from her body.

"You're not making it easy for me to edit," she said breathlessly.

"It's not my fault you get me hot and bothered." He shifted closer.

She giggled. "I need to get this done."

"Okay," he whispered against her neck, loving her so much that his chest physically ached.

"You edit, and I'll just…" He slid his hands along her soft body. She sighed as he kissed her shoulder.

"Blue…" She craned her neck to the side, giving his mouth better access to nip at her warm skin. "I'll never get this done." A sweet sound of surrender slipped from her lips as she rolled onto her back, smiling up at him. "You're distracting me."

"That's the point."

"But…the video." She wound her arms around his neck.

"I'll help you edit after I love your body like it deserves to be loved." He pressed his lips to hers.

"But your parents," she whispered.

"I don't think they want to edit your video," he teased as he moved down her body, kissing as he went. "But I can go ask them if you want."

"Blue." A wanting whisper.

She sighed dreamily as he slowly undressed them both. As their bodies came together, and the world went dark, until there was only him and Lizzie.

After, as they came down from the clouds, "Love you" was all he could manage. Only it wasn't. He'd make darn sure that he fulfilled his promise and edited the video if it took the last of his energy. Seeing Lizzie with his family, watching her beautiful smile as she laughed and joked with them, and her confidence as she talked about her webcast with each of them, answering their questions and soaking in their support, had made him love her even more. He'd never been more proud of anyone—of Lizzie's determination and of his family's unconditional support. His family tended to open their hearts along with their arms, and he wished Lizzie could have that with her own parents. Even though Lizzie took life by the horns and never let anything, or anyone, keep her down, Blue wasn't done trying with her father. He'd make it his mission to set things straight so the woman he loved felt complete.

Blue's thoughts turned to what his mother had said right before she'd gone up to bed, when she'd pulled him away from the others and asked, *What stage are you in?*

The very best one, he'd answered, knowing she was referring to the stages of love.

Not even close, she'd said. *Time brings more happiness. One day you'll look back and realize the two of you have history. That's when it becomes magical.*

He lay beside Lizzie, listening to her breathing settle. If this wasn't the very best love could be, then sign him up for a lifetime of it, because he couldn't imagine being happier than they already were.

Chapter Thirty-Two

AFTER THEY RETURNED from New York, real life came back in earnest. Orders for a bridal shower and a wedding came in on short notice, and Lizzie would be busy for the next few weeks meeting with the bride and groom. She'd reluctantly fallen back into the routine for the *Naked Baker*, and that bothered her. She hadn't been reluctant before. Even if she hadn't necessarily wanted to spend her evenings filming, editing, and analyzing the show, she'd always gone in willingly. She knew that was because there'd never been an inkling of a way out from under the show while still making enough money to help Maddy. But the network's email had changed that. She'd dared to hope for more of a life with Blue, for evenings spent doing whatever they felt like doing rather than structured by her webcast schedule.

The bright light to the whole situation was that, true to his word, Blue had been amazingly supportive of her efforts with the show and supportive of her in every other way as well. They'd been staying at her place, and she felt him everywhere. His clothes were in her closet and in two of the dresser drawers. His toiletries were in her bathroom, and he'd hung a hook on the wall by the kitchen door for their keys. It felt like they'd always been together, but even stronger than his tangible possessions, his love filled every nook and cranny of her life. It was in the air she breathed and in the look in his eyes. And when he wasn't with her, his love remained.

Blue was up early every morning, which she loved, because they got ready for work together, making love in the shower, dressing and teasing each other—sometimes leaving late for work because they couldn't resist falling back into each other's arms. Blue had taken to coming by the shop every afternoon, bringing her lunch or coffee, or just coming by to check on her. She loved that he made the time to do that, but then again, that was Blue. He gave and gave and gave. He even offered to work with Duke to see if they could drum up interest with another prospective buyer for the business, but Lizzie had had enough. She didn't want to hope to find a way out from under the webcast anymore. It was easier to accept her fate and move forward, even if it was taking her a little longer to accept it than she'd hoped.

The only dark cloud in her life was her relationship with her stubborn father. She'd called him several times, and still he wouldn't come to the phone. She'd even taken an hour off yesterday and stopped by the inn, hoping to speak with him, but he'd refused to see her. Her mother had said he was meeting with someone, which she assumed was an excuse. How was she supposed to handle the fact that her mother was covering for him?

She was sure that asking her mother to tell her father that she was about ready to give up trying hadn't been the best way to handle it, but she'd been at such a loss, had felt so devastated by his refusal to see her, that she was at her wit's end with the whole situation. There was only so much denial a person could take before they broke down or walked away. And there was no way she was letting his conservative views mess up things for Maddy or for her. She had an incredible man who adored her and friends and family—aside from her father—who accepted and supported her. This was his loss.

If only it didn't hurt so bad.

It was true what people said about going through difficult times together and how struggles could bring people closer together. For her and Blue, that was definitely true. She'd never felt so loved, cherished, or supported.

It was Thursday night. She'd texted Blue earlier to tell him that she was taking the flowers to the cemetery and then she'd meet him at home. She packed up the flowers and walked out to her car thinking about the show she had to tape tonight. Maybe she'd go a little crazy and make a cake shaped like butt cheeks. Her mind shifted back to Blue—he was never far from it. She shivered with memories of crossing off the mile-high club from her Naughty-Places list on the way back from New York. She'd never imagined the bathrooms on airplanes were so small, but that had made it all the more fun when they'd snuck in together.

She smiled to herself as she unlocked her car door. It was a good thing her father didn't know about her lists. That might just push him to an early grave.

"Peanut?"

Lizzie froze. Tears sprang to her eyes at the sound of her father's voice and the endearment she hadn't heard in a decade. She gripped the car door for stability as she turned to face him in the hazy darkness of the evening. His eyes were sad, his shoulders drooped in a way she'd never witnessed, jumbling the powerful image of her father she carried with her.

Blood rushed to her ears. She'd seen him angry, happy, and nonplussed, but the remorse riding his deep-set eyes and draining the strength from his shoulders was so shockingly unfamiliar, it momentarily numbed her.

"Dad?" she finally managed.

He stepped closer, and when he spoke, his tone was tender and forgiving.

"When you were a little girl, you told me that I was cock-eyed. I wasn't sure what you meant, and when you tried to explain it, the best you could come up with was that I saw things crooked." His lips curved up with a tentative smile.

She couldn't remember saying that to him, but it didn't surprise her. It must have been before she'd learned to hold her tongue.

"My whole life I've stood strong in my convictions about morals and ethics and the way we should live our lives," he said without even a hint of his typical confidence.

"I know, and I'm sorry I've let you down." She felt her heart tearing in half, wanting to please him and not wanting to back down at the same time. "But I'm not going to change what I'm doing. Not even for you."

He nodded, his face solemn. "I know that. Elizabeth, it seems I've misjudged you, and it took someone other than my own family to show me how badly I had."

"What do you mean?" *Other than family?*

"Do you know why I couldn't meet with you when you came by the inn yesterday?"

Because you didn't want to. She couldn't bring herself to respond.

"I've had a visitor every day this week. Someone who obviously cares for you a great deal, someone who wanted me to fully understand the daughter I raised." Her father dropped his eyes again. "I'm ashamed to admit that it took another man to make me see exactly how crooked my views were. A man who refused to take no for an answer. A man who came to the inn nearly every day and sat in the parlor until I finally really heard what he had to say."

Tears sprang to her eyes. *Blue.* She tightened her grip on the cold metal door.

"He forced me to listen, Lizzie, and not even your own mother could do that. Your mother hasn't spoken more than two words to me since this mess began other than to tell me that I'm a stubborn old fool." He smiled at that. "She's right, and I'm not proud of it."

"Dad, don't let anyone force you to accept who I am." She was trembling, and it took all of her determination to drag the words from her lungs.

"Blue didn't force anything…but the truth. He told me about the things you did for others, and he told me about how hard you worked day in and day out. And he pointed out one very important thing that I somehow managed to miss." He held her gaze then, and it made her heart ache even more. "He pointed out that it shouldn't matter if you're the Naked Baker or not, which, Elizabeth, I'm ashamed to say that you, too, pointed out to me. I think you might have cracked my hard head, and he simply drove the point home."

"But it does matter. That's why you're so mad, and honestly, Dad, I'm ashamed of doing it, too. That's a big part of why I didn't tell you."

"You're probably ashamed because of my beliefs, honey, but your boyfriend was right. It shouldn't matter. When you love a person, you love who they are on the inside, and you have to trust that the decisions they're making are the best ones for them. He made me see that my turning you away for doing this webcast was the same as if *you'd* turned me away for not having the same beliefs as you. But you didn't throw our relationship away, peanut. You kept coming back. I was the idiot. I was the one who messed up."

Lizzie wiped tears from her cheeks. "So, you're not mad?"

"Mad? No. A little embarrassed that I couldn't provide for my daughters and monumentally ashamed of myself for how I've treated you, but now that I see things more clearly, I'm proud that you could do what I was unable to. I was wrong to say you weren't the daughter I raised. You're a hundred times stronger than the person I thought I raised, because you stand true to your convictions even at the cost of losing others—and you did it not just for yourself but for your younger sister. That, Elizabeth, makes you a stronger person than anyone I have ever known. I was just too wrapped up in my own beliefs to see it."

Lizzie could barely push air through her throat. Tears streamed down her cheeks as she forced her voice to work. "Thank you, Daddy."

"Don't thank me. I'm an old fool, and it took me way too long to come around. Thank that boyfriend of yours, who I didn't even know existed until he showed up at the inn. I'm sure that's another one of my failings. If you feel like you can't tell me things, well, I'll work on that, too, peanut. I only hope that it's not too late for you to forgive me."

He opened his arms and she walked right in.

"I forgive you."

"That boyfriend of yours…"

"Blue, Daddy. His name is Blue." *And I love him so much.* She didn't want to keep silent anymore about anything. She'd seen what hurt that could cause. "I love him, Dad. I love him so much."

"I saw it in your eyes, baby girl. But I have to ask, what kind of a name is Blue?"

"Dad!" She tried to pull out of his arms, and he held her too tightly for her to escape.

"I'm kidding." His laughter stitched up the tear in her heart. "He...*Blue* told me how hard of a time he had with your videos, too, and how his love for you gave him the strength to overcome his own insecurities. It takes a strong man to admit his weaknesses."

"You're seeing crooked again, Dad. Those are his strengths."

Chapter Thirty-Three

BLUE HEARD THE front door close and knew Lizzie had finally made it home. He tugged on the bottom of the apron he was wearing and glanced at the kitchen, where he'd worked all afternoon.

"Blue?" she called as she passed by the door to the basement.

"Down here," he called up. His stomach dipped as he walked to the bottom of the stairs, nervously putting one hand on his hip. Then, feeling ridiculously self-conscious, he shook it out, only to put both hands on his hips again as she came into view.

Her jaw gaped and her eyes nearly bugged out of her head, but the appreciative smile and the heat that pinked her cheeks made it all worthwhile.

"You're wearing my apron." She descended the steps, staring hungrily at his bare legs.

"Yup."

She circled him, and knowing she'd see his bare butt turned him on.

"You're not wearing any underwear."

"Nope." He laughed.

She finished circling him and stepped in close, running her

hand up his thigh. "I like this welcome-home attire."

He chuckled. "*We* have a show to tape."

She froze. "What?"

"Your apron's in the bathroom. I suggest you go change before I strip you bare and have my way with you, because once I do that, I promise you, you're not getting back up to film a thing."

She shuddered against him.

"How can we do that with…?" She lowered her gaze to his tented apron.

"Angles, baby. It's all in the angles."

"Are you sure you don't want to play first, tape later?"

Heck yeah, I want to play first. "Nope. Work, then pleasure. My girl taught me that."

She made that sexy pouty face that made him want to forget what he had planned. He forced himself to point to the bathroom. "Go."

She came out of the bathroom wearing heels and her apron, without the flesh-colored thong she normally wore.

"Damn, you're sexy." He pulled her in close again, and this time he sealed his lips over hers, soaking in the feel of her hot, wet mouth, her tongue tangling with his. He backed her up against the wall, holding her hands above her head as he devoured her mouth, pressing his hips to hers.

She broke away suddenly, breathing hard. "You went to see my dad."

This time it was Blue who froze. After his initial visit with Lizzie's father, it was clear that the man hadn't really heard what he'd had to say. Blue had returned three more times, unwilling to give up until he'd not only heard him out, but really listened and understood what Blue had to say—and hopefully changed his mind. He wasn't sure where things stood with the man. Vernon had sat stoically, listening to every word, but he hadn't given any indication as to where his mind was. For all Blue knew, it would take another week, month, year of visits before the man opened his eyes.

Lizzie must have read his confusion, because she said, "He came to the shop and apologized."

Blue let out a breath he hadn't realized he'd been holding. "He did? Are you upset with me for talking to him?"

She ran her finger along his collarbone, making his entire body aware of that one sensual touch. "No, not upset with you at all, but it kind of bothers me that it took you talking to him to make a difference. Then again, he's stubborn, and I'm glad that he finally came around."

"He loves you, Lizzie."

"I know. I think Sky was right when she said that my father loves me too much, and that's why he was so upset."

"Love can really mess with a person's mind." He stepped back and waved at his apron. "As you can see, people do weird things for love."

They both chuckled, and he kissed her again before leading her into her newly renovated kitchen. "I took the liberty of fixing things up for you. I couldn't stand the idea of you working with an oven that was older than dirt or counters that looked like they belonged to your grandmother."

Again her eyes widened. "You redid my kitchen?"

"I tried to match the look of your old appliances so it wouldn't be too noticeable in your videos. I hope you don't mind."

"You did this in a day? Why did the upstairs one take weeks?"

He smiled, slightly embarrassed that her quick inhalation meant she'd just figured it out. "It was my chance to be closer to you. Do you blame me?"

"For dragging out a job so you could see me?" She laughed. "Hardly. But I do blame you for making me get up even earlier than usual so I could leave before you saw me."

"Why did you do that?" He folded her into his arms.

"Because I knew that if I was alone with you I'd have a hard time saying no when you asked me out. And I also knew you'd see that on my face, or sense it in my vibes or something."

He nuzzled against her neck, drinking in her sweet floral scent. "I do love your sexy vibes."

She threw her arms around his neck and went up on her toes, striking his favorite position with their bodies and mouths pressed together. They kissed like it was their first time, a slow, intoxicating kiss that made him want to forgo the baking altogether.

"Thank you," she said before she pressed her lips to his again. "Thank you for loving me, for everything you do for me, and"—she shifted her eyes to the baking supplies on the counter—"for baking with me."

He forced himself to pry his mouth from hers, and she giggled as her eyes dropped to his arousal.

"We'd better get cooking before I bend you over the counter and have my way with you."

"That's number thirteen on my Naughty-Places list," she said as she dragged her finger across his jaw.

He cursed under his breath. "How am I supposed to function with *that* on my mind?"

She smiled and said, "I could say the same. Are you sure you want to do this? You said you couldn't watch me film, that it was too hard."

"I realized while I was talking with your father that I needed to cross this line. It's the only one we have left, so let's do this."

"Only one? I can think of a dozen or more." She raised her brows.

"Really, Lizzie? That's *all*? Baby, I'm going to show you lines you haven't even thought of yet." He lowered his lips to hers in a kiss that left his entire body throbbing. "I meant lines relating to your webcast."

"What if I can't do it?" She bit her lower lip nervously.

"What do you mean? You do this several times a week."

"I've never had to seduce a camera in front of you. It's embarrassing."

He slid his hand to the nape of her neck and brought her in close again. Man, he loved her. "Not half as embarrassing as it is for me wearing an apron while fully aroused. Together we can do anything. Haven't you learned that yet?"

LIZZIE WONDERED WHAT she'd done in life to deserve to be this happy. Blue had put on black-framed glasses like the ones she wore and a baseball cap. She didn't have the heart to tell him that she thought her viewers were probably mostly men and might not like watching a guy. Then again, what did she know? Maybe they would.

She and Blue laughed the whole time they baked, and she found she didn't like him seducing the camera *at all*. It made her even more jealous than she cared to admit to herself. She'd never been on the other side of the fence, and now she understood why it had made Blue's skin crawl. She had the urge to stand between him and the camera, so women wouldn't see his gorgeous biceps and chest peeking out from the apron, or the hard planes of his back, and want him the way she wanted him.

He moved with confidence, every muscle coming to life with the smallest of motions, and that made him even sexier as he stirred the frosting they'd made.

"Everyone knows you need a taste test," he said in a husky voice as he dipped his finger into the frosting and brought it to Lizzie's mouth.

As he slid his finger into her mouth with a scorching-hot look, her body smoldered from the inside out. She swirled her tongue around his finger as she dug her own finger into the frosting, then stroked it over his lower lip, following it with her tongue. She nibbled at his lip, making him groan before stepping back and bending over to take a tray out of the oven. She sensed his heat before she felt him press against her. It took all of her focus not to let on to the camera that she was suddenly madly aroused.

She set the hot tray on top of the oven and turned a seductive gaze to the camera while she fanned her face. "It sure is getting hot in here."

Blue moved beside her again, dipping his finger into the frosting and sucking it off with a look that could melt steel. She narrowed her eyes again, this time taking him up on the obvious challenge. No way was he going to do a better job of seducing the camera than she was.

She stuck three fingers into the frosting, eyeing the camera, and said, "There are so many good uses for frosting, and as we all know, it's the little lusty surprises that bring us the most pleasure." She slid her hand beneath his apron, knowing that all the audience would see was her hand disappearing below the counter.

Blue's chin dropped to his chest as he uttered a curse.

"Why, it looks like my baking partner is having a hard time." She picked up the towel from the counter and wiped her hands. Blue's gaze burned through her, filled with wanton desire she could practically taste—and *oh, how she wanted to taste him*!

"Let's see those big, strong arms in action." She turned her eyes to the camera again. "Watching a man in the kitchen is such a turn-on, isn't it?"

She handed him the spatula. "You spread the frosting, and I'll—" She dramatically dropped the towel to the floor. "Whoops!" She bent over in front of him.

"Lizzie," he said through gritted teeth.

"Camera's rolling," she whispered, though she'd already turned it off with the remote she kept beneath the counter. He tried to frost the cake, stopping every few seconds to breathe heavily or mutter a curse as she wiggled her butt, taunting him.

She rose up and pointed to the spatula in his hand, which had stilled over the cake. "What's wrong? Camera shy?" She licked her lips playfully.

He tore off his hat and glasses and tossed them aside. "I'll delete the tape, but I've got to be close to you."

She swiped her fingers in the frosting and rubbed it over her lips. "Enjoy."

"God, I love you," he said between frantic kisses, knocking the flour and sugar off the counter with his elbow and showering them in white powder. They both laughed as he kissed the sugar and flour from her lips, her neck, her jaw, scrambling her brain into love-soaked mush.

"Marry me, Lizzie," he panted out, gazing into her eyes.

And what she saw there, all that love, for *her*, bowled her over. "Marry me. I want you to be mine. I want to be yours. I'll support your naked baking on every level."

She could barely breathe, but a smile tugged at her lips. "You want to marry the Naked Baker?"

"More than I want anything else in this world. Say yes, and I'll be right here by your side every moment of every day. We'll fix up the lighthouse just the way you want it. And after two years, if you want to stop filming the show, we'll start a family, or we'll keep filming. Whatever you want, as long as we're together."

She smiled up at him. "I'd say yes, but I think you're just asking me because of my mad baking skills."

He laughed, narrowed his eyes, as if to say, *Really? You're going to tease me at a time like this?* But he played along with it, and that made her fall even harder. "It's that obvious?"

"Yeah, but you're kind of cute, and you are a really good kisser, so…" She wanted to remember this moment, the look in his eyes, the flour hanging in the air, the aroma of love and freshly baked cake surrounding them. She wanted to remember the fullness of her chest and the way her heart was so happy that there was no room for doubt.

"Wait," Blue said. "I almost forgot."

"Wait? You don't want my answer?" She laughed as he reached into the pocket of his apron and pulled out the most elegant diamond band she'd ever seen. Her heart nearly stopped. It, too, was peppered in white dust. He blew the dusting of white powder off the beautiful ring and gazed into her eyes again.

"I've never seen you wear jewelry, and I assumed it was because you don't want it to get hooked on things while you work. I hope this isn't too cumbersome, and if I was wrong, and you want a different ring, something bigger, flashier—"

With fresh tears streaming down her cheeks, she pressed her finger to his lips. "You've never read me wrong a single time since we've met. Yes, I'll marry you, Blue. Yes, yes, yes!"

As he slid the ring on her finger, he said, "I love you, Lizzie, and I will spend the rest of our lives making sure you are the happiest woman on earth."

"That's all well and good, but can we get back to making out, please, because I really want to knock another item off my list."

He laughed and kissed her again. "Which item is that?"

"Make Blue happy."

"Baby, you've just made me the happiest man on the planet."

"Oh? I think we can make you even happier." She wiggled out of his arms, opened the fridge, and held up two cans of whipped cream.

"You just got even sexier." He scooped her into his arms, and his lips came lovingly down over hers, sealing their vows as he carried her toward the stairs.

Epilogue

BLUE COULDN'T TAKE his eyes off Lizzie, standing across the room with Trish and Susan. They say that the bride should always be the most beautiful woman at her wedding, but Blue knew, at least in this case, that wasn't true. Despite how gorgeous Susan looked, no one compared to his stunning fiancée. Lizzie was a vision in a blue dress that hugged every lush curve, her hair pinned up, with sexy tendrils framing her beautiful face. It was after midnight, and many of the guests had already left the reception. Blue couldn't wait to get Lizzie back into his arms.

"Bro, you're going to burn a hole through her, staring like that," his older brother Gage said as he came to his side with Jake, Cash, and Duke.

Across the room, Jeremy was talking with his siblings. He winked at Blue and mouthed, "You're next."

"There are worse things in life than being attracted to the woman you love." *The woman I love.* Blue hadn't imagined thinking those words, and now he couldn't imagine a day going by when he didn't think them at least a dozen times. "I hope you guys find what I have someday."

Jake snickered before taking a swig of his drink. "Don't hold your breath. Cash and Gage haven't dated in forever and Duke? Well, he likes to reel them in and toss them back."

"Says the man who can't settle down with one woman long enough to buy her a drink." Duke lifted his chin with the barb.

"Why buy a drink when you can get the liquor for free?" Jake eyed a brunette standing by the bar. "Speaking of which, I'll catch you guys later. I see a lonely lady just asking for a good time."

Lizzie caught Blue's attention from across the room with a smile, sending his heart into a frenzy. He'd never tire of seeing her smile, those adorable dimples, or the love in her eyes. He lifted his chin and crooked his finger. She said something to Trish and Susan, and the three of them approached.

"You guys put everyone else to shame. The Ryder hunks, line 'em up and roll 'em out," Susan teased. "And I have the hunkiest of them all."

"I beg to differ." Lizzie wrapped an arm around Blue. "Mine looks the best in an apron."

Blue uttered a curse.

"An apron? Do share," Trish teased as her eyes skittered away, landing on a guy across the room. His shirtsleeves were pushed up to his elbows, exposing heavily inked forearms. Before Lizzie could elaborate, Trish said, "*Who* is that?"

"Firefighter, off-limits to you," Cash said.

"That just made him even more interesting." Trish raised her brows and headed in the handsome man's direction.

Cash moved to follow her, and Susan held him back. "Leave her alone. She's a big girl."

"This is what happens at weddings. Women lose their minds, and men lose their ability to make decisions."

"Speaking of decisions, don't you two want to use that honeymoon suite I booked for you?" Duke asked.

Blue snaked an arm around Lizzie's waist and pulled her in tight against him. "Tired?"

"Not *too* tired," she said with a seductive glint in her eyes.

He pressed his cheek to hers and whispered, "If we leave now, we can sneak into the pool and skinny-dip."

She trapped her lower lip between her teeth and smiled. "In the hotel?" she whispered. "The pool is closed."

He reached into his pocket and pulled out the pool key, which Duke had given him earlier.

She feigned a yawn aimed at the others. "The champagne is hitting me hard. I think I need to call it a night."

"Oh, really?" Susan said.

Blue feigned a sigh. "Yeah, I'm beat, too."

"I bet you are," Duke said under his breath.

Blue and Lizzie congratulated Jeremy and Susan, and said their goodbyes to the rest of his family, then hurried down the hall toward the pool.

"I can't believe you arranged this," she said, clinging to his arm.

"Baby, there's nothing I won't do for you." He unlocked the door to the pool. The room was dark, save for the lights from the hallway streaming in through the interior window. Blue pushed a code into a keypad hidden behind a picture on the wall—*Thank you, Duke*—and black curtains lowered over the interior windows.

"Oh my gosh, that's amazing," Lizzie said, already taking off her heels.

Blue unzipped her dress and pushed it from her shoulders, bringing his lips to her heated skin as the fabric tumbled to a pile at her feet, leaving her in silk and lace, a vision of beauty he couldn't resist as he took her in his arms.

She smiled up at him, those beautiful dimples in full force. She unbuttoned his dress shirt, pressing a kiss to every inch of skin as she revealed it.

"I want to give you everything you've ever wanted, Lizzie." He slipped from his pants as she took off her lingerie, and he pulled her in close again, running his hands over her hips. "Do you have any regrets about telling our families about your show or the deal with FCN not coming through?"

"My only regret is that I waited a year to go out with you," she said as she stripped off her bra. "Do you have any regrets about being with me? You really don't mind being naughty like this with me? I think I've corrupted you," she said as they walked into the pool.

They dunked under the water, and he brought her body flush against him.

"Baby, you couldn't corrupt me if you tried. Remember when I said love came in stages, and that we'd get to each stage when we were ready?"

"Yeah," she said, a little breathless and incredibly sexily.

"You have your lists. I have my stages. Tonight my stage one is going to blow your list out of the water."

"Funny," she said as her legs wound around his waist and their bodies joined together. "I have a feeling my list will win."

"I love you, Lizzie Barber." He sealed his lips over hers, and there, in the darkness of the heated pool, with Lizzie in his arms and love in his heart, he knew he'd been right—every moment of his life had been leading him to *her*—and every moment of his future would be spent loving her.

The End

Please enjoy a preview of the next *Sweet with Heat* novel
Embraced at Seaside

Chapter One

THE SCENT OF patchouli hung in the air as Jana Garner slid silently from the sheets in the unfamiliar room. A thin glow from the streetlights seeped between the heavy curtains, cutting a path across Hunter Lacroux. She couldn't help but admire his powerful physique one last time. Something to draw upon later when she would surely berate herself for hooking up, yet again, with the unfairly irresistible pigheaded man.

One beautifully sculpted arm arched across his forehead, and the other stretched across the pillow on which she'd slept, revealing the tattoo of the four essential life elements wrapping around his bicep. She'd asked him about it once, and he'd said he was an *earthy* guy. She didn't linger on his tattoo for long. His broad chest was too tantalizing, and it led to ripped abs. Abs that, even when he was sleeping, were perfectly defined. The sheets were bunched across his danger zone, which was an ideal location for them, because there were two things about Hunter Lacroux that drove Jana wild: his wickedly dark eyes that made her forget all the reasons why she should never touch him and that certain part of his anatomy that brought such immense pleasure, and kept her coming back for more.

Hunter Lacroux was the one man on the planet she should stay away from and the only one she seemed unable to deny. She tiptoed around the bed and picked up her miniskirt and top, searching for her bra and panties and wondering how she'd ended up here again. She'd been out with her sister, Harper, her friend Sky, and Sky's fiancé, Sawyer, at a bar in Provincetown, when Sky's brothers Hunter and Grayson and their friend Clark had shown up. She vaguely remembered getting into a heated debate with Hunter. *Don't we always?* Hunter knew Jana had been training under her brother Brock, a local boxing champ, for almost three years, and he'd been intent on giving her a hard time about women infiltrating a *man's* sport.

Jerk.

The next thing she knew they were several shots of tequila to the wind and stumbling along Commercial Street to…? She looked around the room. *This place*, wherever that was. It looked like a motel bedroom, but in reality, knowing Hunter, it could have been a friend's house where they'd crashed for the night.

Tequila. It was always her undoing. She should know better than to do shots of it anytime—but especially when *he* was around. She momentarily wondered why her sister hadn't dragged her away from him. Harper knew she had fallen into bed with him before and had sworn off him. Darn her.

She glanced at her reflection in the mirror above the dresser. Her long blond hair was knotted and tangled, and her eyes were bloodshot. *I really need to stop doing this.* Her eyes dropped to the reflection of Hunter. *Especially with you.*

If she were honest with herself, she'd admit that she needed to stop blaming Harper, too, and take some responsibility for her actions. She was twenty-five, for goodness' sake, not sixteen.

She stole another glance at Hunter, remembering the way he'd fisted his hands in her hair, tugging until her scalp stung, and nearly growled her name when they were fooling around. The man was an animal in the sack, better than any man she'd ever been with. She didn't do relationships, not after a string of horrible breakups and hurt feelings. She'd sampled enough men over the years to be certain of two things. Men as talented in bed as Hunter were hard to come by, and if she were looking to settle into a monogamous relationship, which she definitely wasn't, it wouldn't be with a player like him.

She pulled on her clothes and sank down to her knees, looking under the furniture for her panties. *Where the heck were they?*

She tiptoed back around the bed, grabbed her purse from the chair and picked up her flip-flops. She glossed over his jeans lying by the foot of the bed and his T-shirt by the door in one last search for her lingerie. Her eyes danced over the chair in the corner, the dresser, the...*Ohmygosh.*

Her stomach dipped as she plucked her bra from the top of the lampshade in the corner of the room, where he must have tossed it last night. He was definitely an aggressive and fun lover. Two admirable traits—if they weren't attached to bullheaded Hunter. She didn't know what it was about him that pissed her off, but every time they were together they clashed like oil and water, then tangled in the sheets like starving castaways fed for the first time in years.

One last sweep of the room confirmed that her panties were a lost cause. It wasn't the first time she'd left panties behind—and it probably wouldn't be the last.

She opened the door as quietly as she could and stepped into the brightly lit hallway, tiptoeing out the front door. The sign out front read, WE RENT ROOMS BY THE HOUR! GRAB A DATE AND COME ON IN!

Holy cow. That was a new low, even for her. She ducked her head and continued on her thankfully short walk of shame to her car, where she found a piece of paper shoved in the crack of the door. She recognized Harper's perfectly scripted writing.

J, I tried to dissuade you. Call me later, you big ho! Xox, H

Jana climbed into her car and closed her eyes, letting her head fall back against the headrest. She probably should have thought about the busy day she had today before she'd picked up the first shot last night. She had boxing practice at seven with Brock, and she'd agreed to help out this week at Undercover, her brother Colton's bar. She started the car, and a quick glance at the clock told her she had four hours until she was supposed to meet Brock, which meant she might be able to catch two hours of shut-eye if she was lucky.

Her cell phone vibrated with a text. Caller ID revealed the name DO NOT RESPOND! She cringed, remembering that she'd programmed that in after the last time she'd slept with Hunter. She opened and read the text anyway. *You snuck out again? Seriously? At least when I do that I remember my underwear.*

The smiley face at the end of the text told her that she'd now officially hooked up with Hunter too many times. He was getting comfortable, and that was the last thing she needed.

HUNTER PULLED UP in front of Grunter's Ironworks at ten after eight and parked his younger brother's truck. He and Grayson had been in the metalworking business together for years, and he still never tired of seeing the Grunter's Ironworks emblem on the building.

He climbed from the truck and checked his phone one last time. He hadn't expected Jana to respond to his text, but that didn't stop his gut from knotting at the thought of the saucy little blonde ignoring his message. She was a spitfire of annoyance and sensuality that was hard to ignore. He shoved his phone into his front pocket, chuckling to himself about the little package he'd left for her on his way in to work, and headed into his shop.

Clark Shelton was sitting at his desk with his back to the door, talking on the phone. Hunter and Grayson had grown up with Clark, and they'd hired him to run their business after college. Hunter headed to the back of the shop to begin work on a sculpture he was designing for a local competition. He'd been trying to conceptualize the project for a week, and nothing felt right. But the competition was too big to walk away from. The winner would not only have their work featured in a community beautification project, but would also be awarded a major art contract with a national children's foundation.

The beautification project, and the competition, were funded by Parker Collins, an actress who was building a summer home in Wellfleet. The project was her way of appeasing local residents who were dismayed over the size of her sprawling summer home. The project included creating massive gardens and a gazebo for outdoor concerts across from the harbor. Hunter was designing a sculpture for the competition, and Grayson was working on designs for the gazebo.

Grayson was leaning over the drafting table. He lifted serious eyes to Hunter.

"Jana get home okay last night?"

"I assume so. Why?"

"You *assume* so?" Grayson smirked. "She left before you woke up again, didn't she?"

Hunter scoffed. "Why do you care?"

"Maybe because she's like a sister to Sawyer, our sister's fiancé, remember? I don't want you to mess up their relationship."

"Let me worry about that, *little* brother. Trust me, she was all in. It's not like I took her against her will." In fact, she'd been all over him, tearing at his clothes before they'd even made it into the rented room.

"A'right, but if you hurt her, you know Sawyer will go crazy, and I'm not protecting you." Grayson laughed. He and Hunter were both over six feet tall, with athletic physiques, but unlike their other brothers, Pete and Matt, they'd spent their lives out *alpha*ing each other. While their brothers seemed to morph into responsible adults the day they became teenagers, Hunter and Grayson had accepted that role in their professional lives, but their personal lives were a different story altogether.

"Yeah, I'll remember that." He laughed at the idea of Grayson protecting him, but he knew his brother was right. Not only had Sky become close with both Jana and her sister, Harper, but she brought them to almost all their get-togethers, too. It seemed like Jana was always around, and she was the last person he should be hooking up with, considering he usually slept with a woman a few times at most, then closed that door. But flames ignited every time he and Jana were in the same room, and she had some kind of crazy hold over him that he'd been unable to escape.

Grayson lowered his gaze to the designs again. "I drew up the plans for the detail around the arches." While neither Grayson nor Hunter was interested in settling down in their personal lives, when it came to their business, they had a whole different attitude. They'd worked hard to build a reputable business that they could be proud of. Their love of their craft showed in their exceptional designs, and that kept them in high demand.

"Cool." Hunter came around the table to check out the designs. The competition required only designs and a small scale model of the gazebo, while the sculptures were expected to be full-size and ready for display by the competition date, which was a little more than five weeks away.

They had gone back and forth about the finite details for the gazebo, initially thinking about using a seashell theme, then moving to more of an overall oceanic theme, until finally they'd agreed on something more naturalistic. When Hunter had presented the idea of tangled vines interspersed with fish and shells, as well as clusters of berries and leaves, Grayson had loved it.

"You any closer on the sculpture?" Grayson asked.

"I'm working on something, but it still doesn't feel right. I figured I'd fabricate some of the pieces and see if I start to feel good about it."

He needed to get on the ball, but for some reason his creativity was at a standstill. Hunter was a perfectionist. This carried over to his clients to the nth degree. He sometimes spent hours laboring over the slightest angles or twists of metal.

The fact that Hunter did not go to the same lengths for a relationship wasn't lost on him.

To continue reading, buy EMBRACED AT SEASIDE

More Books By The Author

**Sweet with Heat: Seaside Summers
(Includes future publications)**

Read, Write, Love at Seaside
Dreaming at Seaside
Hearts at Seaside
Sunsets at Seaside
Secrets at Seaside
Nights at Seaside
Seized by Love at Seaside
Embraced at Seaside
Lovers at Seaside
Whispers at Seaside

**Stand Alone Women's Fiction Novels
by Melissa Foster** (Addison Cole's steamy alter ego)
The following titles may include some harsh language

Chasing Amanda (mystery/suspense)
Come Back to Me (mystery/suspense)
Have No Shame (historical fiction/romance)
Megan's Way (literary fiction)
Traces of Kara (psychological thriller)
Where Petals Fall (suspense)

Acknowledgments

I've waited a long time to write about Blue Ryder, and it was so much fun being in his world and meeting his siblings. I can't wait to bring you the rest of their stories.

I have endless gratitude for my amazing readers, friends, and fans who continue to inspire me on a daily basis. Aimee Suter, I hope you find Blue Ryder worthy of fulfilling your lists. Thank you for letting me borrow them for this story. I hope I did them justice.

Please note that the Food Channel Network (FCN) is a fictional network, and not an error or misrepresentation of the real Food Network.

The next few years are going to be very busy as I bring you more Sweet with Heat novels. Remember to sign up for my newsletter to keep up-to-date with new releases and special promotions and events. www.AddisonCole.com/Newsletter

If you don't yet follow me on Facebook, please do! We have such fun chatting about our lovable heroes and sassy heroines, and I always try to keep fans abreast of what's going on in our fictional boyfriends' worlds. facebook.com/AddisonColeAuthor

Thank you to my meticulous and patient team of editors and proofreaders: Kristen, Penina, Elaini, Juliette, Marlene, Lynn, and Justinn.

As always, endless love goes to my real-life hunky hero, Les, for supporting my love of too many fictional boyfriends to count.

Addison Cole is the sweet alter ego of *New York Times* and *USA Today* bestselling and award-winning author Melissa Foster. She enjoys writing humorous, and deeply emotional, contemporary romance without explicit sex scenes or harsh language. Addison spends her summers on Cape Cod, where she dreams up wonderful love stories in her house overlooking Cape Cod Bay.

Visit Addison on her website or chat with her on social media. Addison enjoys discussing her books with book clubs and reader groups and welcomes an invitation to your event.

Addison's books are available in paperback, digital, and audio formats.

www.AddisonCole.com
facebook.com/AddisonColeAuthor

CPSIA information can be obtained
at www.ICGtesting.com
Printed in the USA
LVHW010039260619
622381LV00001BA/154